W9-CDH-888

MAY 1995

The Rock
of Tanios

AMIN MAALOUF

The Rock
of Tanios

AMIN MAALOUF

Translated by Dorothy S. Blair

George Braziller   **New York**

First published in the United States of America in 1994
by George Braziller, Inc.

Originally published in French under the title *Le Rocher de Tanios*

Copyright © 1993 by Editions Grasset & Fasquelle
Translation copyright © 1994 by Dorothy S. Blair

For information, please write to the publisher:
George Braziller, Inc.
60 Madison Avenue
New York, New York 10010

ISBN 0-8076-1365-7

A catalogue record of this book is available at The Library of Congress

Typeset in Great Britain by Intype, London
Printed and bound by Haddon Craftsmen, Scranton, Pennsylvania

First Edition

CONTENTS

To the memory of
the man with the broken wings

*C'est un peuple pour qui se
sont montés ces Alleghanys et ces
Libans de rêve!* . . .

*Quels bons bras, quelle belle
heure me rendront cette région d'où
viennent mes sommeils et mes
moindres mouvements?*

Arthur Rimbaud
Illuminations

I

In my native village, the rocks have names. There is the Ship, the Bear's Head, the Ambush, the Wall and the Twins, also known as the Ghoul's Breasts. But, most important, there is the Soldiers' Rock, where they used to keep a lookout in the past when the army was hunting down the rebels; no place is more revered, more replete with legends. And yet, when I happen to dream of the scenes of my childhood, it is another rock which I see. In appearance like a magnificent seat, hollowed out, as if worn away by the pressure of people's buttocks, and with a tall, straight back, sloping down on each side by way of arm-rests – the only one, I think, to bear the name of a man: the Rock of Tanios.

I have gazed long at this stone throne without daring to approach it. Not out of fear of the danger; in the village the rocks were our favourite playground and, even as a child, I used to dare the older boys to climb the most dangerous ones; we had no equipment other than our hands and legs, but we had the knack of clinging to the rock-face with our bare skin and not even the most gigantic crag had us beaten.

No, it was not fear of falling which deterred me. It was something I believed in and a promise I had made. Exacted from me by my grandfather, a few months before his death. 'Any of the rocks, but never that one!' The other youngsters, like me, kept their distance, out of the same superstitious fear. They too must have promised, with a finger on the down of their embryo moustaches. And have obtained the same explanation: 'They nicknamed him

Tanios-*kishk*. He came and sat on that rock. He was never seen again.'

This person was often mentioned in my presence, the hero of so many local anecdotes, and his name had always intrigued me. Tanios, I was well aware, was one of the many local variations of Antoine, like Antoun, Antonios, Mtanios, Tanos or Tannous... But why the ridiculous nickname '*Kishk*'? My grandfather had never been prepared to give me an explanation. He told me only what he reckoned suitable for a child's ears: 'Tanios was the son of Lamia. You have surely heard of her. It was very long ago, long before I was born even, or before my own father's birth. In those days the Pasha of Egypt was making war on the Turks and our ancestors suffered. Especially after the murder of the Patriarch. He was shot right here, on the outskirts of the village, with the English Consul's gun . . .' That was how my grandfather spoke when he didn't want to give me a straight answer, he would toss out scraps of sentences as if to point to a path, then another, then a third, but without setting out on any of them. I had to wait for years before I discovered the true story.

However, I had hold of the right end of the thread, as I knew the name Lamia. We all knew it in the region, thanks to a saying which happened to have been passed down to us for two centuries: 'Lamia, Lamia, how could you hide your beauty?'

Thus, even in our own day, when the young men gathered in the village square happen to see a woman pass, wrapped in a shawl, there is always one who murmurs: 'Lamia, Lamia . . .' Which is often a genuine compliment, but which can sometimes be tinged with the most cruel mockery.

The majority of these youngsters know very little about Lamia, or of the tragedy which this saying still recalls. They simply repeat what they have heard from the lips of their parents or grandparents, and occasionally, like them, they point as they speak to the upper part of the village, now uninhabited, but where the still imposing ruins of a castle can be seen.

Because of this gesture, so often repeated in my presence, I long imagined Lamia to be a sort of princess who sheltered her beauty from the eyes of the villagers behind those high walls. Poor Lamia, if I could have seen her busy in the kitchens, or trotting barefoot through the halls, a pitcher in her hands, a shawl over her head, it would have been difficult for me to mistake her for the chatelaine.

But she was not a servant either. I now know a little more about her. Thanks in the first place to the old people of the village, men and women, whom I questioned untiringly. It was twenty years or more ago, they are all dead now, except for one. His name is Gebrayel, a cousin of my grandfather and now ninety-six years old. If I name him, it is not only because he has the privilege of surviving, it is first and foremost because the evidence of this former schoolteacher, with his passion for local history, is especially valuable; unique in fact. I would sit for hours gazing at him; he had huge nostrils, thick lips and a little bald, wrinkled pate – features that age has most certainly emphasized. I have not seen him recently, but I am assured that he still has the same confident tone of voice, the same eager expression, and his memory is still sound. Through the words which I am about to write, it is often his voice that must be heard.

It was owing to Gebrayel that I soon acquired the deep conviction that Tanios, over and above the myth, had been a creature of flesh and blood. The proofs came later, many years later. When, with the help of chance, I was finally able to lay my hands on authentic documents.

There are three of these from which I shall often quote. Two come from people who knew Tanios intimately. And a third is more recent. Its author is a monk who died just after the First World War, Elias of Kfaryabda – that is the name of my village, which I don't think I have yet mentioned. His work bears the following title: *A Mountain Chron-*

icle or the History of the village of Kfaryabda the hamlets and farms which depend upon it the monuments which there arise the customs which are observed the remarkable people who have lived there and the events which took place there with the permission of the Almighty.

A strange book, uneven, disconcerting. On certain pages the tone is personal, the pen warms up and runs away with itself, the reader is carried along by some lyricism, by some bold flights of fancy, and feels he is in the presence of a genuine writer. And then, suddenly, as if fearing he had committed the sin of pride, the monk retracts, withdraws, the tone becomes flat, and he does penance by retreating into his role as a pious compiler, then he accumulates borrowings from past authors and notables from his own times, preferably in verse, those Arabic verses from the age of Decadence, stiff with conventional images and cold sentiments.

Of this, I became aware only after meticulously re-reading the thousand pages – nine hundred and eighty-seven to be exact, from the preamble to the traditional final line which runs: 'You who will read my book, be indulgent . . .' When I first held this work in my hands, with its green binding simply adorned with a great black diamond, and opened it for the first time, I was struck only by the cramped handwriting, without commas, full-stops or even paragraphs, nothing but the scrolling calligraphy enclosed in its margins like a picture in its frame, with, here and there, a word escaping to recall the preceding page or announce the next one.

Still hesitating to start reading a work whose very appearance threatened to deter me, I flicked through the pages of the monster with half an eye, when the following lines jumped out at me – I copied them immediately and later translated and punctuated them:

The enigmatic disappearance of Tanios-*kishk* dates from 4 November 1840 . . . And yet he had everything,

4

everything that a man can expect from life. The riddle of his past was solved, his future path made smooth. He could not have left the village of his own free will. No one can doubt that a curse is attached to the rock which bears his name.

Immediately, the thousand pages ceased to seem opaque. I began to look at this manuscript differently. Like a guide, a companion. Or perhaps as a steed to carry me forward.

My journey could begin.

First Passage

The Temptation of Lamia

May the Almighty grant me His pardon for the hours and days that I am about to steal from the blessed time of prayer and reading the Holy Scriptures in order to write this imperfect history of the people of my region, my excuse being that not one of the minutes we live would have existed without the thousands of years which have preceded it since the Creation, and that not one of our heart-beats would have been possible had it not been for the successive generations of ancestors, with their encounters, their promises, their hallowed unions, or even their temptations.

Preamble to *A Mountain Chronicle*,
the work of the monk Elias of Kfaryabda

I

In those days the heavens were so low that no man dared draw himself up to his full height. However, there was life, there were desires and festivities. And if one could never expect the best in this world, one hoped every day to escape the worst.

The whole village belonged at that time to one feudal lord. He was the heir to a long line of sheikhs, but when anyone speaks today of 'the time of the Sheikh', without further precision, there is no doubt who is meant, the reference is to the one in whose shadow Lamia lived.

He was not one of the most powerful people in the country. Far from it. Between the eastern plains and the sea there were dozens of more extensive domains than his. His sole possessions were the village of Kfaryabda and a few surrounding farms; he must have had at the most three hundred households under his authority. Above him and his peers there was the Emir of the Mountains, and above the Emir the Provincial Pashas, those of Tripoli, Damascus, Sidon and Acre. And even higher, much higher, near Heaven, there was the Sultan of Istanbul. But the people of my village did not look so high. For them, 'their' Sheikh was already a considerable personage.

Every morning they would make their way in their great numbers to the castle to wait for him to wake, crowding into the corridor leading to his bedchamber. And when he appeared, they welcomed him with a hundred formulas of greeting, loud and soft, a cacophony accompanying his every step.

Most of them were dressed like him in black baggy

trousers (the usual *seroual*), white striped shirt, terracotta-coloured cap, and nearly everyone sported similar thick moustaches, proudly curled at the tip, and had clean-shaven faces. What distinguished the Sheikh? Only the apple-green waistcoat decorated with gold thread which he wore in all seasons, as others wear a sable fur or carry a sceptre. Having said that, even without this adornment, no visitor would have had any difficulty in distinguishing the Master in the midst of the crowd of courtiers, on account of all those heads dipping one after the other to kiss his hand, a cere-monial which continued until he reached the Hall of Pillars, until he took his usual place on the sofa and put the gilded mouthpiece of his hookah to his lips.

When the men returned home later in the day, they would say to their wives, 'This morning I saw the Sheikh's hand.' Not, 'I kissed his hand . . .' That is indeed what they did, and publicly, but they were too modest to say that. Neither did they say, 'I saw the Sheikh' – pretentious words, as if it were a question of an encounter between two people of equal rank! No, 'I saw the Sheikh's hand', such was the hallowed expression.

No other hand had so much importance. The hand of God and that of the Sultan dispensed only global calamities; it was the Sheikh's hand which distributed daily misfortunes. And also occasional crumbs of happiness.

In the language of the local people, the same word, *kaff*, sometimes meant both a hand and a slap. So many feudal lords had made this a symbol of power and an instrument of government. When they talked among themselves, far from the ears of their subjects, a maxim was frequently on their lips: 'A peasant must always be ready for a slap on the back of his head', meaning he must constantly be made to live in fear, with his head bowed. Moreover, 'slap' was often simply a euphemism for 'irons', 'whip', 'forced labour' . . .

No lord was ever punished for ill-treating his subjects; if, in some rare cases, the superior authorities took this amiss, it was because they were determined to cause his downfall for quite different reasons, and were looking for the slightest excuse to overthrow him. For countless centuries people had been living under arbitrary laws, and if there had ever been a former age when justice reigned, no one had any memory of it.

When they were fortunate enough to have a master less greedy, less cruel than the others, they thought themselves privileged, and thanked God for showing them so much consideration, as if they felt He had done the best He could.

This was the case with Kfaryabda; I remember being astonished, and more than once indignant, at the affectionate way certain villagers spoke of this Sheikh and his reign. 'It's true,' they said, 'he liked to have his hand kissed and, from time to time, he would deliver a resounding slap across the face of one of his subjects, but it was never to humiliate him gratuitously; as the Sheikh was the one who sat in judgement in his domain, and had to settle all disputes – between brothers, neighbours, husbands and wives – he was in the habit of listening first to the litigants, then to some witnesses, before suggesting an arrangement; the parties were expected to agree to this and to seal their reconciliation on the spot by the customary embraces; if anyone stubbornly held out, a hearty slap from the Master would put an end to the argument.'

Such a punishment was sufficiently rare for the villagers to speak of nothing else for weeks, doing their best to describe the hissing of the slap, fantasizing about the finger-marks which were said to remain visible for three days, and the wretched victim's eyelids which never stopped blinking afterwards.

The relations of the slapped man would come to visit him, sitting round the room in a circle, silent as if in mourning. Then one of them would speak up, saying one mustn't feel humiliated. What man has never had his ears boxed by his father?

That was how the Sheikh wished to be considered. When addressing the people of his domain, even the oldest, he would say, '*yabni*, my son!' or 'my daughter, *ya binti*!' He was convinced that a close pact bound him to his subjects; they owed him obedience and respect, he owed them his protection in all circumstances. Even at that time, the beginning of the nineteenth century, this sort of fundamental paternalism already seemed incongruous, a survival of a primordial age of childhood and innocence, which the majority of the villagers put up with, and for which some of their descendants are still nostalgic.

For my part, I must admit that, when I discovered certain facets of this person, I felt myself becoming a little less severe towards him. For, if 'our' Sheikh insisted on all his prerogatives, he did not, like so many other overlords, hold his duties cheap. Thus, all the peasants had to bring him a share of their crops; but he was accustomed to say to them in exchange, 'No one in this domain will ever go hungry as long as a loaf of bread and an olive are left in the castle.' More than once, the villagers were able to confirm that these were not vain words.

Equally important in the villagers' eyes was the way the Sheikh dealt with the higher authorities, and that mainly explains why people remember him so favourably. When the Emir or the Pasha exacted some new tax from them, other feudal lords took care not to argue, saying that it was better to pressurize their subjects than to put themselves in bad odour with the authorities. Not so 'our' Sheikh. He stormed, raged, sent supplication after supplication, spoke of drought, frost, locusts, slipped a judicious baksheesh, and sometimes obtained a delay, a remission, or even an exemption. The Treasury agents were then said to extort the shortfall from more docile lords.

He was not often successful. The authorities were rarely disposed to compromise in the matter of taxes. At least he had the merit of trying, and the peasants were grateful to him.

No less appreciated was his behaviour in times of war. Priding himself on an ancient custom, he had obtained for his subjects the right to fight under their own flag, instead of having to enlist with the rest of the army. An unheard-of privilege for such a tiny fief, which could furnish at the most four hundred men. For the villagers the difference was great. To set off with their brothers, sons, cousins, commanded by the Sheikh himself, who knew each one of them by name, with the knowledge they would not be abandoned on the spot if they were wounded, that they would be ransomed if captured, that they would be decently buried and wept over if they had to die! To know also that they would not be sent to the slaughter-house to please some depraved pasha! The peasants were as proud of this privilege as was the Sheikh himself. But naturally it had to be deserved. It was not enough to 'go through the motions', one had to fight, and fight valiantly, much more valiantly than the foot-sloggers at their sides or among their enemies, their courage must be constantly quoted as an example throughout the Mountains, in the whole Ottoman Empire; their pride, their honour, was at stake, but it was also the only means of retaining this privilege.

For all these reasons, the people of Kfaryabda considered 'their' Sheikh as the lesser of evils. He would even have seemed a genuine blessing if he had not had one failing, an outrageous failing which, in the eyes of certain villagers, cancelled out his noble qualities.

'Women!' old Gebrayel said to me, and his predatory eyes lit up in his hawk-like face. 'Women! The Sheikh coveted them all, and he seduced one every evening!'

As far as the last part of this sentence was concerned, this was pure fabrication. But for the rest, which after all is the essential, it does indeed seem that the Sheikh, following the example of his ancestors, and so many other lords, in every latitude, had the firm conviction that all the women in his domain belonged to him. Like the houses, the land, the mulberry-trees and the vines. The men, too, for that matter. And that, any day, at his convenience, he could make the most of his rights.

One must not, for all that, imagine him prowling about the village like a satyr in search of his prey, with his henchmen acting as procurers. No, that is not the way things were. However imperious his desire might be, he never for a moment relinquished a certain dignity, never would he have dreamed of slipping furtively through a secret door, like a thief, to take advantage of a husband's absence. It was on his own premises that he officiated, so to speak.

Just as every man had to go, at least once a month, 'to see the Sheikh's hand', so all the women had to put in a day's work at the castle, to help in the daily or seasonal labours, that was their way of showing their allegiance. Some of them demonstrated particular talents, an unrivalled way of pounding the meat in the mortar, or kneading the dough for the bread. And when a feast had to be prepared, all skills were needed at once. A form of forced labour in brief; but shared between dozens, hundreds of women, it became less onerous.

I have perhaps let it be understood that the men's contribution was limited to the morning hand-kissing. That was not the way things were in fact. They were required to be responsible for the wood and the many repairs to the Sheikh's estate, restoring any crumbling terraces, not forgetting the ultimate duty of all the males – war. But in peacetime, the castle was a hive of women bustling about, chatting and also enjoying themselves. And sometimes, at siesta-time, when the whole village sank into a dimly-lit torpor, one or other of the women would stray between corridors and bedchambers to surface two hours later in the midst of whispers.

Some of them fell in with these games willingly, flattered at being courted, desired. The Sheikh had a fine presence, and they knew moreover that, far from throwing himself at the first female face he saw, he appreciated charm and intelligence. They still repeat in the village this saying of

his, 'Only a donkey would sleep with a she-donkey!'
Insatiable, yes, but difficult to please. That is how he is still
seen today, and that is probably exactly how his contempor-
aries, his subjects, saw him. So, many of the women were
anxious at least to be noticed, this reassured them about
their charms. Even if it meant subsequently letting themselves be led astray – or not. A dangerous game, I agree;
but at the time when their beauty was budding, then flower-
ing, could they, before it faded, give up all wish to attract?

And yet, in spite of what old Gebrayel says, most of them
would have nothing to do with these compromising affairs
which had no future. The only part they would play in these
amorous diversions was to side-step the advances, and it
seems likely that the Master managed to accept defeat when
his 'opponent' proved too cunning. And, what was more
important' – far-sighted, since, as soon as the object of his
desire found herself alone with the Sheikh, she could not
reject him without humiliating him, which no village-woman
would have had the nerve to do. They had to exercise their
skill earlier, in fact by avoiding finding themselves in this
embarrassing situation. They had to think up a variety of
ruses. Some of them, when it was their turn to come to the
castle, arrived with an infant in their arms, their own or
that of a neighbour. Others brought along their sister
or mother, certain that, in this way, they would not be
harassed. Another plan, to escape the Master's attentions,
was to sit right next to his young wife, the Sheikha, and not
leave her side all day.

The Sheikh had not married until he was nearly forty,
and even then it had been necessary to force his hand. The
Patriarch of his community had received so many complaints against the incorrigible seducer that he had decided
to use his influence to put an end to this scandalous situation. And he thought he had found the ideal solution: to
marry him to the daughter of an even more powerful feudal
chief, the Lord of the Great Jord, in the hope that in this
way, out of regard for his spouse, and even more to avoid

annoying his father-in-law, the Master of Kfaryabda would be obliged to behave himself.

No sooner was the first year over than the Sheikha had already given birth to a son, who was christened Raad. However, despite his satisfaction at having an heir, the man quickly resumed his depraved habits, neglecting his spouse during her pregnancy and even more after the confinement.

The which spouse, belying the Patriarch's predictions, was to give evidence of astonishing weakness. No doubt she had in mind the example set by her own family of feudal lords, an unfaithful father, womanizing brothers, and a resigned mother. In her eyes, her husband's behaviour was the result of his temperament and his social rank, two things she could not change. She never wanted to be told about the Sheikh's adventures, so that she would not be obliged to react. But gossip reached her, and she suffered, even if she wept only when alone, or else with her mother, to whom she returned for prolonged visits.

In the castle she feigned indifference or proud irony and drowned her sorrows by indulging her sweet tooth. Sitting for hours on end in the same place, in the little saloon next to her bedchamber, she sported by way of headdress an old-fashioned *tantour* – a sort of tall silver tube, planted vertically in her hair, on which was draped a silken veil, an outfit so complicated that she took care not to remove it even when she went to bed. 'Which,' Gebrayel remarked, 'was scarcely conducive to regaining the Sheikh's favours. Any more than her corpulence, either. She was said always to have within reach a basket full of sweetmeats over which the serving-women and visitors kept permanent watch, for fear it become empty. And the chatelaine gorged herself like a pig.'

She was not the only woman to suffer, but it was among the men that the Sheikh's excesses aroused the most resentment. If some of them pretended to believe that the thing happened only to other men's wives, mothers, sisters and daughters, all lived constantly in fear of seeing their honour tarnished. The village ceaselessly buzzed with women's names, every jealousy, every revenge was expressed by this means. Quarrels sometimes broke out, on futile grounds, which revealed the suppressed rage of various individuals.

People watched each other, spied on each other. A woman had only to dress with a touch of coquetry when she was leaving for the castle for her to be suspected of setting her cap at the Sheikh. And immediately, she was judged guilty, more guilty than the latter, for whom they offered the excuse that 'that was the way he was made'. It is true that there was one infallible procedure available to those women anxious to avoid any adventure: this was to present themselves before the Master looking hideous, dressed like scarecrows, deformed . . .

However, there are some women who cannot manage to hide their beauty. Or perhaps it is their Creator who feels loath to see it hidden; but, Lord! how many passions around them!

One such woman lived in my village at that time. This was Lamia, in fact. The Lamia of the old saying.

II

Lamia bore her beauty like a cross. Any other woman would only have to veil herself, or be draped in some unbecoming material, to cease attracting attention. Not Lamia. She seemed to be drenched in light. Try as she might to conceal herself, to keep in the background, to melt into the crowd, she inevitably gave herself away, she was detected, it only needed a gesture, a trifle – a hand touching her hair, a refrain hummed unthinkingly – all eyes were on her, all ears only for her voice which was limpid as clear water.

If, with the others, all the others, the Sheikh was expressing his vanity and his hot blood, with Lamia it was different, from the very first moment. Her grace and charm intimidated him, a sentiment that he had rarely experienced. His desire for her was all the greater, but his impatience all the less. For his more common conquests, this born warrior had his well-tried stratagems – a tender word, a roguish insinuation, a brief demonstration of power, and he won the day. With Lamia he was resigned to undertaking a siege.

He might possibly not have been able to stick to such a wise approach had it not been for a circumstance which reassured him and constrained him at the same time: Lamia lived under his own roof, in a wing of the castle, since she was the wife of his major-domo, Gerios.

Clerk, chamberlain, treasurer, secretary, sometimes even confidant, the latter did not have exactly defined functions. He had to keep his master informed of the state of the domain, the crops, the sharing out of the water, taxes, the *avania**. He even meticulously entered in a register all the gifts the villagers brought to the castle, for example, 'Toubiyya, the son of Wakim, came at the High Holiday – that is to say, at Easter – with half an *ocka*† of soap and two ounces of coffee . . .' Lamia's husband also drew up the contracts for the tenant farmers.

If it had been a question of a richer, more extensive domain, Gerios would have been an important dignitary; moreover, in the villagers' eyes, his fate was most enviable; he lived secure from want, and the apartments he occupied, modest compared to those of his master, were better appointed than the finest houses in the village.

It was after obtaining this much prized post that Gerios had asked for Lamia's hand. His future father-in-law, a relatively well-off peasant, whose elder daughter was married to the village priest, had accepted him only after long hesitation. The suitor seemed perfectly capable of providing for the needs of a family, but Lamia's father could not bring himself to like him. Few people appreciated him, moreover, although no one was able to find anything to reproach him with, except a certain coldness. He was, as they say in the village, 'one of those people who do not laugh even when presented with bread hot from the oven'. As a result he was considered sly and arrogant. They were even openly hostile to him. If this affected him, he never showed it and never reacted. In his position he could have made life difficult for those who disliked him. He refrained from doing so. But no one showed him any gratitude for this. 'He is incapable of doing either good or evil,' was all they said, quite unkindly.

When Gerios's predecessor quit his post, the Sheikh had accused him of misappropriating large sums of money. Lamia's husband would never have committed such errors

*An extortionate tax levied by the Turks, especially on Christians, during the Ottoman Empire.
†Turkish measure of weight, exactly 2283 gm.

but, if one was to believe his detractors, it was less out of honesty than of cowardice. Difficult to say, now all the witnesses are silent. Yet it seems certain that he was genuinely terrified of his master, that he trembled in his presence more than the humblest villager and gave in to all his whims. The Sheikh was capable of having him write a letter to the Emir and, the next moment, of putting out his foot for him to help him remove his shoes. And Gerios never showed the slightest resistance.

When the village elders speak nowadays of Lamia's husband, there is one story they delight in repeating. It varies slightly from one telling to another, but the substance is the same. The Sheikh, as I have said, had an abundant moustache but was otherwise clean-shaven, and this was a subject which frequently recurred in his conversation. His moustache was for him the symbol of honour, power, and when he made an important promise he pulled out a hair which he entrusted very solemnly to the person concerned, who wrapped it in a clean cloth to return to him the day the promise was kept. Conversely, he was in the habit of mocking those who wore a beard, accusing them of uncleanliness, claiming he had seen them wipe their hands on it; so that, with the exception of the priest, not a single villager dared adorn his chin for fear of being the target of sarcastic remarks. Whereas they all, naturally, cultivated moustaches, just like the Sheikh. Gerios was no exception, his own being the exact replica of his Master's, thick, sometimes oiled, and turned up at the ends in a double kiss-curl. So far, nothing unusual; such forms of imitation have been, since the dawn of time, a mark of deference.

Except that, one day, speaking once more of moustaches in the presence of his visitors, the Sheikh had pointed out, with some irritation, that his major-domo's was more abundant than his own. That same evening Lamia saw her husband standing in front of a mirror, busy chopping at his moustache to thin it out. She had watched this strange mutilation without a word. But she felt diminished.

That was Gerios. He spoke little, ate little, smiled rarely. He had some education but no other ambition than to keep his job and retain his master's goodwill, a master whom he served moreover honestly and diligently.

Lamia would certainly have been happier with a less lack-lustre husband. She who was so merry, so mischievous, so spontaneous by nature, every time she attracted attention in public by a witty remark, a little laugh, every time she hummed a song, Gerios was there, frowning at her, looking surly, anxious. Then she fell silent. And when she met the women who came to work at the castle, when she joined in their laughter, their whispering, when she lent a hand with their tasks, her husband reproached her. He never ceased repeating to her that she had to maintain her rank instead of working like a servant; when she wanted to be agreeable to him, she went off to chat to the Sheikha and stuff herself in her company.

Perhaps he was right. If she had followed his advice, she would probably have avoided many misfortunes for herself and her family. Her existence would not have made waves, she would have lived according to her rank, grown old according to her rank, she would today lie buried according to her rank, and no saying would have arisen to revive the memory of her unwise beauty.

Between the bride and the husband there is a difference of age
She is in her fifteenth spring and he in his thirtieth winter.

On the occasion of what village wedding were these verses composed by a popular poet? The *Mountain Chronicle*, which quotes them, does not give this information; I would not be surprised to discover one day that they were describing Lamia and Gerios.

In fact, the young woman often let herself be guided by her spring-like disposition. She was merry only when in merry company, and derived pleasure from inspiring pleasure in those around her. It was in her nature to please and she did please. The village-women might have been expected to be jealous of her beauty and the famous 'rank' which she was supposed to uphold. Not in the least. They could all detect and appreciate her transparency, her total absence of affectation, conceit, cunning, they could all talk to her as to a sister. Even the Sheikha was friendly to her, in spite of the fact that her incorrigible husband had eyes only for Gerios's wife; true, he addressed all the women as 'my daughter!' but when he said this to Lamia he put so much happiness, so much gentleness into the words that they became a caress. In the kitchens the women joked about this, trying to ape the master's honeyed '*ya binti!*'; they did this, moreover, in Lamia's presence and she laughed wholeheartedly. She was, in all probability, flattered, but never for a moment thought she might possibly fall from grace.

The Sheikh, for his part, doubtless had some ulterior motive. Which does not mean that every one of his smiles, every one of his affectionate words was a calculated move.

To tell the truth, if the incident by which their lives were intertwined obeyed some plan or other, it could only have been that of Providence.

'An incident, just an incident, nothing more,' Gebrayel insisted. There was however a gleam in his eyes when he added, 'Tiny, like a grain of sand, or just a spark.'

And when he began to tell the story, it was with ceremony and flourishes:

'It was one of those July days that are so disliked in the village. The air dry and thin. On the roads, at every step, the flocks send up dust. Windows and doors were endlessly opened, but not a shutter banged, not a gate creaked on its hinges. The still airlessness of summer, you know what that is like!'

It is true that the folk of Kfaryabda cannot resign themselves to living in an oven. They no longer speak, they
scarcely eat. The whole day long they drink straight out of
pitchers, holding them high above their heads and, out
of pique, letting the water spill over their faces, their hair,
their clothes. And, no matter what happens, they don't put
a foot outside the house until it gets cool.

'Nevertheless, that day the Sheikh had some visitors.
Strangers. Lamia made the coffee, and brought it to the
Hall of Pillars, the servants were probably all drowsing in
their corners. Then she came to fetch the empty cups. The
Sheikh was no longer in his usual place. And, strangely
enough, the golden mouthpiece of his hookah was lying on
the floor. Normally, when he got up, he automatically
rolled the pipe round the bowl and removed the tip to
keep it clean.'

As she went out into the corridor, Lamia heard the sound
of heavy breathing coming from a small room, sometimes
used as a private room for intimate discussions. The Sheikh
was there, in the semi-darkness, lolling with his forehead
pressed against the wall.

'Is our Sheikh feeling unwell?'

'Nothing serious, *ya binti.*'

But he spoke as if short of breath.

'You had better sit down,' she said, taking him gently by
the arm.

He stood up, his breath came more evenly, he arranged
his attire and pressed his thumbs to his temples.

'It's nothing. The heat certainly. Most important, not a
word. To anyone.'

'I swear,' she said. 'By the Messiah!'

She took the crucifix which she wore round her neck,
put it to her lips, then pressed it to her heart. Satisfied, the
Master gave her a little pat on the arm, before going off to
join his guests.

Nothing else was to occur that day, nothing other than
this commonplace summer indisposition. But for Lamia,

something had changed in her way of looking at this man. Up till then she had always shown him deference mingled with a certain amount of prejudice and, like so many other women, she feared to find herself alone with him. But now she noticed that the veins of his temples were swollen, that his brow was sometimes furrowed, as if he were assailed by hordes of worries, and she was on the look-out for the opportunity to be alone with him. Simply to be assured that he was not again indisposed.

Quite different feelings, however, up till then kept at a distance, insinuated themselves into her heart, under cover of her legitimate concern. For the Sheikh, for the besieger, a veritable Trojan horse was in place. Without his having raised a finger to introduce it. To inspire a tender compassion is perhaps, for some people, one of the tricks in the game of love; not for him, he would never have wished for this arrow in his quiver!

Several days elapsed before Lamia found another opportunity to see the Sheikh without witnesses, to ask him if he had again felt unwell. He made the moist click with his tongue which, in the village language, signifies 'no', but she was sure he was lying.

And had he mentioned the other incident to his wife?

'To no one! The person is not born who will ever hear me complain!'

To reassure him, Lamia renewed her promise of silence, again putting the crucifix to her lips, then to her heart. While she was accomplishing this brief pious ritual, the Sheikh took her left hand in his and squeezed it for a moment, as if to share her oath. Then he left without a backward glance at her.

She was surprised to find herself smiling affectionately. 'The person is not born who will ever hear me complain!' he had said. He thought to speak like a man, but to a woman's ears this remark sounded like a little boy's boasting. Lamia remembered her youngest brother saying the same thing, word for word, the day he had been cupped. No, there was no doubt about it, she could no longer perceive the Lord of the village such as he wanted to be perceived, nor as the others saw him. And when they spoke of him in her presence, which occurred hourly, the words resounded differently in her head; she was irritated by some, others delighted or worried her, no word left her indifferent, she had stopped taking gossip for what it was, a way of dispelling boredom. And she no longer ever felt inclined to chip in herself.

Sometimes, when the village-women went too far with their bawdy suggestions, she was tempted to shut them up. But she restrained herself, and even forced herself to join in their laughter. If she had even once compelled them to keep quiet, she would have become a stranger to them and they would have made mincemeat of her good name. It was better to remain in their good graces! But if Lamia behaved in this way it was not out of calculation, but because it was her nature, she never felt better than when she retreated into silence amid the gathering of women with wet hands, letting herself be lulled by their cackle and their teasing.

One day, it must have been in mid-September, or soon after – on arriving in the little smoke-filled courtyard where they made the bread, she heard a long ripple of laughter. She went to sit down on a stone, near to the *saj*, the round convex iron baking sheet, under which a fire of broom branches was crackling. A cousin took it upon herself to put her in the picture. 'We were just saying that for the last few weeks he seems to have mended his ways, we no longer hear his adventures mentioned . . .' When, in the village, anyone said 'he' or 'him', without taking the trouble to explain, everyone knew who they were talking about.

'The Sheikha has taken him in hand,' assured a matron,

slapping the dough on to the red-hot metal by means of a large padded cushion.

'The Sheikha, surely not!' said another. 'Only yesterday I was with her and she told me she was leaving in a week's time with her son, to spend the winter in the Great Jord with her mother. If she'd managed to win back her man's affection, why would she be going?'

'Perhaps he's ill,' suggested another.

They turned to Lamia, who had to draw a deep breath to say, in a detached voice, 'If he were ill, it would have been noticed.'

Seated on a stone beside her was a woman, so old and silent that no one thought she was following the conversation. However, she said, 'Or perhaps he's madly in love.'

The others had not heard her correctly.

'What did you say, *hajje?*'

They called her *hajje* because in her youth she had gone on a pilgrimage to Bethlehem, to see the Holy Crib.

'He must be in love, and he's waiting for his wife to turn her back.'

'Her presence has never stopped him doing whatever he pleases!' objected the matron.

'I've known your Sheikh ever since he was still sitting on his mother's lap. If he's madly in love with a woman, he won't make a move as long as the Sheikha is still in the castle . . .'

Then they began to speculate on the identity of the woman in question. They murmured one name, then another, a third . . . Then a man came by and they changed the subject.

However, this gossip went on echoing in Lamia's head throughout that day. And when night came she was still thinking about it.

Could the Sheikh be so seriously ill? Ought she not to mention it to someone, send for the doctor from Dayroun? No, he would be angry with her. Better to wait and watch. In a week's time, if she saw some pretty woman hanging about in the corridors leading to his apartments, she would be reassured.

But was this really what she wished, to see him resume his amorous activities?

The night wore on. She tossed and turned on her bed, unable to find a comfortable position. She no longer knew what she ought to wish for. She turned and tossed again. And why then should she wish for anything to do with this man?

Her husband slept on his back beside her, his mouth open like a fish.

III

The day before the Sheikha was to leave, while all the people at the castle were busy with the final preparations, Gerios was surprised to hear his wife ask him with a childish insistence if he would allow her to take part in the journey.

'You want to spend the winter in the Jord?'

'Not the whole winter, just a few weeks. The Sheikha has invited me more than once . . .'

'You've got nothing to do there.'

'I could be her lady-in-waiting.'

'You're neither a servant nor a lady-in-waiting; how many times have I got to tell you that? You are my wife, and your place is with me. A woman doesn't leave her husband for weeks and months on end. I can't understand how you even dare to think of it.'

She had to accept it. The thought of accompanying the Sheikha had never really appealed to her before, but that morning, after another restless night, she had woken up with this idea in her head. To go away, get away from the castle for a bit, away from the women's whisperings, the men's glances, and her own doubts. She had no illusions about Gerios's reaction, but she was hoping for a miracle. She needed this miracle. And when she was forced to give up any hopes, she suddenly seemed shattered, and shut herself up in her room for the rest of the day, weeping.

'Lamia was just sixteen, and when she wept, two dimples appeared in her cheeks, as if to collect her tears.'

Gebrayel knew every detail about her.

'Do you really believe she was as beautiful as they say?'

My question was almost sacrilegious.

'Even more beautiful! The most beautiful of all women! A picture of grace, from her head to her heels. Long, delicate hands, such sleek black hair falling halfway down her back, huge maternal eyes and her affectionate voice. She scented herself with jasmine, like most of the village girls. But her jasmine was like no other.'

'Why was that?'

'Because Lamia's jasmine took on the scent of her skin.'

Gebrayel did not smile. His gaze was elsewhere.

'Her skin was rosy and so soft that all the men dreamed of stroking it, if only with the backs of their fingers. Her dress was open to the bottom of the crucifix, and even lower. Women at that time revealed their chests without the slightest suggestion of indecency, and Lamia allowed the whole surface of each breast to be seen. I would have liked to rest my head on those mounds every night . . .'

I cleared my throat.

'How can you know so many things? You never saw her!'

'If you don't want to believe me, why are you questioning me?'

My intrusion into his dream had irritated him. But he didn't hold it against me for long. He got to his feet and prepared a large glass of mulberry syrup for each of us.

'Drink it slowly,' he said. 'There is still a long story to tell.'

When the Sheikha's caravan set out, a little before dawn, the castle seemed to empty. Because a great number of guards and maidservants had accompanied the chatelaine, and also because it was right in the middle of the harvest season and nearly all the men and women of Kfaryabda were out in the fields. That morning, the Sheikh had only had three visitors, and none of them stayed to share his midday meal. He had a tray brought to him with the lightest of dishes, bread, olive oil with oregano, curds, drained of the whey. And as Gerios was fussing around in the corridors, the Master invited him to join him. Then he asked where Lamia was.

She had left her quarters only to wish the Sheikha a good journey, then she had returned to shut herself up in her room, as on the previous day. And when Gerios came to tell her the Sheikh had asked for her, she replied that she was not hungry. Her husband raised a threatening hand.

'Put on a shawl and follow me!'

The Sheikh, as always, appeared delighted to see her, and she took care not to seem surly. Soon the conversation became a dialogue between the two of them, Gerios simply letting his eyes roam from one to the other with a blank face, nodding his head non-stop in approval when the Sheikh was speaking; but as soon as Lamia opened her mouth, he began to bite his lower lip as if to tell her to cut it short. He never laughed spontaneously at her witticisms, he waited for the Sheikh to begin to laugh, keeping his gaze fixed exclusively on his Lord and Master as long as he was laughing.

Lamia echoed the Sheikh's humour. She had eyes only for him, occasionally looking down at the dish in which she dipped her bread. And the Master, in the course of their conversation, ventured not the slightest glance at Gerios. Only at the end, at the very end of the meal, did he turn to him suddenly, as if he had only just that minute noticed his presence.

'I nearly forgot the most important thing. You must go urgently to see Yaakoub the tailor. I promised to pay him a thousand piastres before this evening, and I must keep my word. And you must also tell him to come tomorrow morning early, I need him to make me some clothes for the cold season.'

Yaakoub lived in Dayroun, the neighbouring town, two hours' ride away.

Lamia immediately picked up the tray to take it back to the kitchens.

'I'll go and make the coffee.'

'*Khweja* Gerios will not have time for any coffee, he must leave immediately if he's to get back by nightfall.'

He called him that when he wanted to please him – *Khweja*, an old Turko-Persian word which, in the Mountains, was used to refer to people who had some education and wealth and no longer worked the land with their hands. The major-domo rose without more ado.

The Sheikh hesitated for a moment, then went on, 'I won't have coffee now either. I'll have it after the siesta, rather. But if our lovely Lamia could bring me a basket of fruit, such as only she knows how to arrange, I would be grateful to her to the end of my days.'

She did not expect such a request. She seemed embarrassed, troubled, not knowing what to reply. Her silence lasted only a fraction of a second, but it was too much for Gerios who, with a look at her that could kill, hurried to answer for her.

'Of course, our Sheikh! Immediately! Lamia, get a move on!'

While the Lord and Master quietly made his way to his bedchamber, Gerios hurried to the little room he used as an office. It was there that he kept his register, pens, inkwells, and also the large metal safe from which he had to take the money for the tailor. Lamia followed him.

'Stop, I must speak to you!'

'Later! You know I have to leave!'

'I'm going to prepare the basket of fruit for the Sheikh, but I'd prefer you to take it to him. I don't like to go into his bedroom, I wouldn't like him to ask me for anything else.'

'What else could he ask you for?'

'I don't know, he's so difficult to please, he'll want me to peel the fruit, cut it up . . .'

She stammered. Gerios had let go of the door of the safe, which he had opened, and turned to her.

'If you'd managed to keep to your station, as I've constantly begged you to do, the Sheikh would not have asked you for anything.'

And what about you? she might have said. Do you keep to your station? Couldn't he have sent any one of his servants to tell Yaakoub to come tomorrow morning? But she had no desire to start an argument. Her tone became imploring and contrite.

'I was wrong, I admit, and you were right. But let's forget the past . . .'

'Yes, let's forget the past, and in future see you remember your rank. But for today, our Master has made a request and you must obey him.'

Then Lamia grabbed her husband by his sleeves. Her eyes were filled with tears.

'You must understand me, I'm afraid of going into that room!'

Their eyes met for a long moment, a very long moment. Lamia was under the impression that her husband was hesitating, she noticed how he was torn, and for one second she imagined he was going to say, I understand your anxiety, and I know what I have to do! She so much wanted to rely on him at this time. She wanted to forget all the pettiness that she reproached him with, and only remember that he was her husband, that she had been given to him for life, and that she had sworn to obey him for better or for worse.

Gerios said nothing and Lamia remained silent, for fear of annoying him. He seemed undecided, hesitant. For a few seconds, but long seconds. Then he pushed her away. And then he moved off.

'You've already made me late enough. I shan't have time to get back before nightfall.'

He didn't look at her again. But she watched him leave. He stooped, and his back was one enormous black hump. Lamia had never seen him appear so squat.

She felt betrayed, abandoned. Deceived.

She took her time preparing the tray of fruit. With a bit of luck, when she got to the Sheikh's room, he would already be asleep.

As she passed along the last corridor, she felt a tingling, a sort of numbness spreading through her thighs. Was it fear? Was it desire? Or perhaps fear had given rise to desire?

Her hands were trembling now. She moved more slowly. If there were a Heaven to watch over God's creatures, It would see to it that she never reached that room.

The door was ajar, she pushed it gently with the edge of the basket and looked in. The man was lying on his mat, with his back to her. He was holding his amber worry-beads in his right hand. When he was not smoking his hookah, he would run his fingers over the beads; he used to say that their clicking brought him a feeling of serenity, like the trickle of water running over stones and the crackle of wood in the fire.

Lamia looked neither at the amber beads nor at the seal which the Master wore on his ring finger. She simply made sure his big masculine fingers were not moving. Then she was emboldened, took two steps into the room, bent down to put the basket on the floor. Just as she was straightening up something made her start. A pomegranate had slipped out and was rolling away with a dull sound, which to Lamia's ears echoed like a roll of drums. Holding her breath, she waited for the fruit to come to a standstill, a hair's breadth from the sleeper's hand. She waited another second before stooping down over the basket to pick up the rebellious pomegranate.

The Sheikh had moved. He had turned over. Slowly, drowsily. But, as he turned, he took hold of the pomegranate without looking at it, as if he sensed its presence.

'You took your time, I was nearly asleep.'

He looked towards the window as if to guess the time.

But the curtains were drawn and the sky was overcast. In the half-light of that autumn afternoon it could have been any time.

'What good things have you brought me?'

Lamia stood up with difficulty. In her voice a tremble of fear.

'Grapes, camel-figs,* medlars, some apples and that pomegranate.'

'And, in your opinion, of all the fruits you have brought me, which is the most delicious? The one that I can bite into with my eyes shut and have nothing but a taste of honey in my mouth?'

Outside, a thick cloud must have hidden the sun, for the room had become infinitely darker. It was early afternoon and it already seemed far into the night. The Sheikh rose, selected the plumpest grape from the finest bunch and brought it close to Lamia's face. She opened her lips.

Just as the grape slipped into her mouth, he whispered, 'I'd like to see you smile!'

She smiled. And so he shared with her all the September fruits.

---

*The local term for a particularly large, juicy fig.

Second Passage

The Summer of the Locusts

*In the year 1821, towards the end of the month of June, Lamia,
the wife of Gerios, the major-domo of the castle, gave birth to a son,
to whom the name of Abbas was first given, and then Tanios. Even
before he had opened his innocent eyes, he had drawn down on the
village a torrent of undeserved malevolence.*

It was he who was later nicknamed Kishk, *and whose fate is
known. His whole life was but one succession of passages.*

A Mountain Chronicle,
the work of the monk Elias of Kfaryabda

[Before picking up the thread of the story, I would like to
linger a moment on the quotation that forms the epigraph
to this chapter, and in particular on this enigmatic word,
oubour, which I have translated as 'passage'. Nowhere did
the monk Elias find it necessary to provide a definition for
this word: however it occurs constantly in his writing, and
by cross-checking I have managed to pinpoint its meaning.

The author of the *Chronicle* says, for example: 'Fate passes
back and forth across our path, just as the cobbler's needle
passes through the leather which he fashions.' And, elsewhere: 'Destiny, whose fearsome passages punctuate our
existence and fashion it . . .' So 'passage' is both a manifest
sign of fate – an intrusion which can be cruel, or ironic, or
providential – and also a milestone, a stage in an exceptional existence.

In this sense, the temptation of Lamia was, in the destiny
of Tanios, the preliminary 'passage'; the one from which all
the others were to stem.]

I

When Gerios returned from his errand, the night was well advanced. His wife was already lying on the couch in their bedchamber, and no word was spoken.

In the following weeks, Lamia experienced the first bouts of nausea. She had been married for more than two years, and her intimates, worried that her belly remained flat, were considering having recourse to saints and simples to exorcize the spell. The pregnancy was a source of joy to all, and the women rallied round the mother-to-be to express the fullness of their affection. You could have looked in vain for the slightest suspicious glance, the slightest malicious gossip. Only, when the Sheikha returned to the castle in March, after a prolonged stay with her family, Lamia had the feeling that their relationship had suddenly cooled. It is true that the Master's spouse behaved differently with everyone, was irascible and scornful towards the village-women, who began to avoid her; what is more, her features seemed fallen in, somewhat emaciated, and yet she was still as obese as ever.

The local people did not spare their ribald comments about her. From 'their' Sheikh, they were prepared to accept many a caprice, but as for this foreigner, this 'skinful of sour milk', this 'thorn-in-the-flesh, born from the moons of Jord', if Kfaryabda didn't suit her, she could just go back to where she came from!

Lamia, however, was not convinced that the chatelaine was angry with the whole village; somebody must have alerted the Sheikha about her, and she wondered what her mistress could have been told.

The child was born on a bright, balmy summer day. A light cloud modified the heat of the sun and the Sheikh had had carpets spread out on a roof terrace overlooking the valley, to lunch in the open air. With him were the priest, *Bouna* Boutros, two other village notables, together with Gerios; and at a little distance, seated on a stool, the Sheikha, with her *tantour* on her head and her son on her lap. With the help of the arak, everyone seemed in a good mood. No one was drunk, but merriment had enlivened actions and words. In her room, not far away, Lamia was groaning and pushing, encouraged by the midwife. Her sister – her big sister, the *Khouriyya*, the wife of the village priest – held her hand.

A little girl came running to the guests, prepared to announce the news they were waiting for; but their expressions must have intimidated her, for she blushed, hid her face, and simply whispered a word in Gerios's ear before running off. But the messenger's haste had given her away, everyone understood, and Lamia's husband, emerging for once from his reserve, announced loudly: '*Sabi!*'

A boy!

The goblets were filled to celebrate the event, then the Sheikh asked his major-domo, 'What are you going to call him?'

Gerios was about to mention the name he had in mind when he felt, from his Master's expression, that the latter had his idea also. So he thought it wiser to say, 'I haven't decided yet. As long as he wasn't born . . .'

He accompanied this white lie with a characteristic grimace, meaning that, out of superstition, he had not dared choose a name in advance, since this would presume it was going to be a boy, and that he would be born alive, as if one took for granted what had not yet been vouchsafed, a presumption which Heaven scarcely appreciated.

'Well,' said the Sheikh, 'for my part, there's a name that's always been a favourite of mine, and that's Abbas.'

As soon as the Master's first words were out of his mouth, Gerios had, out of habit, begun to nod his head in agreement, and when the name was proposed, his decision was already taken.

'Then it shall be Abbas! And later the boy will be told it was our Sheikh in person who chose his name!'

Letting his delighted gaze roam over the people present to receive the customary approval, Gerios noticed that the priest was frowning and that the Sheikha had suddenly begun to clutch her child tightly to her, in an inexplicable rage. She was ashen white, you could have slashed her face and hands without a drop of blood being shed.

Gerios's eyes lingered on her for a moment. And suddenly he understood. How the devil could he have accepted that name? And above all, however could the Sheikh have suggested it? Joy and arak must have fuddled the minds of both of them.

The scene had lasted only a few seconds, but for the child, for his family, for the whole village, it had upset the applecart. 'That day,' wrote the author of the *Mountain Chronicle,* 'the fate of everyone was inscribed and sealed; like a parchment that it only remained to unroll.'

So much lamenting because of a blunder committed by the Sheikh, and in any case repaired immediately?

It must be said that, for generations in Kfaryabda, there had been precise customs regarding forenames. The villagers, 'the folk from the valley', as they were known, gave their sons the names of saints: Boutros, Boulos, Gerios, Roukoz, Hanna, Frem or Wakim to honour Saints Peter, Paul, George, Roch, John, Ephraim or Joachim; and sometimes biblical names too, such as Ayyoub, Moussa and Toubiyya, for Job, Moses and Tobias.

In the Sheikh's family – 'the folk up above on the hill' – there were other customs. The boys had to have names suggesting power or past glory. Like Sakhr, Raad, Hosn, which mean 'rock', 'thunder', 'fortress'. And also certain names from the history of Islam; the Sheikh's family had been Christians for centuries, which had never prevented them from claiming Abbas, the Prophet's uncle, as one of their ancestors, as well as a good dozen Caliphs; moreover, on the wall in the Hall of Pillars, just behind the Sheikh's usual seat, was a high, wide panel on which was traced a genealogical tree which would have caused many a crowned head to pale with envy, including that of the Sultan of Istanbul, whose origins did not go back to the noble Meccan family, but were lost, Caliph that he was, in the steppes of Eastern Asia.

The Sheikh had named his son Raad, after his own father. As for himself – this is not going to be easy to explain, but that's how it was – he was called Francis. Yes, Sheikh Francis. A Christian name which clearly belonged neither to the warrior's panoply, nor to the Prophet's family, but which strongly resembled the saints' names current among the villagers. But that was only how it appeared. The name did not refer specially to the saints of the Christian calendar, neither Saint Francis of Sales nor Saint Francis of Assisi, except insofar as Francis the First had been named in honour of the latter. There had been a 'Sheikh Francis' in every generation since the sixteenth century, since the day Süleyman the Magnificent had granted the King of France the right to keep an eye on the fate of the Christian minorities in the Levant, as well as the Holy Sites, and the French king had written to the chiefs of the great families in the Mountains assuring them of his protection. Amongst these recipients was one of our Sheikh's ancestors. He is said to have received the message the day his first child was born. The child was immediately christened Francis.

If the explanations I have just given seem necessary today, the villagers at that time would not have needed them. Not a single one would have deemed it insignificant that the Sheikh could give Lamia's child the most distinguished name of his own lineage. Gerios already thought he could hear the huge snigger that would shake Kfaryabda! Wherever could he hide his shame? As he rose from the table to go to see the child, he did not look in the least like a proud and happy father; his moustache seemed to droop, and he could scarcely walk straight as he made his way to the room where Lamia was dozing.

There were a good dozen women of all ages fussing around. Not seeing in his dazed appearance anything other than overwhelming joy, they pushed him towards the cradle where the infant was sleeping, his head already covered with a linen bonnet.

'He looks healthy,' they murmured. 'May God permit him to live!'

Only the priest's wife noticed the man's expression.

'You look upset; could it be because your family is growing?'

He neither moved nor spoke.

'What are you thinking of calling him?'

Gerios would have liked to hide his discomfort, but he had to speak to her, the *Khouriyya*. Because of the influence she alone had over all the inhabitants of the village, including the Sheikh. Her name was Saada – but no one called her that, not even her husband – and in her day she had been the most beautiful girl in Kfaryabda, just as her sister Lamia was to be ten years later. And if her eight or nine pregnancies had since deprived her of her slender figure and her bloom, her charm, far from deserting her, had in some way risen completely to the surface of her eyes, which were mischievous and authoritative.

'We were at lunch, and ... the Sheikh suggested we should call him Abbas.'

Gerios tried hard to control his emotion, but the end of the sentence slipped from his lips like a groan. The *Khouriyya* took care not to start. She even managed to seem amused.

'That's just like your Sheikh, he's a man who never hesitates to give way to the impulses of his great heart. He appreciates your collaboration, your devotion, your honesty, he thinks of you now as a brother, and he wants to honour you by giving your son one of his family's names. But in the village, people won't take the matter in the same way.'

Gerios opened his lips to ask how people would react, but no sound came, and the priest's wife went on, 'They will whisper: "This Gerios turns his back on us, because he lives 'up at the top of the hill', he doesn't want to give his son a name like ours." They will hold it against you and your wife as well, and their tongues will wag. They are already jealous of your situation . . .'

'Perhaps you are right, *Khouriyya*. Only I've already told the Sheikh I was honoured by his gesture . . .'

'You must go and see him and tell him Lamia had secretly made a vow. What would you like to call the child?'

'Tanios.'

'Perfect. You will say his mother had promised to give him *mar* Tanios's name, if the saint caused him to be born healthy.'

'You're right. That's what I must tell him. I'll speak to him tomorrow, as soon as we're alone.'

'Tomorrow it will be too late. You must go to him immediately, otherwise the Sheikh will start trumpeting Abbas to right and to left, and he won't want to back down.'

Gerios went off, sickened at the idea of having, for the first time in his life, to thwart his Master's wish. He strove to prepare in his head a long, detailed explanation, full of eternal gratitude and humble apologies. He did not need to use them. The matter was simpler than he foresaw.

'A vow is sacred,' said the Sheikh, after the first words. 'Say no more. Tanios it shall be!'

The Lord and Master of the village had, for his part, also had time to reflect. Especially when the Sheikha had risen to her feet, snatched up her son so abruptly that the child had begun to howl, and then had withdrawn without a word to the guests.

She took refuge in her room, or, to be exact, on the

balcony of her room, where she spent the rest of the day pacing up and down, muttering violent curses. Never had she felt so humiliated. She who had spent her life pampered in one of the grandest houses in the Mountains, what the devil was she doing with this skirt-chaser? She was angry with everyone, even with the Patriarch, her confessor. Was he not the one who had had the idea of this marriage?

She swore to leave this accursed castle the very next day, before dawn, and if anyone tried to stop her she'd send a message to her father and brothers who would come to deliver her, fully armed, with all their men, who'd lay waste the Sheikh's domain! Up till then she had always seemed resigned, she had accepted everything in silence. But this time it was no longer a question of tumbling one of the village girls, this was different: this man had fathered a child to a woman who was living under their roof, and, not satisfied with that, he wanted to acknowledge it openly, he wanted to give the child the name of his illustrious ancestor, so that no one would have the slightest doubt about its paternity!

No matter how she tried to explain it, no matter what excuses she sought in an attempt to appear once more conciliatory and submissive, no, this was more than she could bear. Even the humblest peasant-woman would have tried to avenge herself if she had been made to suffer such an affront, and she, the daughter of a powerful lord, should she let herself be trodden on?

Then, grabbing the tall *tantour* in both hands, she snatched it off and threw it on the ground. Her hair fell down in dark locks. And her fat, childish face lit up with a smile of victory through her tears.

In the kitchens of the castle the village-women, their hands deep in cinnamon and caraway, were lightheartedly preparing the *meghli* in honour of the newborn son.

II

The day after Tanios's birth, the Sheikh left early to shoot partridge, accompanied by Gerios and a few other Kfary-abda notables. On his return, in the early afternoon, a serving-woman came to announce loudly, in front of the whole household gathered to receive him, that the Sheikha had left suddenly for the Great Jord, taking their child with her, and she had been heard to mutter that she'd be in no hurry to return.

Few people were unaware that the Sheikha's prolonged absences suited her husband admirably; if she had told him of her intention to leave, he would not have tried to stop her. But to let the matter be announced publicly like that, and be taken for an abandoned husband, that he could not tolerate! He'd bring her back to the castle, even if he had to drag her by the hair!

Saddling his best mount, a chestnut mare which he called Bsat-er-rih, 'Flying carpet', accompanied by two of his body-guard, excellent horsemen, he set out without even washing his face, lay down in the open country, more to rest the animals than himself, so much did his fury keep him awake, and reached his father-in-law's home before the horses of his wife's carriage had even been unsaddled.

She had retired sobbing to the room she had occupied as a girl, where her father and mother followed her. The Sheikh soon joined them. He made the first move.

'I have come to say one word only: My wife is the daughter of a powerful man, whom I respect as much as my own father. But she has become my wife, and even if she were

44

the daughter of the Sultan, I could not agree to her leaving my home without my permission!'

'And I,' said the father-in-law, 'I too have only one word to say: I gave my daughter to the descendant of a distinguished family, for him to treat her honourably, not for me to see her returning to my home in tears!'

'Has she ever asked for a single thing without getting it? Has she not as many servants as she wishes, and dozens of village-women who at the slightest word from her hasten to attend to her every need? Let her say it, let her speak, since she is in her father's house!'

'It may well be that you have deprived her of nothing, but you have humiliated her. You see, I did not marry my daughter to keep her from want. I married her to the son of a great family so that she should be as respected in her husband's home as she was in this one.'

'Could we speak man to man?'

The father-in-law indicated to his wife that she should take their daughter into the adjacent room. He waited till they had shut the door and then added, 'We'd been warned that you didn't leave a single woman in peace in your village, but we hoped that marriage would make you begin to see reason. There are unfortunately some men who don't settle down till they're dead. If that's the only cure, we have thousands of doctors in this region who can administer it.'

'You threaten me with death in your own house? Well then, go ahead. Kill me! I have come here alone, unarmed, and your supporters are everywhere. You have only to call them.'

'I do not threaten you. I want only to know what language you understand.'

'I speak the same language as you. I have done nothing you have not done. I have already walked through your village, and through the vast domain you own, where half the children look like you and the other half resemble your brothers and your sons! I have in my village the same reputation that you have in yours. Our fathers and grandfathers had the same in their time. You are not going to point a finger at me as if I had committed the unthinkable, simply because your daughter has returned in tears. Did your wife ever leave this house because you bedded the village-women?'

The argument must have carried, as the Master of the Great Jord remained thoughtful for a long moment, as if he could not make up his mind what attitude to adopt.

When he finally spoke, it was a little more slowly and slightly more softly.

'We all have things to reproach ourselves with. I am not Saint Maroun and you are not Simon the Stylite. But I, for my part, have never abandoned my wife and become infatuated with my local constable's wife, neither have I ever got another woman pregnant under my own roof. And if a woman had a son by me, I'd never have thought of giving him the name of my most distinguished ancestor.'

'That child is not mine!'

'Everyone seems to think so.'

'What everyone thinks is of no importance! I know. When all is said and done, I can't have slept with this woman without knowing it!'

The father-in-law paused again, as if to sum up the situation once more, then he opened the door and called his daughter.

'Your husband assures me that there has been nothing between this woman and himself. And if he says so, we must believe him.'

The Sheikha's mother, who was just as obese, and dressed all in black like certain nuns, intervened for the first time.

'I want that woman to leave, with her child!'

But the Sheikh of Kfaryabda replied, 'If this child were my son, I would be a monster to drive him out of my house. And if he is not my son, what do they reproach me with? What do they reproach this woman with? What do they reproach her husband and their child with? For what crime would people wish to punish them?'

'I shall not return to the castle till that woman has gone,' the Sheikha said with great assurance, as if the matter did not brook any discussion.

The Sheikh was about to reply when his host forestalled him.

'When your father and husband are deliberating, you keep quiet!'

His daughter and wife gazed at him in horror. But without paying·them the slightest attention, he had already turned to his son-in-law and put his arms around his shoulders.

'Your wife will have returned to your home in a week, and if she's obstinate, I shall bring her back myself! But we've chatted long enough. Come, my visitors will think we are quarrelling! And you women, instead of standing there like crows, staring at us, go to the kitchens and see if dinner is ready! What will our son-in-law think if we leave him to starve after this long journey? Send for the girl from Sarkis to sing us an *ataba*! And get them to bring the hookahs with the new tobacco from Persia! You'll see, Sheikh, you'd think you were smoking honey!'

When the Master returned, the whole village was agog with rumours about his wife's departure, about his own precipitate departure, and naturally about Lamia, her son, and the name which had nearly been given him. But the Sheikh scarely paid any attention, he was worried about something else. His father-in-law. This person, so feared throughout the Mountains, by what miracle had he been won over when, only a moment before, he had been threatening him with death? He could not believe that his arguments had convinced him; men like him do not seek to convince or be convinced, everything for them is an exchange of blows, and if he did not immediately give as good as he got there was reason to be anxious.

To the many villagers who came to express their good wishes on his safe return, the Sheikh replied by brief, empty formulas, and mentioned his wife and father-in-law only in the most discreet terms.

He had been back only a few hours when the *Khouriyya* was seen to make her appearance in the Hall of Pillars. She was carrying something covered with a mauve silk veil, and when she was some distance from the Master, she said in a loud voice, 'I have something to ask our Sheikh, in private.'

All those present rose simultaneously to leave. Only the *Khouriyya* could thus empty the castle reception hall without the Master thinking to say a word. He was amused even, and retorted to the intruder, 'What do you want to ask me this time?'

Which had the result of giving rise to a cascade of laughter among the men as they dispersed, continuing outside.

For they all knew what had happened the last time.

It was more than twelve years ago, when this plump woman was a young girl, and the Sheikh had been surprised to see her arrive at his home without her parents, and demand to see him without witnesses.

'I have a favour to ask,' she had said, 'and I shall not be able to give anything in return.'

Her request was not simple: she had been promised to her cousin Boutros, the son of the old priest at that time, but the young man had left to study at the monastery, to prepare to take over from his father, and had been noticed by an Italian priest who had persuaded him to pronounce his vows without marrying, as in Europe, explaining that no sacrifice was more pleasing to Heaven than celibacy. He had even promised him that, if he abstained from taking a wife, he would be sent to the great seminary in Rome, and on his return he might well become a bishop.

'To give up a pretty girl like you, to become a bishop, this Boutros must be out of his mind,' said the Sheikh, without smiling.

'That's what I think too,' the girl agreed, with scarcely a blush.

'But what do you want me to do?'

'Our Sheikh will find some way of talking to him. I know Boutros is coming up to the castle tomorrow with his father . . .'

The old priest turned up in fact, leaning on his son's arm, and undertook to explain proudly to the Sheikh that the boy had been so brilliant in his studies that his superiors had noticed him, and an Italian visitor had even promised to take him to 'Roumieh', to the Pope's own city, no less.

'Tomorrow,' he concluded, 'our village will have a much more deserving priest than your humble servant.'

The old man expected his Master to react with a beaming face and some words of encouragement. He simply received black looks. Followed by a clearly embarrassed silence. And then these words: 'When you have left us, *Bouna*, after a long life, we shall have no more need of a village priest.'

'How is that?'

'The matter has been agreed upon for a long time. I and my whole family, and all the tenant farmers, have all decided to become Muslims.'

The Sheikh and the four or five villagers who were with him at that moment exchanged a furtive glance, and then began to nod their heads sadly in unison.

'We do not want to do this as long as you are alive, so as not to break your heart, but as soon as you are no longer with us the church will be transformed into a mosque, and we shall have no more need of a priest.'

The young seminarist was thunderstruck, the whole world seemed to collapse around him. But the old priest did not appear unduly perturbed. He knew 'his' Sheikh.

'What is wrong, Sheikh Francis?'

'Everything is wrong, *Bouna*! Every time one of us goes to Tripoli, Beirut, Aleppo, he has to put up with vexations; he's reproached for wearing this colour instead of that, walking on the right instead of on the left. Haven't we suffered enough?'

'To suffer for one's Faith is pleasing to the Lord,' said the seminarist excitedly. 'One must be ready for every sacrifice, even for martyrdom!'

'How can you expect us to die for the Pope's religion, when Rome does not even respect us?'

'In what way?'

'They have no respect for our traditions. One day, you'll see, they'll end up sending us celibate priests who'll lust after our women, not one of whom will dare go to confession, and our sins will heap up on our heads.'

The seminarist was only just beginning to understand the real object of the discussion. He thought fit to expose his arguments.

'In France, all priests are celibate, and they are good Christians!'

'France is France, here is here! We have always had married priests, and we have always given them the prettiest girl in the village, so that their eyes would be satisfied and they would not covet other men's wives.'

'There are men who can resist temptation.'

'They resist better if their wives are at their sides!'

The visitors nodded their heads even more vigorously, all the more since they were now reassured about their Sheikh's real intentions, knowing that his ancestors had become Christians only to conform to the Faith of their subjects.

'Listen, my son,' the Master went on, 'I will now speak plainly to you, but I shall not go back on anything I say. If you are seeking to become a holy man, your father, married man as he is, has more holiness in him than the whole city of Rome; if you seek to serve the village and its faithful, you have only to follow his example. If, on the other hand, your aim is to become a bishop, if your ambition is greater than the village, then you can leave, for Rome, for Istanbul, or anywhere else. But know that, as long as I am not dead and buried, you will never set foot in these Mountains again.'

Thinking that the discussion had gone too far, the old priest wished to find a loop-hole.

'What does our Sheikh desire? If we came to see him, it was in fact to ask his advice.'

'What is the use of lavishing advice when no one wants to listen?'

'Speak, Sheik, we will do as you wish.'

All eyes were turned towards Boutros. Who, under so much pressure, had to nod in assent. Then the Sheikh beckoned to one of his guards and whispered three words in his ear. The man was absent for a few minutes, to return accompanied by young Saada and her parents.

The future priest left the castle that day, duly betrothed, with his father's blessing. There was no more question of his continuing his studies in Rome, no question of his becoming a bishop. For this, for some time, he bore a grudge against the Sheikh. But as soon as he began his life with the *Khouriyya*, he vowed infinite gratitude to his benefactor.

This was the episode to which the Sheikh alluded when the priest's wife arrived to see him that day. And when they were alone, he continued, 'The last time, you wanted *Bouna* Boutros's hand, and I gave it to you. What do you want this time?'

'This time I want your hand, Sheikh!'

Before he could get over his astonishment, she had grasped his hand, then removed the veil which covered the object she was carrying. It was a copy of the Gospels. She placed the Sheikh's hand upon it as if she had every right. If it had been any other person, he would have rebelled, but with her he let himself be guided obediently. This woman's self-assurance had always inspired him with amused admiration.

'Consider yourself in the confessional, Sheikh!'

'Since when does one confess to a woman?'

'Since today.'

'Because women have learned to keep a secret?'

'What you say will not leave these four walls. And if I, outside these premises, am obliged to lie to protect my sister, I shall lie. But I want you to tell me the truth.'

It seems that the Sheikh kept silent for a long time. Before, feigning fatigue, he came out with, 'That child is not mine, if that is what you want to know.'

Perhaps he was going to add something else, but she did not give him the chance and said no further word herself. She replaced the silken veil over the Gospels and carried the basket away.

Could the Sheikh have lied, with his hand on the Holy Scriptures? I do not think so. On the other hand, we have no way of confirming that the *Khouriyya* reported his words faithfully. She had promised to tell the village-folk only what she deemed necessary to tell them.

Did they believe her? Perhaps not. But not one of them would have wished to doubt her word.

Because of the 'locusts' . . .

III

When the Sheikha returned to Kfaryabda in the first week of August she was accompanied by her father and her five brothers, as well as sixty horsemen and three hundred men on foot, together with grooms, ladies-in-waiting, men and women servants – in all nearly six hundred people.

The castle guards wanted to scatter through the domain to summon the villagers to arms, but the Sheikh told them to calm down, to put a good face on it; it was only a visit, in spite of appearances. He himself went to the top of the front steps to receive his father-in-law worthily.

'I have come with my daughter, as I promised. These few cousins insisted on accompanying me. I told them that on the Sheikh's lands they would always find a shady corner to lay their heads, and two olives to assuage their hunger.'

'You are at home, among your own people!'

The Lord of the Great Jord then turned to his followers.

'You heard, you are at home here. In this I recognize the generosity of our son-in-law!'

Words greeted by cheers that were too joyous not to be disquieting.

The first day there was a banquet of welcome, as custom demands. On the second day everyone had to be fed again, and also the third day, the fourth, the fifth ... The provisions for the new year had not yet been got in, and with a feast everyday, sometimes two, the stocks of food in the castle were soon exhausted. Not a single drop of oil, wine or arak remained, no flour, no coffee or sugar, no conserve of lamb. The harvest bade fair to be poor that year, and at the sight of the beasts being slaughtered every day – calves, goats for the ground meat, sheep by the dozen, and whole poultry yards – the folk of my village felt famine was upon them.

Why did they not react? It was certainly not for want of the wish to do so, nor was it the alleged 'untouchability of guests' which restrained them – oh, no, they would willingly have roasted them all on the spit, down to the very last one, with an easy conscience, from the moment when they had knowingly infringed the laws of hospitality. But the event was too unusual to be measured by the conventional yardstick. For it was – let us not forget – a family quarrel. Grotesque, disproportionate, but a family quarrel just the same. The Lord of the Great Jord had come to teach a son-in-law who had offended him a harsh lesson in his own manner, and no one could have expressed that better than the Sheikha, when she had retorted to a village-woman, who was complaining about what was happening, 'Go and tell your master that if he hasn't got the means to entertain a great lady's retinue, he'd have done better to marry one of his peasants!' For this is what these 'visitors' had in mind: they had not come to massacre the population, to set fire to the village, to sack the castle. They were simply attempting to exhaust their host's resources.

Moreover, their heroes were not their most valiant warriors, but their finest trenchermen. At every banquet, the latter were assembled in the midst of the troops, who encouraged them with their acclamations and laughter, and they vied with each other to see who could swallow the most hard-boiled eggs, who could quaff a whole bowl of golden wine, or consume an entire dish of *kebbe*, a dish as wide as a man's outstretched arms. Getting their revenge through a good blow-out, so to speak.

And what if they were to take advantage of one of the banquets, when wine was flowing freely, to fly at the visitors' throats? They adored warlike exploits in Kfaryabda, and more than one warrior came to whisper in the Sheikh's ear that he need only say the word, he need only make one sign . . . 'We wouldn't massacre them, oh no! We'd simply knock them senseless, strip off their clothes and tie them naked to trees, or hang them up by their feet till they brought everything up.'

But the Sheikh invariably replied, 'I'll disembowel with my own hands the first one of you who unsheathes his weapon. What you feel, I feel too; what hurts you, hurts me; what you wish to do, I wish even more to do. I know you can fight, but I don't want slaughter, I don't want to start an endless vendetta with my father-in-law who has twenty times more men at his disposal than I have. I don't want this village to be full of widows, generation after generation, because one day we lacked patience with these unspeakable folk. Let us trust in God, he will make them pay!'

Some young men left the castle, grumbling. Usually it was the priest who called on God and the Sheikh who led the troops into battle . . . But most of them agreed with the Master and no one, in any case, wanted to take the initiative and be the first to shed blood.

So they fell back on another form of revenge, that of people without arms; the village began to hum with cruel anecdotes about the man who, by a slight twist of a word, began to be called, not the Lord of the Jord – which means 'the arid heights' – but the Lord of the *Jrad* – which means 'locusts'. There were many jokes at that time, consisting of popular verses like the following:

> *I am asked why I lament on my fate,*
> *As if I had never before suffered from locusts!*
> *It is true they invaded my field last year*
> *But the locusts last year did not devour my sheep.*

At every evening gathering reciters would launch their barbed verses against the people of the Great Jord, mocking their accents, their attire, ridiculing their country and their chief, casting doubts on their virility, reducing all their past and future feats of arms to those of the packs of gluttons, who had made a permanent impression on everyone's imagination. But their favorite victim was the Sheikha, whom they depicted in the lewdest of postures, without worrying that children were present. And they laughed till they forgot their troubles.

On the other hand, no one dared to make the slightest joke, cast the slightest aspersion on Lamia, utter the slightest offensive observation on her husband, or the doubtful paternity of her son. There is no doubt that, if all these events had not taken place – if the Sheikha had not sought to have her revenge, if she had simply left with some provocative remark – whispering and sly glances would have made life intolerable for Gerios and his family and have forced them into exile. But by thus declaring war on the whole village, by going to such lengths to impoverish, starve and humiliate them, the Lord of the Great Jord had achieved the opposite result. Henceforth, to cast doubts on Lamia's virtue and the paternity of her son was to recognize the validity of the arguments of the 'locusts', it was to justify their extortions, and anyone who adopted such an attitude would have appeared as an enemy of the village and its inhabitants, he would have no more place among them.

Even Gerios who, after the episode of the boy's name, had felt himself becoming the village laughing-stock, now found people rallying round him, embracing him warmly as if to congratulate him. Congratulate him on what? Apparently on the birth of a son, but the truth was different, and if no one was capable of explaining it, they all understood it in their hearts: the villagers had set up this crime for which they were being punished, out of bravado, as an act of defiance, for which each of the protagonists was henceforth absolved and must be defended, be he the imprudent lover, unfaithful wife or cuckolded husband.

Speaking of the latter, it has to be said that, as soon as the 'locusts' arrived, and until they left, Gerios had wisely

left the castle with his wife and the six-week-old infant, to
take up temporary residence with the priest, his brother-in-
law, in a room adjacent to the church. There, an endless
procession of attentive visitors arrived – more than they had
received in two years in their quarters 'up on the hill' – in
particular mothers who insisted on suckling the babe, even
if only once, to give physical expression to their support.

Many people must have wondered if this excessive good
will would last when the 'locusts' were no longer there to
nurture it.

'For their ill-fated swarm,' states the *Chronicle*, 'was eventually to fly away, to the arid heights of the Great Jord.'

On the eve of this blessed day, there had been rumours,
but the villagers had not believed them; for six painful
weeks rumours had been circulating daily, only to be refuted
by nightfall. Frequently, moreover, they emanated from the
castle, and from the lips of the Sheikh himself, whom no
one, however, blamed for these lies. 'Is it not said that in
dark times one lives from false dawn to false dawn, just as
when, in the mountains, in Spring, one finds oneself in the
middle of a stream, and must leap towards the bank from
one slippery stone to another?'

This time, however, the Sheikh was under the impression
that his 'guests' were really about to depart. More or less a
prisoner in his own castle, he had nevertheless made an
effort to keep up appearances, and every morning he
invited his father-in-law to join him for coffee on the *liwan*,
the inner balcony overlooking the valley, the only place
where it was possible to see anything except the dozens
of tents pitched chaotically by the visitors and which had
transformed the approaches to the castle into a veritable
nomad camp.

For some moments, father-in-law and son-in-law had been
exchanging barbs dipped in honey, when the Sheikha came
to tell her father that she was missing her son, who had

been left behind with his grandmother during this 'visit', and would like to see him again. The 'Lord of the Locusts' pretended to be frankly indignant.

'What! You ask my permission to leave when your husband is present?'

The said husband then had the feeling that the business had finally been completed, that the punishment visit was nearly over. He was both pleased and worried. He was afraid in fact that, just as they were about to depart, by way of a last straw, and to leave a souvenir behind, the horde would indulge in an orgy of looting and burning. Many people in the village had the same fear, so much so that they did not dare wish for the fateful day of the departure, preferring to see the weeks of peaceful pillaging prolonged.

In the event their fears were not realized. Contrary to all expectations, the locusts retreated in good order, or nearly; it was the end of September, and on their way out they 'visited' vineyards and orchards and stripped them clean – but no one had thought that could be avoided. On the other hand, there was no death to be mourned, no destruction. They too had no wish to trigger off a *thar*, a cycle of revenge; they simply wished to inflict a costly humiliation on the son-in-law, and this had been done. The Sheikh and his father-in-law even exchanged embraces on the steps of the castle, as on the arrival, in the midst of the same mocking cheers.

The last words heard from the Sheikha's lips were, 'I shall be back at the end of the winter.' Without making clear whether she would be escorted as lavishly.

That winter there was famine throughout the whole region, and our village suffered more harshly than others. The lower the stocks of provisions grew, the more they cursed the 'locusts'; if those people ever took it upon themselves to return, no one, not even the Sheikh, would have been able to prevent a massacre.

For years they waited for them, keeping watch on all the roads and on the mountain-tops; plans were drawn up to exterminate them, and, if some people feared their return, many others hoped for it resolutely, unable to console themselves for having been so patient the first time.

They did not return. Perhaps they had never intended to do so. But perhaps it was because of the illness that attacked the Sheikha, said to be consumption, which was naturally seen by the people of my village as a just punishment. Visitors returning from the Great Jord, and who had caught a glimpse of her in her father's home, reported that she had grown weak, emaciated, was aged, unrecognizable, and that she was clearly fading away . . .

Gradually, as the danger retreated, those who had always had their doubts about the birth of Tanios, and who deemed that the amorous adventure had cost too dear, ventured to raise their voices.

At first, Lamia's son caught no echo of this, no one would have wanted to mention it in his presence. Although he had grown up, like all the villagers of his generation, haunted by the 'locusts', he could not have suspected that it was his birth that had brought down this catastrophe upon his people. His childhood was happy, peaceful, he was greedy, merry and wayward and even became something of a village mascot, and in all innocence he made the most of it.

As the years went by, it sometimes chanced that an ignorant or ill-disposed visitor, seeing this handsome child, dressed in new clothes, playing freely in the castle corridors, would ask him if he were the Sheikh's son. And Tanios would reply, laughing, 'No, I'm Gerios's son.' Without hesitating and without thinking anything wrong.

He seems never to have had the slightest suspicion concerning his birth until that most cursed day when someone yelled three times in his face, 'Tanios-*kishk*! Tanios-*kishk*! Tanios-*kishk*!'

Third Passage

Destiny from the Lips of a Fool

The words of a wise man flow clearly. But at all times men have preferred to drink the waters which gush forth from the darkest caves.

Nader,
Wisdom on Muleback

I

I can pinpoint the exact spot where Lamia's child was standing when this incident occurred. The place has changed very little. The main square has the same aspect and the same name, '*Blata*', which means 'Slab'. People arrange to meet, not 'in the square', but 'on the Slab'. Today, just as in former times. Nearby is the parish school, which has been in use for three centuries, a fact about which no one thinks of boasting, however, because the oak tree in the courtyard will soon be in its six-hundredth year and the church can pride itself on being twice that age, at least as far as its oldest stones are concerned.

Just behind the school, the priest's house. His name is *Bouna* Boutros, the same as the one who lived in Tanios's day; I would have liked to be able to say that he is one of his descendants, but the fact that they are namesakes is pure coincidence; the two men are in no way related, except insofar as all the village-folk are cousins as soon as one climbs four rungs up the ladder of ancestry.

The urchins of Kfaryabda still play in front of the church and under the tree. In those days they used to wear a sort of overall, the *koumbaz*, as well as a cap; you had to be completely impoverished or out of your mind, or at the very least quite eccentric, to go out *ksheif* – bare-headed – a word which sounded like a reprimand.

At the far end of the square, there is a spring which runs from deep inside the hill, through a cave; it is the same hill whose summit was formerly crowned by the castle. Even today, you feel you must linger to admire the ruins; in former times the sight must have been quite overwhelming.

I recently saw an engraving done in the last century, the work of an English traveller, which a local artist had coloured; at that time the side of the castle which overlooked the village was one unbroken façade, you'd have thought it a cliff face built by man, from the stone known as Kfaryabda stone, hard and white with purplish lights.

The people had countless names for the Lord's dwelling. They would say they were going 'to the harem', 'up the hill', 'to the house up there', or even 'to the needle' – for a reason which I was to discover only later – but mostly they would be going 'to the castle', or simply 'up the hill'. Very uneven steps led up from the *Blata*; that was the way the villagers took when they went 'to see the Sheikh's hand'.

Over the entrance to the cave was an arch adorned with Greek inscriptions, an impressive shrine for a precious, venerable spring, for it was around this that the village was constructed. Its water, ice-cold in every season, flows for the last cubits over the surface of a rock which is hollowed out like a funnel, then runs through a wide crenellated mouth into a small basin; from there it irrigates a few surrounding fields. The village youngsters have always used this spot to play at a test of endurance: the game consisted of seeing who could keep his hand the longest under the icy shower of water.

I have tried it more than once. Any child of Kfaryabda can hold out for fifteen seconds; after thirty a dull ache spreads from the hand along the arm up to the shoulder and a sort of general numbness overwhelms you; after a minute the arm feels amputated, severed, you risk losing consciousness at any moment; you have to be a hero or suicidal to persist any longer.

In Tanios's time, they liked to arrange competitions. Two boys would put their hands under the water simultaneously and the one who pulled out first lost and had to hop all round the square. All the village idlers who happened to be in the only coffee-house, watching a game of *tawle*, or lingering in the neighbourhood of the 'Slab', would wait for this time-honoured attraction, clapping, urging on the hopping and jeering at the same time.

On that particular day Tanios had challenged one of the priest's sons. When they came out of school, they had made their way together to the duelling spot, followed by a crowd of schoolmates. Followed also by Shallita, the village idiot, an old, retarded, skeletal individual, long-legged, barefoot, bareheaded, who stumbled when he walked. He was always hanging around the children, harmless but sometimes irritating, laughing when they laughed without even knowing why, seeming to enjoy their games even more than they did, listening to their conversations without anyone bothering about his presence.

When they reached the spring, the two youngsters took up their positions, lying on the ground one on each side of the basin, with raised hand, ready to start their test of endurance as soon as the signal was given. At that moment, Shallita, who was standing right behind Tanios, took it into his head to push him into the water. The lad lost his balance, toppled over, felt himself falling into the basin, but hands reached out to fish him out in time. He stood up, wet through, picked up a bowl which happened to be lying there, filled it with water, grabbed the wretch by his rags and was about to empty the basin over his head, when Shallita, who up till then had been laughing at the joke, began to yell incoherently. And when Tanios let him go, hurling him violently to the ground, he was heard to shout, in a voice suddenly intelligible, 'Tanios-*kishk*! Tanios-*kishk*! Tanios-*kishk*!' while banging his right palm with his left fist as a sign of revenge.

Revenge, it certainly was. Which could be read very clearly in the eyes of all those standing round Tanios, even more than in his own. Some of the urchins had begun to laugh, but immediately thought better of it when they noticed the general consternation. Lamia's son took a little time to understand the name he had just been called. The elements of the terrible charade fitted together in his mind only slowly, one after the other.

The word *kishk* was never meant to be used as a nickname; it refers to a sort of thick, bitter soup whose basic ingredients are curdled milk and corn. It is one of the oldest and greatest culinary achievements still extant and is still prepared in Kfaryabda in the same way as a hundred years, a thousand years, seven thousand years ago. The monk Elias refers to it at length in his *Chronicle*, in the chapter on local customs, detailing the way in which the corn is first ground, then left for several days in huge earthenware pans to 'drink up' the milk. 'In this manner a paste is obtained, called green *kishk*, that the children adore, and which is spread on a tanned sheepskin and left to dry on the terraces; then the women crumble it in their hands before sieving it to obtain a whitish powder which is kept in linen sacks throughout the winter . . .' Then a few ladlefuls only have to be mixed with boiling water to make the soup.

The taste may seem strange to the uninitiated, but to a child of the Mountains, no food is better to help withstand the rigours of winter. The *kishk* has long been the normal fare for a village meal.

As far as the Sheikh was concerned, he had without doubt the means of eating other things than this poor man's nourishment, but from preference, and perhaps also out of political acumen, he made a veritable cult of *kishk*, proclaiming ceaselessly that it was the king of foods and comparing in front of his guests the different ways of preparing it. It vied with moustaches as his favourite subject of conversation.

The first thing Tanios remembered, on hearing Shallita calling him by that name, was a banquet which had taken place two weeks previously, in the course of which the Sheikh had announced to all and sundry that no woman in the whole village could make *kishk* as perfectly as Lamia; she herself was not present at the banquet, but her son was, as well as Gerios, to whom he had turned on hearing these words, to see if he felt as proud as he did himself. Well, no! Gerios had seemed appalled rather, keeping his eyes down and turning quite pale. Tanios had put his reaction down to courtesy. Was it not correct to appear embarrassed in the face of praise from the Master?

But now the boy put a quite different interpretation on Gerios's extreme embarrassment. He knew in fact that it was said of several village boys, and also of some other slightly older people, that the Sheikh was in the habit of 'summoning' their mothers to prepare some dish or other, and that these visits were not without reference to the children's births; then the name of the dish in question was bracketed to the individual's name: for example Hanna-*ouzi*, Boulos-*ghamme* . . . These nicknames were extremely insulting, no one would wish to make the slightest reference to them in the presence of the person concerned, and Tanios blushed when they were mentioned in front of him.

Never, in his worst nightmares, could he have suspected that he himself, the darling of the village, could be one of those wretches to whom such a disgrace could be attributed, or that his own mother was one of those women who . . .

How can one describe what he felt at that moment? He was angry with everyone, with the Sheikh and Gerios, his two 'fathers', with Lamia and all those who, in the village, knew what was said about him, and who must regard him with pity or derision. And his companions who had witnessed this scene, even those who had appeared scared, found no grace in his eyes, for their attitude proved conclusively that they shared a secret with the others, a secret which the village idiot had been the only one to reveal in a moment of anger.

'In every age,' comments the monk Elias, 'there has always been a madman among the people of Kfaryabda, and when one disappeared another was ready to take his place, like an ember that goes on smouldering under the ashes, so that the fire is never extinguished. No doubt

Providence needs these puppets, which she manipulates to rend the veils that man's wisdom has woven.'

He was still standing on the same spot, shattered, unable even to look around, when the priest's son came over and announced to Shallita that the next time he saw him in the village he would hang him with the church rope, which he clearly pointed out to him; the terrorized wretch never dared to follow the urchins again, or even to venture near the *Blata*.

He now took up his abode outside the village on a vast sloping stretch of land known as the Landslip, because it was strewn with a large number of insecure rocks which shook on their foundations. Shallita lived among them, dusting them, sweeping them, preaching to them; he claimed that they moved at night, that they groaned and coughed, and also that they gave birth to young.

These strange ideas were to leave a trace in the villagers' memories. When we played, as children, if one of us bent down to look at the foot of a rock, the others shouted in chorus, 'Well, Shallita, has the rock had its baby?'

In his own way Tanios was also to distance himself from the village. No sooner had he opened his eyes each morning than he went off on long, solitary walks, thinking and recalling episodes from his childhood which he interpreted in the light of what he could no longer ignore.

No one, seeing him pass, asked him what was wrong; the incident near the spring had in two short hours gone the rounds of the village. Perhaps only the people directly implicated – his mother, Gerios, the Sheikh – had heard no echo of it. Lamia noticed that her son was different, but he was more than thirteen years old, nearly fourteen, the age when a boy becomes a man, and in the extreme calm which he affected everywhere she saw only a sign of precocious maturity. Moreover, there was never the slightest argument between them any more, voices were never raised, Tanios even seemed to have become more polite. But it was the politeness of the person who feels himself a stranger.

At the priest's school, it was the same thing. He attended assiduously the lessons in calligraphy or catechism, he answered correctly when *Bouna* Boutros questioned him, but as soon as the bell rang he made off at full speed, avoiding the *Blata*, slipping away by the least-frequented paths, to wander far from all eyes until nightfall.

Thus it was that, one day, having walked straight before him till he was on the outskirts of the little town of Dayroun, Tanios spotted a little way off a procession approaching: a man on horseback with a servant on foot, holding the bridle, and circling around him a dozen other horsemen, apparently his bodyguards. All carried rifles and wore long beards which were visible from a distance.

II

Tanios had already come across this person two or three times in the past, always in the neighbourhood of Dayroun, but had never greeted him. Those were the orders in the village. You didn't speak to the outlaw.

Roukoz, the Sheikh's former major-domo. The same whose place Gerios had taken some fifteen years earlier. The Sheikh had accused him of appropriating the income from the sale of crops; it was in a sense money that belonged to the Lord, since it was a question of the share of the crops which the tenant farmers owed him; but it was also the peasants' money, since it was meant to be used to pay the tax – the *miri*. Because of this crime, all the villagers had had to pay an extra contribution that year. So their hostility to the former steward was motivated as much by their obedience to the Sheikh as by their own resentment.

The man had been compelled to leave and had remained in exile for many years. Not only from the village and its surroundings, but from the whole mountain region, since the Sheikh had sworn to apprehend him. So Roukoz had had to flee to Egypt, and on the day Tanios met him he had been back in the area for about three years. A return which had not gone unnoticed, since he had purchased, right on the borders of the Sheikh's domain, vast lands on which he had planted mulberry trees to breed silkworms, and built a house and a cocoonery. With what money? The villagers had not the slightest doubt that it was their money which this scoundrel had caused to fructify on the banks of the Nile!

All that was however only one version of the facts; Roukoz

had another one, which Tanios had already heard whispered in the village school: the story of the theft had simply been a pretext invented by the Sheikh to discredit his former collaborator and prevent him returning to Kfaryabda; the real cause of their quarrel was the Master's attempt to seduce Roukoz's wife and so he had decided to leave the castle to preserve her honour.

Who was speaking the truth? Tanios had never had any hesitation in accepting the Sheikh's version: not for anything in the world would he have wanted to appear well-disposed towards the exile, it would have seemed like treachery! But things appeared to him now in a quite different light. Was it so unthinkable that the Sheikh should have tried to seduce Roukoz's wife? And could he not have invented the story of embezzlement to prevent the village siding with the steward, so forcing the latter to flee?

As the procession approached, Tanios felt his heart go out to the man who had dared to leave the castle, slamming the door behind him, for the sake of his honour, this man who had occupied the same post as Gerios, but who, for his part, had not resigned himself to grovelling for the rest of his life, who, on the contrary, had preferred to go into exile, and had returned to defy the Sheikh even on the very borders of his fiefdom.

The day his former major-domo returned to the region, the Master of Kfaryabda had ordered his subjects to capture him forthwith and hand him over. But Roukoz had armed himself with a letter of protection from the Emir of the Mountains, and another bearing the signature of the Viceroy of Egypt, and a third written by the Patriarch in his own hand, which documents he took care to show to all and sundry; the Sheikh was not quite up to confronting all these high authorities at once, and he had had to swallow his wrath and a little of his dignity.

What is more, the former steward, not wishing to rely solely on these written protections, and fearing to fall victim to an attack, had attached to his person some thirty men whom he paid liberally and furnished with firearms; this little troop guarded his property and escorted him as soon as he set foot outside his own home.

Tanios now observed the procession with delight, he revelled in the display of so much wealth and power, and when he finally came level with them, he shouted cheerfully, 'Good day *Khweja* Roukoz!'

A young rascal from Kfaryabda addressing him so respectfully, and with such a broad smile! Roukoz ordered his bodyguard to halt.

'Who are you, young man?'

'They call me Tanios the son of Gerios.'

'The son of Gerios, the Sheikh's major-domo?'

The boy nodded, and Roukoz did likewise, several times, incredulous. A quiver of emotion passed over his pockmarked face, half hidden by his grey beard. It must have been years since any villager had wished him good day . . .

'Where are you off to, in these parts?'

'Nowhere. I've just come out of school and felt like reflecting, so I started walking straight ahead.'

The escort could not help spluttering with laughter at the word 'reflecting', but their master silenced them before saying to the boy, 'If you are not going anywhere in particular, perhaps you would honour me with a visit.'

'The honour is all mine,' Tanios replied ceremoniously.

The former steward ordered his astounded escort to turn around, and despatched one of the horsemen with a message to the notable whom he was on his way to visit.

'Tell him there has been a hitch and the visit is postponed till tomorrow.'

Roukoz's men could not understand how he could change his plans just because this lad had told him he was free . . . They could not understand the extent to which their master suffered by being outlawed from the village, and how much it meant to him that someone from Kfaryabda should greet him and agree to cross his threshold, even if it was only a youngster. So he sat Tanios down in the place of honour, offered him coffee and cakes, talked to him of the past, of his quarrel with the Sheikh, telling him about the harassment his wife had suffered at the latter's hands, the unfortunate woman who had since died, in the prime of life, soon after giving birth to their only child, Asma, whom Roukoz sent for to be introduced, and whom Tanios embraced warmly just as adults embrace their children.

The 'outlaw' talked and talked, with one hand placed on his honoured visitor's shoulder, the other gesticulating to emphasize his words.

'Your only ambition can't be to go and kiss the Sheikh's son's hand every morning, just as your father kisses the Sheikh's hand. You must study and grow rich if you wish to have a life of your own. Study first, then money. Not the other way round. By the time you have money you'll neither have the patience nor be the right age for studying. First must come studies, but real studies, not just the school of our good priest! Then you can come with me. I am building new cocooneries for silkworms, the biggest in all the Mountains, and I have neither son nor nephew to succeed me. I am over fifty, and even if I remarried and eventually had a son I would not have time to prepare him to take over from me. Heaven sent you to meet me, Tanios . . .'

On his way back to the village the lad let these words re-echo in his head. And his face lit up. This day had for him the taste of revenge. Doubtless he was betraying his people by siding with the outlaw, but he found comfort in this feeling of having betrayed. For fourteen years the whole village had been sharing a secret that he alone ignored, and yet this execrable secret concerned him alone, and affected him in his very flesh! And now, by a just reversal of things, he was the one who had a secret from which the whole village was excluded.

This time he no longer sought to avoid the *Blata*, he even made a point of crossing right through it, stamping his feet noisily and hurriedly greeting those he met.

After passing the spring, he began to climb the steps leading to the castle, then turned, gazed down on the square, and noticed that the crowd was denser than normal and the discussions more lively.

He imagined for a moment that his 'betrayal' was already known; but the people were commenting on a quite different piece of news: the Sheikha had died after her long illness, a messenger had come to announce this that very evening and the Sheikh was preparing to leave for the Great Jord with a few notables to attend the funeral.

No one in the village pretended to feel grief. Doubtless this woman had been deceived, held up to ridicule, doubtless her marriage had been one long humiliating ordeal, but since that last 'visit' no one was prepared to grant her the slightest extenuating circumstance. What the 'Sheikha of the Locusts' had suffered at her husband's hands during the short years they had been together was, according to the folk on the *Blata*, nothing but her just deserts. And at the very moment of her funeral, the only comment certain village-women could make was the terrible curse, 'May God bury her even deeper!'

Whispered very softly, for the Sheikh would not have greatly appreciated such vindictiveness. He seemed to show more compassion, and, in any case, more dignity. When the messenger brought him the news, he summoned the most important villagers to tell them, 'My wife gave you what remained of her life. I know we have had to suffer from the actions of the dead woman's family, but in the face of death these things are forgotten. I want you to go with me to attend the funeral, and if anyone there utters a word out of place, we hear nothing, we turn a deaf ear, we do our duty then we come home.'

In the Great Jord they were received coolly, but no one was molested.

On his return, the Sheikh announced that he would be

receiving condolences for three days, this time at his home, in the castle; for the men, in the Hall of Pillars, and for the women, in the saloon where the Sheikha used to sit, surrounded by the village-women who came to take refuge with her from the Sheikh's attentions, a large room with bare walls, furnished merely with low benches covered in blue cotton.

But whoever was to receive the women's condolences? The author of the *Mountain Chronicle* explains that, 'the dead woman having in the village neither mother, sister, daughter or sister-in-law, it was incumbent upon the wife of the major-domo to assume the functions of hostess at the castle'. The worthy monk makes no comment, leaving us to imagine the atmosphere which must have reigned when the village-women, who came out of pure social propriety, veiled in black or white, but with no grief in their hearts, entered the room, turned towards the place formerly occupied by the chatelaine, discovered Lamia seated there, and had to walk up to her and stoop down to embrace her, saying, 'May God give you the strength to bear this misfortune!' Or else, 'We know how great is your suffering!' Or some other untruth befitting the occasion. How did many of these women manage to accomplish with dignity this ritual full of pitfalls? The chronicler does not relate.

Things happened quite differently with the men. There, no one had any illusions about his neighbours' feelings either, but there was no question of compromising on appearances, out of respect for the Sheikh, and even more on account of his son, the fifteen-year-old Raad, the only person to mourn sincerely, whom he had brought back with him from the Great Jord. The villagers – and even his own father – looked on him as a stranger. Which he was in fact, not having set foot in the village since he was one year old; his maternal family scarcely encouraged him and the Sheikh dared not insist too much for fear his father-in-law should decide to 'escort' him in his own way . . .

Discovering this young man was an ordeal for the people

of Kfaryabda. An ordeal renewed every time he opened his mouth and they heard the Jord accent, the detested accent of the 'locusts'. Which was inevitable, since he had always lived there. 'God only knows what is hidden behind that accent,' they said to each other, 'and what ideas his mother has put into his head about the village.' They had never given it a thought as long as Raad was far away, but they realized now that their master, who was nearing sixty, could disappear overnight, leaving his lands and his men in enemy hands.

If the Sheikh too was worried, he did not show it, and treated his son like the man he was growing into, and the heir that he already was. He seated him on his left to receive the condolences, and from time to time named the men as they entered, and watched him out of the corner of his eye to make sure he had carefully noted his father's actions and managed to imitate them.

For it was not enough to welcome each visitor according to his rank, the finer shades of his position had also to be respected. With the tenant farmer Bou-Nassif, who had in the past tried to cheat about shares of the crops, he had to be allowed to stoop down, take the Master's hand in his own, place a long kiss on it and then get up. With Toubiyya, an honest servant of the overlord's family, once he had kissed the Master's hand, he had to be taken by the elbow in a pretence of helping him to rise.

As for the tenant farmer Shalhoub, a long-time comrade-in-arms and hunting companion, he too began to bend down, but with scarcely perceptible slowness, expecting to see the Master withdraw his hand, then help him to rise while embracing him briefly; he would then go to take his place while smoothing his moustache. When it was the turn of the tenant Ayyoub, who had grown rich and had just had a house built in Dayroun, he also must be helped to his feet and given a brief embrace, but only after he had lightly touched the Lord's fingers with his lips.

So much for the tenant farmers; there were other

standards for the townsfolk, the priest, the notables, the comrades-in-arms, the equals, the castle servants . . . There were those who must be greeted by name, those whose formulas of condolence must be answered by another personal formula, not the same for all, naturally, and not with the same intonation.

And then there were other still more special cases, such as that of the muleteer and pedlar, Nader, who had been driven out of the castle four years previously and was taking the opportunity of seeking forgiveness. He had come to mingle with the crowd, looking more affected than was strictly necessary; at this, the Sheikh had whispered at length in his son's ear; then the muleteer had approached, bent down, taken the Sheikh's hand, raised it to his lips and let it linger there for a long moment.

If the Master did not desire such a reconciliation, which would be quite exceptional in a period of mourning, he would have turned away, pretending to speak to Gerios, who was behind him, and he would have continued to ignore the person in question until he had withdrawn, or been 'assisted out'. But the Sheikh could have adopted such an attitude only in the case of an extremely serious misdemeanour, for example if an individual such as Roukoz, considered by the Master as a thief and a rogue, had calmly come to seek an easy absolution. Nader's error was not 'of the same carat', as they say in the village; so the Sheikh left him hanging on to his hand in this way for a few seconds, then finally touched his shoulder with a tired sigh.

'God forgives you, Nader, but you have got far too ready a tongue!'

'I was born that way, Sheikh!'

In the Sheikh's eyes, the muleteer had been guilty of a gross impertinence. He had been a regular visitor to the castle, where both his conversation and his learning were appreciated; he was in fact one of the best-educated men in the whole mountain region, even if you wouldn't suspect this from his appearance and his trade. Always on the

look-out for any news or any novelty, he readily lent his ear
to his most enlightened customers, but he took even more
pleasure in hearing himself speak, and the quality of his
audience mattered little to him.

People say that he would seat himself on his mule, with
a book propped against the animal's neck, and travel the
roads in this posture. When he heard of a book which
interested him, in Arabic or Turkish – the only languages
he could read fluently – he was ready to pay a high price
to acquire it. He was accustomed to say that this was the
reason why he had never married, as no woman would have
wanted a man who spent every piastre he earned on books.
Village rumour had another version, his preference for
beautiful young men, but he had never been caught in the
act. In any case it was not because of these undisclosed
leanings that the Sheikh had quarrelled with him, but on
account of the French Revolution.

Since childhood, Nader had admired this uncon-
ditionally; to the Sheikh, on the other hand, and all his
peers, it was nothing but an abomination, an aberration,
fortunately short-lived; 'our' Frenchmen had lost their
heads, they said, but God had quickly guided them back on
to the right path. Once or twice the muleteer had alluded to
the abolition of privileges, and the Sheikh had replied
ambiguously, half joking, half threatening, and the visitor
had left it at that. But one day, when he had been to sell
his wares to the dragoman at the French consulate, he had
gathered such an extraordinary item of news that he had
been quite unable to keep it to himself. It was 1831, there
had been a change of regime in France the previous year,
Louis-Philippe had acceded to the throne.

'Our Sheikh will never guess what a Frenchman told me
last week.'

'Get it off your chest, Nader!'

'The new king's father supported the Revolution and he
even voted for the death of Louis XVI!'

The muleteer was certain he had scored a point in their

interminable debates. His fat, beardless face shone with pleasure. But the Sheikh did not find this amusing. He had risen to his feet in order to shout the louder, 'No one utters such words in my house. Get out, and never set foot here again!'

Why this reaction? Gebrayel, who reported this episode to me, remained puzzled. It is certain that the Sheikh had judged Nader's words highly improper, impertinent, perhaps he had even thought them subversive in the presence of his subjects. Was it the information itself which had shocked him? Had he deemed it an insult to the new king of the French? Was it the tone which he had found offensive? No one dared ask him, the muleteer less than anyone; he could have kicked himself for his indiscretion, as the village was his village where he had his home and his books, and the Sheikh was one of his most generous customers. So he had taken advantage of the first day of condolences to come to obtain forgiveness.

I have not yet mentioned the most important thing about this man: he was the author of the only book which offers a plausible explanation of Tanios-*kishk*'s disappearance.

Nader was, in fact, in the habit of noting down in an exercise-book his own personal observations and maxims, sometimes long, sometimes succinct, transparent or sibylline, generally in verse, or otherwise in fairly mannered prose.

Several of these texts begin with, 'I said to Tanios', or else, 'Tanios told me', without its being possible to establish with certainty whether this was a simple trick of presentation or the record of authentic conversations.

Doubtless these writings were not intended to be published as they stood. In any case, it was long after Nader's death that an academic discovered them and published them with a title that I have translated as *Wisdom on*

Muleback. I shall frequently have recourse to his invaluable evidence.

III

No sooner had he obtained his pardon than the muleteer went to sit next to Tanios, and whispered in his ear, 'What a life! To have to kiss hands to be able to earn your daily bread!'

Tanios approved discreetly. While he kept his eyes glued to the group formed by the Sheikh, his son and Gerios, standing one step behind them, he was just thinking the same thing and wondering if, in a few years' time, he would find himself in the same position as the major-domo, bowing obsequiously, hanging on Raad's orders. 'I'd rather die,' he swore to himself, and his lips quivered with repressed rage.

Nader came close again to whisper, 'It was really something, the French Revolution, the heads of all those sheikhs falling!'

Tanios did not react. The muleteer fidgeted on his seat, as if he were on the back of his mule which was not moving quickly enough. And he twisted his neck like a lizard, to examine the carpets on the floor, the arched ceiling, his hosts and their visitors, all at the same time, while pulling comical faces and winking. Then he leaned again towards his young neighbour.

'The Sheikh's son, doesn't he look a bit of a lout?'

Tanios smiled. But at the same time warning him, 'You're going to get driven out for a second time!'

At the same moment the boy met Gerios's eyes, and the latter beckoned to him to come and speak to him.

'Don't stay next to Nader! Go and see if your mother wants anything!'

While Tanios was wondering whether he should obey or defy him by going back to his place, a clamour arose outside. Someone came and whispered a few words in the Sheikh's ear, and the latter rose and went to the door, beckoning to Raad to follow. Gerios went after them.

A distinguished visitor was on his way, and tradition demanded that the Sheikh should go to meet him. It was Said *beyk*, the Druse lord of the village of Sahlain. Clad in a long striped *abaya*, which fell from his shoulders down to his calves, adding to the majesty of his face which was dignified by a fair moustache.

Following the custom, he began with the words, 'News has reached me, would that it were not true!'

The Sheikh gave the correct reply. 'Heaven has wished to try us.'

'Know that you have brothers at your side in your ordeal.'

'Since I have known you, Said *beyk*, the word "neighbour" has been more agreeable to my ears than the word "brother".'

Formulas, but not just formulas: the Sheikh had had nothing but trouble with his own kin, whereas there had been no cloud on his relations with his neighbour for twenty years. The two men took each other by the arm and entered together.

The Sheikh sat his guest on his right and introduced him to Raad with these words: 'Know that the day when I die, you will have another father here, to watch over you!'

'May God prolong your life, Sheikh Francis!'

Still more formulas. But eventually they got down to the main business. To the strange person who was standing at a little distance and whom all present were examining from head to foot. Even in the women's room, the rumour had spread, and some of them had hurried in to see him. He had neither beard nor moustache and wore a sort of flattened hat which covered his neck and ears. The little hair which was visible was grey, almost white.

Said *beyk* beckoned to him to come closer.

'This honourable man who accompanies me is an English clergyman. He was anxious to do his duty on this painful occasion.'

'He is welcome!'

'He has come to live in Sahlain with his wife, a virtuous lady, and we have cause to congratulate ourselves on their presence.'

'It is your noble blood which speaks through your mouth, Said *beyk*!' said the parson in Arabic, the rather stilted Arabic of oriental scholars.

Nothing the Sheikh's admiring glance, Said *beyk* explained, 'The reverend gentleman lived for seven years in Aleppo. And after getting to know that fine metropolis, instead of going to Istanbul or London, he chose to come and live in our humble village. God will reward him for this sacrifice!'

The parson was about to reply when the Sheikh motioned him to a seat. Not right next to himself, which would have surprised nobody, in view of the exceptional character of such a visit, but at a little distance, to one side. For, to tell the truth, the Sheikh already knew everything he had just heard – everything that happened in Sahlain was known in Kfaryabda before nightfall – and the arrival of an Englishman, clergyman or not, who had chosen to live in Sahlain, was not a common occurence. Now our Sheikh needed to know more, without the reverend gentleman being able to overhear. His head bent towards Said *beyk*'s, and everyone present could appreciate the extent of their collusion.

'I was told he intended to open a school.'

'Yes, I have lent him premises. We have no school in Sahlain, and I have wished for one for some time. Even my sons are going to attend it; he has promised to teach them English and Turkish, in addition to Arabic poetry and rhetoric. I wouldn't like to speak for him, but I think he has great hopes of your son attending too.'

'Would he not try to convert our children, by any chance?'

'No, we have spoken of this, and he has given me his promise.'

'So you trust him?'

'I trust his intelligence. If he tried to convert our sons, he'd be driven out of the village within the hour, and why should he do such a stupid thing?'

'He would not dare try it with your children and mine, it is true. But he will want to convert the peasants.'

'No, for that, too, he has given me his promise.'

'Well, then, who is he going to convert?'

'I don't know, some merchants' sons, some of the Orthodox . . . There is also the Jew Yaakoub and his family.'

'If he manages to convert my tailor, that will be a real feat . . . But I'm not sure that would please *Bouna* Boutros; for him a Jew is better than a heretic!'

The priest had been there the whole morning, but had left an hour ago, taking leave of the Sheikh and of all those present. But now he was back, someone must have warned him that the wolf was in the fold and he had hurried back, resumed his seat and was staring unashamedly at the clergyman in his funny hat.

'As a matter of fact,' Said *beyk* continued, 'I don't think the reverend gentleman is out to convert people.'

'Indeed,' said the Sheikh, surprised for the first time.

'He's particularly anxious for us not be prejudiced against him, and he will do nothing to embarrass us.'

The Sheikh leaned even closer.

'Perhaps he's a spy.'

'I thought of that too. But we in Sahlain are not privy to the Sultan's secrets. After all, he is not going to write to his consul that Halim's cow has given birth to twins!'

The two men began to chuckle, gasping for breath but keeping their lips and jaws tightly compressed in a solemn mourning expression till it hurt. Their eyes met those of the clergyman, who smiled at them respectfully, to which they responded with kindly nods.

When, after an hour, Said *beyk* rose to take his leave, the

Sheikh said to him, 'The reverend gentleman's plan does not displease me. I shall think it over. Today is Tuesday . . . if he comes to see me on Friday morning he shall have his answer.'

'Take your time, Sheikh, I will tell him to come much later if you like.'

'No, it is not necessary. My mind will be made up by Thursday evening, and I shall let him know my decision without fail the next morning.'

When the Sheikh resumed his seat, after accompanying his distinguished visitors to the front steps, the priest came to sit in the place of honour next to him.

'An English clergyman in our village! As the proverb says, "If you live long enough, you will see many miracles!" I must return with holy water to purify the castle before any other misfortunes occur!'

'Wait, *Bouna*, don't waste your holy water. The clergyman is coming back to see me on Friday and then you can come once and for all with your sprig of hysop instead of troubling yourself twice!'

'He's just been and he's returning in three days time!'

'Yes, the climate in the village must suit him.'

The priest began to sniff the air ostentatiously.

'Could there be some sulphur in our air?'

'You are wrong, *Bouna*, it seems he is a godly man.'

'And what did this godly man come here for?'

'To present his condolences, like everyone else.'

'And on Friday, what is he coming for? To present more condolences? Could he be anticipating another death? Mine perhaps?'

'God forbid! This man is going to open a school in Sahlain – '

'I know.'

' – and he merely came to suggest I send my son!'

'Is that all! And what was our Sheikh's reply?'

'I told him I would think it over until Thursday night. And I shall give him my answer on Friday.'

'Why Thursday night?'

Up till then a slightly mocking smile had played round the Sheikh's lips; it amused him to tease the priest. But suddenly his expression grew severe.

'I will explain everything, *Bouna*, so that tomorrow you do not reproach me with taking you unawares. If, by sunset on Thursday, your Patriarch has not come to express his condolences, I shall send my son to the English school.'

The Prelate had not visited our village for a good fourteen years – since Tanios's birth. He had sided with the Sheikha to the bitter end, perhaps because he had been thought responsible for this disastrous marriage, and he had it in for the Sheikh for having put him in such an embarrassing position. He had shown himself so partisan in the conflict, so insensitive to the villagers' sufferings at the time of the expedition by the men from the Great Jord, that, without any respect for his white beard or his rank, he had been given the same nickname as his protégée; 'the Patriarch of the Locusts' had then sworn never to set foot again in Kfaryabda.

People had grown resigned to his absence. It was the done thing to say they did not miss him, either at the Feast of the Cross or at the confirmation ceremonies, when the Prelate's slap was supposed to leave a lasting memory on the faces of the adolescents; *Bouna* Boutros's slap had to do just as well. All the same, this sort of curse weighed heavily on the shoulders of the faithful; every time there was a death, a serious illness, the failure of a crop – these everyday misfortunes which inspire the question, 'What have I done to Heaven?' – the quarrel with the Patriarch was like an old knife twisting in an old wound. Was it not time to put an end to it? Were not these condolences the ideal opportunity for a reconciliation?

At the time of the Sheikha's funeral in the Great Jord,

the Prelate, who presided over the ceremony, had a word of consolation, in front of the vault, for all the members of the family. Except the Sheikh. Who had nevertheless forgotten his grievances and those of the village, to join them, and who, after all, was the husband of the deceased.

Feeling the insult was all the greater since his in-laws, as well as the notables from Kfaryabda, had witnessed this contemptuous behaviour, the Sheikh had immediately gone to see the Patriarch's verger to let him know, with a hint of threat in his voice, that the next three days would be devoted to condolences at the castle and he expected to see *Sayyidna*, the Patriarch, arrive, otherwise . . .

Throughout that first day, as the visitors filed past, the Sheikh had had but one question in mind: 'Will he come?' And he repeated the message to the priest.

'If your Patriarch does not come, don't even think of blaming me for what I intend to do.'

Bouna Boutros vanished from the village for two days. A last-minute mission which led to nothing. He returned, saying that *Sayyidna* was absent on a visit to the villages of the Great Jord, and he had not been able to get in touch with him. It is also possible that he had found him, but had been unable to persuade him. Be that as it may, on Thursday evening, when the Sheikh left the hall, surrounded by the last visitors, who had come to express condolences, there was no sign of a mitre on the horizon.

The priest slept little that night. Two vain days on muleback had left him stiff and aching, without allaying his anxiety.

'And what's more,' he said to the *Khouriyya*, 'with that mule you know where you're going, she wouldn't even dream of plunging straight over a precipice. Whereas this

Sheikh and this Patriarch carry all the Christians on their backs and they butt at each other like a couple of billygoats.'

'Go and say a prayer in the church,' his wife said. 'If God is good to us, tomorrow he'll install a mule in the Sheikh's castle and another in the Patriarch's palace.'

Fourth Passage

The English Clergyman's School

In reply to your letter, I am pleased to confirm that there was indeed, among the very first pupils at the Sahlain school, one Tanios Gerios, from Kfaryabda.

The founder of our establishment, the Reverend Jeremy Stolton, had come with his wife to settle in the Mountains at the beginning of the 1830s. There is, in our library, a box where the school archives are preserved, in particular letters, as well as annotated Journals for each year. If you wish to consult them, you are very welcome, but you will understand that there can be no question of our allowing them to be removed . . .

Extract from a letter from the Reverend Ishaac, present principal of the English school in Sahlain

I

Bouna Boutros could not have prayed with sufficient fervour, for the next day, on his arrival with his unkempt beard in the Hall of Pillars, the Sheikh was still there, his clothing not transformed into a harness, his ears not having pierced the top of his cap and, beneath his hoary moustache, his lips and jaw not having lengthened.

He had clearly been awake for some time, perhaps he had not even been able to sleep because of his own anxiety. Gerios and some villagers were already with him. The priest greeted the assembly with a surly gesture and took a seat near the door.

'*Bouna* Boutros,' the Sheikh called out jovially, 'come and sit near me rather, the least we can do is to welcome him together.'

The priest felt a moment of hope. Perhaps at least one of his prayers had been answered!

'So he is coming!'

'Of course he is coming. And indeed, here he is.'

He had to swallow his disappointment. It was not the Patriarch who was making his entrance, but the clergyman. He greeted his host with many well-turned Arabic formulas, under the villagers' astonished gaze. Then, at a sign from the Master, he took a seat.

'Heaven arranges things well, *Bouna*, the reverend gentleman has taken the very place that you have just vacated.'

But the priest was not in the mood for appreciating pleasantries. He begged the Sheikh to come and speak privately with him, in the *liwan*.

'If I understand rightly, our Sheikh has made up his mind.'

'Your Patriarch has made it up for me, I did all I could, my conscience is at peace. Look at me, do I look like someone who has slept badly?'

'You have perhaps done everything necessary, as far as *Sayyidna* is concerned. But for your son, are you doing what your duty commands? Can your conscience really be at peace when you send him to people who will make him read falsified gospels and who respect neither the Virgin nor the saints?'

'If God had not wished me to make this decision he would have ordered the Patriarch to come and show his beard at the condolences.'

Bouna Boutros was ill at ease when the Sheikh mentioned beards, and still more so when he spoke of God, for his words then gave the impression of excessive familiarity. So he retorted, with dignity, 'It sometimes happens that God directs his creatures towards the path of their perdition.'

'Would He have done that to a patriarch?' said the Sheikh, most disingenuously.

'I was not thinking only of the Patriarch!'

As soon as their little discussion was over, the priest and the Sheikh returned to the Hall of Pillars. Where the person was waiting for them with some anxiety. But his host immediately reassured him.

'I have thought it over. My son will go to your school, Reverend.'

'I shall be at pains to show myself worthy of this privilege.'

'You must treat him like all the other pupils, without any special consideration, and not hesitate to beat him mercilessly if he deserves it. But I have to make two conditions, which you must promise me here, before witnesses, to respect. The first is that no one mentions religion to him; he will remain in his father's Faith, and go every

Sunday to *Bouna* Boutros, whom you see here, to learn the catechism.'

'I promise this,' said the clergyman, 'as I have already promised Said *beyk.*'

'The second thing, I am called Sheikh Francis and not Sheikh Anklis, and I insist on a French teacher for this school.'

'That also I promise, Sheikh Francis. Rhetoric, poetry, calligraphy, science, Turkish, French, English. And everyone keeps his own religion.'

'Under these conditions, there is nothing more to say. I am even wondering if *Bouna* Boutros isn't now thinking of sending his own sons to your school, Reverend . . .'

'The year when figs ripen in January,' muttered the priest between his teeth.

Then he rose, slammed his cap on his head and left.

'While waiting for those figs,' the Sheikh resumed, 'I know at least one boy who would be happy to accompany my son to this school. Eh, Gerios?'

The major-domo nodded in agreement, as always, and thanked his Master for his constant kindness to himself and his family. But in his heart of hearts he had many reservations. To remove Tanios from the school of the priest, his brother-in-law, to send him to this Englishman, and incur the wrath of the Church, he would not do this with a light heart. However, neither could he oppose the Master's will and refuse the favours granted him.

He forgot his objections at the sight of the boy's reaction. When he reported the Sheikh's suggestion to him, his face lit up, and Lamia judged the moment opportune to restore some warmth to the bosom of the family.

'So, don't you embrace your father for this news?'

And Tanios embraced him, and his mother also, as he had not embraced them since the incident at the spring.

Which did not mean that he was giving up his rebellion. On the contrary, he felt that his metamorphosis, initiated by the fool's words, and strengthened by his visit to Roukoz, the outlaw, had set him free. As if Heaven were only waiting for an act of will on his part to open up new paths for him . . . It was not to the parson's school that he was going, but to the threshold of the whole vast universe, whose languages he would soon speak, and whose mysteries he would unveil.

He was still there, with Lamia and Gerios, but he was far away, he was gazing on the scene which he could imagine as if it were already imprinted on his memory. He was sailing beyond this place, beyond its constraints and its resentments, beyond his most agonizing doubts.

At the same time, two corridors away, in the main building of the castle, the Sheikh was struggling to convince his son that it would be no humiliation for him to go to learn other things besides horse-riding and how to handle weapons.

'Suppose one day you received a message from the King of France, as our ancestor did . . .'

'I would get my secretary to translate it.'

'And what if it were a confidential message, would it really be wise to let your secretary know the contents?'

It did not take the Reverend Stolton long to realize the difference between the two pupils who arrived every morning from Kfaryabda, a journey which took them about an hour by the short cut through the pine forest. In his Yearbook for 1835, there is this entry:

Tanios. An immense appetite for learning and a lively intelligence, imperilled by the agitations of a tormented soul.

Then, two pages later:

The only thing that really interests Raad is for him to be shown the respect due to his rank. If one of the teachers or pupils, at any moment of the day, speaks to him without using his title of 'Sheikh', he behaves as if he had heard nothing and begins to look behind him for the churl to whom such words might have been addressed. As a pupil, I am afraid he belongs to that most discouraging of all categories, the one whose maxim seems to be: 'Teach me if you can!' I would never dream of making an effort to keep him at this establishment if academic considerations were the only ones I had to take into account.

These last few words were almost an admission. For, if the parson was sincerely concerned with the training of young minds, he was also not indifferent to the Eastern policy of His Gracious Majesty.

But how the devil could the education of an adolescent, in a village in the Mountains, be of the slightest import-ance in the eyes of a European power? I can understand people chuckling, shrugging their shoulders – I myself refused to believe this for a long time, until I consulted the archives. But the facts are there: the presence of these two youngsters in the Reverend Stolton's school was known and grimly commented upon even in the office of Lord Pon-sonby, the Ambassador to the Sublime Porte, and doubtless in Paris too, in the Chamber of Deputies, at the initiative of Alphonse de Lamartine – 'Yes indeed,' 'Professor' Gebrayel observed indignantly, 'that oaf Raad had probably never heard of his contemporary Lamartine, but Lamartine had certainly heard of Raad!'

By what miracle? It must be said that, at that time, the European chanceries were concerned about an exceptional event: Mehmet Ali Pasha, Viceroy of Egypt, had undertaken to build in the Middle East, on the ruins of the Ottoman Empire, a new power which was to stretch from the Balkans to the sources of the Nile, thus controlling the route to India.

This, the English would not have at any price, and they were ready to go to any lengths to prevent it. The French, on the other hand, saw in Mehmet Ali the man sent by providence to shake the East out of its lethargy and build a new Egypt, taking France as its model. He had sent for French doctors, French engineers, he had even appointed to his army staff one of Napoleon's former officers. French Utopians had gone to live in Egypt in the hope of building the first socialist society, bringing unheard-of plans – such as cutting a canal from the Mediterranean to the Red Sea. Undoubtedly, this Pasha had everything to commend him to the French. And what is more, if he irritated the English to this extent, he could not be fundamentally bad. There was no question of letting London dispose of him.

In this battle of giants, what weight could the inhabitants of my village carry, and in particular the English clergyman's two pupils?

More than one might imagine. You could say that their names were engraved on the beam of the scales, and if you stooped close enough you could read them. That is what Lord Ponsonby had done. He had bent over the map, and had placed a finger on one exact spot: 'This is where Mehmet Ali's empire will be made or unmade, this is where the battle will be waged!'

For this empire which was being established had two wings: one to the north – the Balkans and Asia Minor – the other to the south – Egypt and its dependencies. Between the two, only one link, by the long coastal route from Gaza to Alexandretta, passing through Haifa, Acre, Sidon, Beirut, Tripoli, Latakia. It was a question of a strip of land sandwiched between the sea and the Mountains. If this escaped the Viceroy's control, the route would become impassable, the Egyptian army would be cut off from its rear, the new empire would be split in two. Still-born.

And overnight, all the chanceries had eyes only for this corner of the Mountains. There had never been seen so many missionaries, merchants, artists, poets, doctors, eccentric ladies and amateurs of old stones. The Mountain folk were flattered. And when they understood, a little later, that the French and English were waging war on their land, so as not to have to fight each other directly, they were more flattered than ever. A destructive privilege, but a privilege all the same.

The aim of the English was clear: to incite the people of the Mountains to rebel against the Egyptians; which the latter, with the support of France, naturally were doing their best to avoid.

As the *Mountain Chronicle* relates: 'When the Egyptian army arrived near the borders of our country, their general-in-chief sent a messenger to the Emir asking him to join him.' Judging it extremely unwise to take part in this confrontation, which far outstripped his tiny principality and his meagre resources, the Emir had sought to procrastinate; so the general had sent him a second message, saying: 'Either you come with your army to join me, or I will come to you and raze your palace to the ground and plant figs on the site!'

The wretched man had had to comply and the Mountains had passed under the authority of Egypt. 'Wretched', in a manner of speaking; he remained a man much feared; peasants and sheikhs alike trembled at the mere mention of his name; but in the face of the Pasha and his representatives, he was the one who trembled.

Mehmet Ali hoped that by bringing the Emir over to his side, he would find himself master of the country. Such would no doubt have been true in other lands, not here. The Emir had authority, to be sure, and influence, but other things counted in the Mountains. There were the religious communities, with their clergy, their leaders, their notables, there were the great families and the lordlings. There were whisperings in the main squares and village quarrels. There was the fact that the Sheikh was on bad terms with the Patriarch, because the Patriarch was convinced that the Sheikh had fathered a child to Lamia, who still lived at the castle, and that, under these circumstances, the Patriarch would not set foot in the castle, and that the

Sheikh, to make it quite clear that a man of his rank was not to be treated like this, had sent his son, out of bravado, to the English clergyman's school!

When Lord Ponsonby stooped over this tiny point on the map, his colleagues had not explained matters in such detail. They had simply said that the Druse community, which had been hostile to the Emir since he had had one of their principal leaders killed, was ready to rebel against him and his Egyptian allies, but such a rebellion would lead nowhere if the Christians, who formed the majority in the country, did not take part.

'And have our people not had any success yet with the Christians?' asked the Ambassador.

He was reminded that for these people, the majority of whom were Catholics, the Englishman was above all a heretic.

'Not one of our people has been able to make any significant contact . . . with the exception of one clergyman who has opened a school.'

'One of our schools in a Catholic village?'

'No, indeed, he would have been driven out within an hour, or else his school would have been burnt down. No, he settled on the land of an old Druse chief, Said *beyk*, but he managed to enrol two Catholic pupils in his school, including the son of the Sheikh of Kfaryabda.'

'Kfar what?'

A more detailed map had to be sought, on which could be read, with the help of a magnifying glass, the names of Kfaryabda and Sahlain.

'Interesting,' said Lord Ponsonby.

In the report drawn up for the Foreign Office, he did not mention Kfaryabda by name, but instanced 'encouraging signs'. That the descendant of one of the greatest Catholic families, a family which boasted of three hundred years of links with France, should find himself at the English clergyman's school was decidedly a success, a breakthrough.

And naturally, there was no question of Sheikh Raad being expelled because of a bad mark!

II

No one in the other camp was prepared to take the matter as seriously as Lord Ponsonby. Neither the Emir, nor Monsieur Guys, the French Consul, nor Sulayman Pasha, alias Octave Joseph de Sèves, who was in command in Beirut, in the name of Egypt. They were engaged in a major conflict and no one had time to devote to this village quarrel. No one except the Patriarch. He alone kept explaining, till he was blue in the face, that the significance of the two children's presence in the clergyman's school should not be neglected. And finally, so as not to offend him, it was decided to penalize the presumptuous Sheikh: an agent from the Emir's Treasury was sent to him with an endless list of overdue taxes, from which in fact he had managed in the past to get himself exempted by all kinds of subterfuges; and now all the past debts were being remembered, with more new taxes added, in particular the *ferde*, instituted by the Egyptian occupying administration. The pretext for this step was the need to replenish the Emir's coffers, depleted by the current conflict. But no one was deceived about the real reasons. And in case anyone had any doubts, the Patriarch had summoned the priest to tell him that, if the Sheikh withdrew the two boys from this heretic school, he would intercede with the Emir on his behalf . . .

The Master of Kfaryabda was indeed in a quandary. The harvest had been disastrous that year and the sum demanded of him – three hundred 'purses', in other words one hundred and fifty thousand piastres – far exceeded the amount he could collect, even if he forced all his subjects to hand over their savings.

So, he couldn't possibly pay, but the other solution was doubly humiliating: first of all the Sheikh would have lost face by removing the boys from the English clergyman's school, and then he would have had to go begging at the Patriarch's feet, requesting this 'Patriarch of the Locusts' to deign to speak to the Emir . . .

Before leaving the village with his escort, the agent from the Treasury made it clear that, if the sums due were not paid in their entirety in the following month, the Sheikh's lands would be confiscated and added to the Emir's domain. A prospect which did not exactly delight the inhabitants of Kfaryabda, who were conscious of having, in the person of their overlord, the least bad master.

The strange thing was the way Tanios reacted to these events. They reconciled him for a time with the village and even, one might say, with his presumed illegitimacy. For what was happening before his young eyes was in fact nothing but the continuation of that same quarrel which had previously provoked the invasion of the 'locusts', a quarrel the cause of which was his own birth. And now he understood it perfectly, he knew why the Patriarch reacted in this way, he also understood the Sheikh's attitude and that of the villagers. And he shared it. If only for one reason: the school. For him, that was what counted more than anything. He studied with enthusiasm, with fury, he soaked up like a sponge every word, every scrap of knowledge, he refused to see anything except this bridge between himself, Tanios, and the rest of the universe. For this reason he sided once more with the villagers, with the Sheikh, against all the enemies of the village, against the Emir, against the Patriarch . . . He espoused all present and past causes.

He had even distanced himself from Roukoz, because the latter had said to him, 'Why should I grieve if the Sheikh's lands are confiscated? Don't you also want feudal privileges to be abolished, just as I do?' The lad had replied, 'That is my dearest wish, but I don't want it to happen in this way!' And Roukoz had retorted sententiously, 'When you cherish a wish whose realization would overwhelm you with delight, you can ask God to grant it, but you can't dictate to Him the way He must set about doing this. For my part I have asked Heaven to punish the Sheikh of Kfaryabda. It's up to him to decide which instrument He will use, some catastrophe, locusts, or the Egyptian armies!'

This reasoning put Tanios ill at ease. For his part, he sincerely wished the Sheikh's privileges to be abolished, and he certainly had no wish to see himself, in fifteen years' time, helping Raad off with his boots . . . But in the trial of strength which was taking place, he knew perfectly well which side he was on, and the wishes he wanted to see fulfilled.

'Today, at noon,' the clergyman wrote in his Yearbook under the date 12 March 1836:

Tanios came to see me in my study to explain the dramatic situation in which his village found itself, a situation which he compared to a mongoose caught in a trap and waiting for the hunter's knife . . . I recommended him to pray, and promised to do whatever was in my power.

I immediately wrote a detailed letter to our Consul, which I hope to entrust tomorrow to some traveller leaving for Beirut.

It was most probably as a result of this letter, a veritable appeal for help, that a strange visitor was seen arriving at the castle. In Kfaryabda they still speak to this day of the English Consul's visit. According to the facts, Richard Wood was not yet Consul – he became so later; at the time he was Lord Ponsonby's official emissary and he had been living for a few weeks in Beirut with his sister who happened to be the real English Consul's wife. But this detail has no effect on the events, nor on the way they have been reported.

'That year,' The *Mountain Chronicle* states, 'our village received a visit from the English Consul, bringing valuable gifts which filled young and old with delight. He was received as no other visitor had ever been before, he attended high mass and he was feasted for three days and nights.'

Overdoing it, wasn't it, for the visit of a pseudo-consul, so much feasting, so many superlatives? Not when the nature of the 'valuable gifts' is known. The monk Elias says no more, but Wood himself recalls his visit in a letter he addressed shortly afterwards to the Reverend Stolton, preserved by the latter in the archives of the Sahlain school. The emissary remains vague on the object of his mission, which his correspondent obviously knows as well as himself; but he explains in detail the nature of the gifts he had brought and the way he was received. The clergyman had certainly mentioned in his own letter the exact amount which the Emir was demanding, since Wood began by having money bags brought into the great hall of the castle and placed just behind his host's hookah; and these bags contained exactly one hundred and fifty thousand piastres. The Sheikh made as if to protest, but his visitor did not give him time for this.

'What has just been placed at your feet is not our gift to you, but for your Treasurer, so that he can meet the Emir's demands without having to importune you.'

The Lord of Kfaryabda noted this with dignity, but he was flattered and his heart leapt like a child's.

There were indeed three other 'genuine' gifts, which Wood described in his letter: 'For the Sheikh, a monumental clock inscribed with the arms of the House of Hanover, transported by camel from Beirut.' Why a clock and not a thoroughbred, for example? Mystery. Perhaps it was meant to symbolize a timeless friendship.

The other two gifts were for the clergyman's pupils. For Tanios, 'a superb mother-of-pearl writing-case which he immediately fastened to his belt'. And for Raad – who already possessed a gold writing-case which he hid as soon as he came out of school for fear of whispers that the Sheikh had been demoted to the rank of secretary – 'a hunting rifle, a Forsyth shot-gun worthy of a royal hunt, which his father immediately took from him to weigh up and caress enviously – perhaps it should have been given to him, rather than to his son, he would have been overwhelmed and the weapon would have been in safer hands'.

This sentence was by no means prophetic, but gives rise to thought when one knows what misfortunes were lying in wait at the muzzle of that gun.

The 'Consul' had arrived one Saturday afternoon, and the Sheikh suggested he spend the night at the castle with his retinue. The village-women did their best to prepare the finest dishes – Wood mentions a stuffed neck of lamb, praises a '*kebbe* cooked with bergamot', clearly the result of some confusion, for if there certainly exists a dish consisting of minced meat with bitter oranges, bergamot is unknown in the cookery of the mountain region. The emissary also mentions elsewhere that Sheikh Francis smiled with amusement at seeing him add water to his wine . . .

The following day, after a brief friendly conversation in the *liwan*, overlooking the valley, with coffee and dried fruit placed before them, the Lord of Kfaryabda asked leave to absent himself for an hour.

'Mass is about to begin. I should not leave my guest like this, but God has been good to me these last two days, He has almost accomplished miracles, and I am anxious to give thanks to Him.'

'I will accompany you, if you do not see any objection . . .'

The Sheikh simply smiled. He himself saw no objection, but he feared a scandal from *Bouna* Boutros if he turned up at church accompanied by an Englishman.

In fact, the priest was waiting for them in front of the building. Polite but firm.

'Our village is grateful for what you have done. That is why, if you will be so good as to honour me with a visit, my wife has made coffee for you in my humble house, whose entrance is at the back. She will keep you company with my eldest son, until I have finished mass. Then I shall join you.'

He glanced briefly at the Sheikh, as if to say, 'I could not have been more polite with your English friends!'

But the 'Consul' replied, in his approximate Arabic, 'It is not necessary to give me special treatment, Father, I am a Catholic myself and I shall attend mass with the rest of the congregation.'

'An Englishman and a Catholic! You are the eighth wonder of the world!' *Bouna* Boutros could not help commenting.

Before inviting this true believer to enter.

To send an Irish agent to this Catholic nation, such had been Lord Ponsonby's supremely clever move, a stratagem which won for long the Mountain folk's admiration for 'those Angliz devils'.

III

That night, the Patriarch slept 'flat on his face', as the people of Kfaryabda say, and his muttered prayers were far from charitable; he condemned so many bodies and souls to Hell, you might well ask which kingdom he was trying to serve. The Sheikh's moustache was like a thistle in his bed, no matter how he tossed and turned, he only rolled the more on to it.

Yet he was at the height of his power. Between the Emir, the Egyptian military staff, the French diplomats and the principal lords of the Mountains, he was the recognized intermediary, the pivot of the coalition, and also its bone-setter – as it was endlessly necessary to mend fractures. The French Consul had no good word for Mehmet Ali, 'an Oriental despot who passes himself off as a reformer in order to lure European liberals'; and when he was asked about de Sèves, his former compatriot, he would say, 'Sulayman Pasha? He serves his new masters faithfully,' and turn up his nose in a grimace. As for the Emir, he secretly rejoiced in the setbacks of his Egyptian protectors, who said of him, almost audibly, that he would remain their most loyal ally as long as their armies were encamped under the windows of his palace.

The Patriarch sometimes had the impression that he was holding up this rickety coalition by the strength of his wrists, and throughout the Mountains he was respected and sometimes revered. No door was shut to him, no favour refused him. Except in one village. In Kfaryabda, even the parish priest turned his back on him.

So his night was troubled, but at dawn he seemed more confident.

'I'll find a way to make them recite the act of contrition,' he promised the verger who was helping him to dress. 'They'll fall at my feet like a coin in the church collecting-box. For every illness there is a cure, and I have the right one for them.'

A few days later a messenger from the Great Jord arrived at the castle to say that Raad's grandmother was dying and wished to see him. The Sheikh did not attempt to oppose the journey, on the contrary he saw in it the opportunity to patch things up with his in-laws, and he gave his son a letter of good wishes, written by Gerios, to take to them, together with some small gifts.

If the grandmother was dying, she was in no hurry. The *Chronicle* does not mention her demise until one hundred and thirty pages – and seventeen years – later, at the age of seventy-four. No matter; doubtless she really wished to see her grandson. But it was the Patriarch especially who had insisted on Raad being sent for. He had grave matters to entrust to him.

Their conversation began like a riddle for children in the catechism class.

'If you were a knight of the Messiah, and you found yourself suddenly a prisoner in Satan's dwelling, what would you do?'

'I'd try to escape, but not before destroying everything, not leaving a stone standing!'

'That is a fine reply, worthy of a true knight.'

'And I'd massacre Satan and all his offspring!'

'Don't let us exaggerate, Sheikh Raad. No mortal can slay Satan. However, it is possible to cause confusion in his house, as he causes confusion in ours. But your zeal pleases me, and I was right to place my trust in you, and I'm sure your Faith and your noble blood will inspire you to actions as they have just inspired you to words.'

Taking the boy's hands in his own and closing his eyes, the Prelate murmured a long prayer. Raad could not understand a single word, but he seemed to feel the incense rise up in his nostrils. The room was windowless, submerged in darkness, and the Patriarch's white beard was the sole source of light.

'You are in the house of Satan!'

The young Sheikh did not understand. He began to look around him, not a little frightened.

'I am not referring to your grandfather's house.'

'The castle . . .'

'I do not mean your father's house either; God forgives him. I am speaking of the English school, the home of heresy and depravity. Every morning, you go to the house of Satan, and you do not know it.'

His face was as solemn as a tombstone. But gradually he smiled.

'But they do not know who you are, either. They simply think they are dealing with Sheikh Raad, the son of Sheikh Francis; they do not know that in you is concealed the knight who is the instrument of their punishment.'

When Raad returned to the village a few days later, taking as usual the short cut through the pine forest, Tanios noticed his chin was beginning to sprout an embryonic beard, and his eyes wore an unaccustomed expression.

At the Reverend Stolton's school, classes were held in the oldest part of the building, the *kabou*, comprising two long vaulted rooms, more or less identical, rather dark for classrooms. Later other rooms were to be added, but in Tanios's day there were scarcely more than thirty or so pupils and the school simply consisted of these two rooms and a third adjoining one, where the clergyman kept his books and which served as his study. On the upper floor were his private quarters. The house was not large, but with its tiled roof rising in a perfect pyramid, its symmetrical balconies, its delicately arched windows and its ivy-clad walls, it managed to give the impression of charm combined with solidity. What is more, it possessed vast enclosed grounds where the pupils could play and where, many years later, for very commendable reasons – the arrival of over a thousand pupils – new buildings would be built, which were, alas, much less attractive. But that is quite another story . . .

A part of these grounds had been set aside for the clergyman's wife to devote herself to the one real passion of her life: gardening. She had a little vegetable garden, as well as flower beds, with daffodils, carnations, a lavender bush and a whole bed of roses. The pupils never ventured there; she had even built a low wall with her own hands, simply a few stones laid on top of each other, but which established a symbolic enclosure.

However, the day of Raad's return to school, he rushed to jump over the wall. He went straight to the rose bushes, which in that month of April were just coming into flower; then, taking his knife from his belt, he began systematically to cut off the finest roses, just below the petals, as if decapitating them.

Mrs Stolton was in the vegetable garden, not far away. She saw the whole thing, but the boy acted with such assurance, such effrontery that she remained dumbstruck for several minutes before yelling something unintelligible. Which impressed the young Sheikh not a whit. He continued his task, until the last rose had dropped into his open handkerchief. Then, putting his knife away, he calmly stepped back over the wall to go to show his booty to the other pupils.

The clergyman rushed up, found his wife in tears, and summoned the culprit to his study. He looked hard at him for some time, trying to find any expression of remorse, before saying, in his preacher's voice, 'Do you realize what has happened to you? When you arrived here this morning, you were a respected Sheikh, and now you have turned into a thief!'

'I haven't committed any theft.'

'My wife saw you take her roses, how can you deny it?'

'She saw me, and I could see that she saw me. So it wasn't theft, it was plunder!'

'What's the difference?'

'Thefts are committed by miserable wretches, whereas plunder is like war, it's practised at all times by noblemen, by knights.'

'I seem to hear someone else speaking through your mouth. Who taught you to answer like that?'

'Why should I need anyone to teach me such a thing? I have known it all my life!'

The clergyman sighed. Pondered. He thought of the Sheikh. Of Mr Wood. Of Lord Ponsonby. Perhaps even of His Gracious Majesty. He sighed again. Then he continued, the force of his words now tempered by resignation, 'You should know, in any case, that if people are to plunder, it should only be in the case of enemies, those whose lands have been conquered, or gates forced by an act of war. And certainly not in houses where you are received as a friend.'

Raad seemed to sink into thought, and the clergyman deemed this attitude, for want of better, as a gesture of repentance. He asked the young Sheikh not to consider himself any longer at war with his establishment and decided to forget the matter.

So to betray his mission as a teacher, so as not to betray the interests of the Crown? Reading between the lines of his Yearbook, it seems the Reverend Stolton felt some slight sense of shame.

In the following days, Raad seemed to have turned over a new leaf. But the demon – pardon, the angel – of temptation was not to let go of him.

This time, the instrument provided by Providence was

a string of worry-beads made of precious wood which a merchant's son from Dayroun had brought to school; it had this special property that, when you ran the beads through your fingers, or, better still, rolled them up in the palm of your hand to let them rub against each other, they gave off a scent of musk. Raad badly wanted them, but when his classmate spoke of selling them to him he was offended. It would have been so much simpler to appropriate them by a noble act of plunder! Or else, as one boy jokingly suggested, to win them. By means of a game widespread among the pupils, called *aassi*, which, loosely translated, means 'dare'. It consisted of challenging someone to a daring act, and if he carried it out, he took possession of the stake.

Sheikh Raad shouted, '*Aassi!*' and his schoolfellows, delighted with this distraction, repeated, '*Aassi! Aassi!*' until the owner of the precious object decided to utter the magic word in his turn, followed by the challenge.

'*Aassi!* I dare you to go over to Mrs Stolton and pick up her dress with both hands and throw it over your head as if you were looking for something, and shout, "Where are the beads, I can't find them anywhere!" '

The merchant's son was delighted with his brainwave. He was certain he had found the ultimate challenge, something that no pupil could possibly carry out. But Raad immediately set off in the direction indicated. The others – seven of them – followed him from a distance, convinced he would soon turn back. Mrs Stolton was stooping over her flower beds, wearing a long dress, the hem of which was black with mud. A dress which the valiant Sheikh grasped in both hands and pulled up so sharply that the lady fell forward with her head in her flowers.

'Wherever are the worry-beads, I can't find them anywhere!' he proclaimed victoriously.

No one else laughed.

This time, the clergyman, forgetting the superior interests

of his country, came yelling at the lout in English. 'Out! Leave this establishment immediately and never set foot here again! Your presence here is a disgrace to us all, and even if King William came in person to Sahlain to ask me to keep you, I'd reply, never, never, never, and never!'

How else could he have reacted? What respect would he have maintained otherwise, for himself and his mission? However, in the ensuing hours, remorse began to grow in him, lacerating remorse, the feeling that he had, with his own hands, destroyed the building that he had undertaken to erect. He felt the need to go and explain things to Said *beyk*, his host and protector.

The lord of Sahlain, who had already heard echoes of the incident, did not make the least attempt to reassure his visitor.

'God has given you all the good qualities, Reverend. You have intelligence, knowledge, integrity, virtue, devotion . . . But you lack patience.'

Patience? The parson heaved a long sigh and strove to give a semblance of a smile.

'You are doubtless right, Said *beyk*. But one needs a quite special variety of patience to put up with Sheikh Raad. And I fear that variety does not grow in England.'

'That is the way things are in our Mountains, Reverend. You thought you were punishing an insolent pupil; all you have done is to punish his father, who is our friend, and who has had to confront half the universe because of his friendship for us.'

'I regret that sincerely, and if I could repair the wrong I have done him . . . Perhaps I should go to see him.'

'It is too late. The only way you can show your friendship to him is not to take amiss what he will have to say to get out of his embarrassment.'

IV

Extract from the *Mountain Chronicle*:

At the end of the month of April, shortly after the Great Feast, Sheikh Francis, the Master of Kfaryabda, decided to withdraw his son Sheikh Raad from the English heretics' school. It is said that an incident had occurred some days previously when the clergyman had surprised his spouse with the young Sheikh in a compromising situation. The flesh is weak in the springtime of nature and also in its autumnal years.

On the third day, which fell on a Friday, *Sayyidna*, the Patriarch, arrived in the village with an important retinue. He had not been there for fifteen years, and everyone rejoiced at his return. He said he had come to hear the young Sheikh's confession, just as he had been his mother's confessor.

Sheikh Francis and the Patriarch exchanged embraces in the presence of all the people gathered on the *Blata*, and in his sermon *Sayyidna* spoke of pardon and reconciliation, and cursed heresy and aberration, the causes of division and rifts in the ranks of the faithful.

There was feasting in the village until dawn. And the next day the Patriarch and the Sheikh left together for the palace at Beit ed-Din, to renew their allegiance to the Emir, the Governor of the Mountains, and announce their reconciliation. He received them with full honours.

'Lord, what an outsider I feel in the midst of all this rejoicing!' Tanios's feelings had swung once more, firmly on the side of anger and contempt. From time to time, to seek distraction from his black thoughts, he imagined the clergyman's wife, a bashful lover in Raad's arms, or else the latter, in the confessional, receiving the Prelate's warm congratulations for the sins he was claiming. Tanios caught himself sniggering aloud, only to return immediately to his silent indignation.

And he walked and walked, as he did whenever his fury was too much for him.

'So, Tanios, you think with your feet?'

The lad was not in the mood to let himself be addressed like this, but the voice was familiar and the silhouette even more so. Not so much that of Nader, as of his inseparable mule, piled up with his wares to the height of a man.

Tanios was about to throw his arms spontaneously around the muleteer, when he remembered the man's reputation and stepped back. But the other pursued his idea.

'I too think with my feet. Inevitably, as all I do is to travel the roads. The ideas which you forge with your feet and which rise to your head comfort and stimulate you; the ones which descend from your head to your feet weigh you down and discourage you. Don't smile, you should listen to me seriously . . . But after all, you may smile, like all the others. No one wants my wisdom. That's the reason I'm forced to earn a living as a pedlar. In former times, the Arabs would give a camel as a reward for every word of wisdom.'

'Oh! If only you could sell your words, Nader . . .'

'I know, I talk a lot, but you must understand me, when I go from village to village, quantities of things pass through my head without my being able to talk to anyone. Then, when I reach the village, I make up for lost time.'

'You do this so successfully that you get yourself driven out . . .'

'That has sometimes happened, but it won't happen any more. Don't count on me to go telling on the *Blata* how Sheikh Raad was expelled from school for hacking off the roses and lifting that lady's skirt like a filthy lout. And I shan't tell either how his father boxed both his ears before parading him like a hero in front of the whole village, in the midst of their cheers.'

Tanios turned round and spat three times. An action which Nader approved.

'You'd be wrong to hold it against these people! They know as well as you and me what happened, and they judge Raad like you and I do. But this quarrel with the Patriarch and the Emir was becoming costly and dangerous, this alliance with the English was a burden, he had to get out of it and without losing face . . .'

'Without losing face?'

'A daring seducer can be blamed, he is never despised. That's the way it is. His father can laugh about his exploits.'

'I don't feel like laughing. When I think about Mrs Stolton and the rumours which will reach her, I'm ashamed.'

'Don't worry about the clergyman's wife, she's English.'

'So what?'

'She's English, I'm telling you; the worst thing that can happen to her is to be obliged to leave the country. Whereas, for you and me, leaving this country is the best thing that can happen.'

'Get away with you, Nader, I'm miserable enough without your wise owl's words!'

In spite of everything Tanios drew a certain satisfaction from the indignation, shame, sadness that he felt at the village rejoicings: the satisfaction of knowing he was right, where they were all wrong, knowing that he had his eyes wide open when the others, all the others, were blinded by cowardice and subservience. He promised himself that, as soon as he returned to school on Monday morning, he would go and see Mrs Stolton, he would kiss her hand like the noblemen he had read about in English books, and express his 'deepest respect and filial devotion' or some other such fine-sounding formula, and he would tell her that the whole village knew the truth about what had happened . . .

Not for one moment did Tanios realize that he too was blinded, not by subservience but by hope. The hope of leaving the castle early the next day, to return to the fresh serenity of his classroom. Not for one moment did he suspect what was so simple, so obvious: there was no longer any question of any boy from the village attending the English clergyman's school. The Sheikh and the Patriarch had made this clear to Gerios before leaving arm-in-arm for the Emir's palace.

Since then, the major-domo had put off daily, hourly, the dreaded moment when he had to announce the news to Tanios. Perhaps the boy would understand the matter himself and be resigned to the situation . . . No, that was impossible, unthinkable. This school was all his hope for the future, all his joy, he lived for nothing else. It was the English school which had reconciled him with his family, with the castle, the village, with himself and his birth.

On Sunday evening, the family was gathered round a dish of *kishk*, dipping pieces of bread in the thick soup. Gerios was telling what he had heard about the conflict between the Pasha and the Sublime Porte; there was talk of a battle which was soon to be waged on the banks of the Euphrates.

From time to time Lamia asked a few questions and gave some instructions to the girl who was waiting on them. Tanios simply nodded, his mind was on other matters, what he was going to say to the clergyman and his wife the next day, when he saw them for the first time after the incident.

'You should perhaps tell Tanios,' his mother suggested when there was a pause.

Gerios nodded.

'I am quite prepared to repeat what was said to me, but I shall not be telling him anything new, a boy as intelligent as he is has no need of lengthy explanations, he must certainly have understood everything for himself.'

'What are you talking about?'

'About the English school. Do I need to tell you there is no question of your attending any more?'

Tanios's teeth suddenly began to chatter, as if a torrent of cold water had flooded the room. He could barely utter the word, '*Laysh?* – why?'

'After what happened, our village can no longer maintain any links with this school. Our Sheikh told me this quite plainly before he left. In the presence of our Patriarch.'

'Let the Sheikh decide for his idiot of a son, but not for me.'

'I will not allow you to speak like that while we live under his roof.'

'Raad never wanted to learn anything, he went to school against his will, because his father insisted on it, and he's delighted not to go any more. For my part, I go there to study, I have learned a great deal and I want to continue learning.'

'You've learned enough. Trust my experience, if you study too much you'll not be able to tolerate life among your own people. You must just be sufficiently educated to fulfil your duties satisfactorily. That is true wisdom. You will help me in my work, I shall teach you all you need to know. You are a man now. It is time for you to begin to earn your daily bread.'

Tanios rose like a zombie.

'I shall eat no more bread.'

Then he went up to the raised alcove where he slept, lay down and did not move again.

At first, it was thought to be a fit of childish sulks. But when next day the sun rose and then set again without Tanios unclenching his teeth, neither to speak, nor to eat, nor to take a sip of water, Lamia began to panic, Gerios shut himself up in his office, with the excuse that he had to bring his register up to date, but mainly to hide his anxiety. And the news spread through the village.

On Wednesday evening, the fourth day of his fast, Tanios's tongue was thick, his eyes staring and dry, and the village-people filed past his bed, some trying to speak to him – in vain, he would not listen – others come to watch the strange sight of a young man allowing himself to slide gently down the slope to death.

They tried everything. The terror of Hell which awaits the suicide, the ban on Christian burial . . . he no longer believed in anything, he seemed to await death as if it were a question of setting out on a marvellous voyage.

Even when Gerios, with tears in his eyes, came to promise he would let him return to the clergyman's school, if only he would accept this glass of milk, he answered, without even looking at him, 'You are not my father! I don't know who my father is!'

A few people overheard him and one of them hurriedly said, 'Poor boy, he's delirious!' For they were afraid now of seeing Gerios kill himself – out of sorrow and shame – at the same time as Tanios.

It was Thursday, already the fifth day of the fast, and some visitors suggested forcing his mouth open to feed him, but others advised against this lest he die of suffocation.

Everyone was at their wits' end. Everyone, even the priest. But not the *Khouriyya*. When Lamia, her young sister, came in tears to fling herself into her arms, like when she was a child, she rose and said, 'There is only one thing to be done, and I will be the one to do it. Lamia, give me your son!'

Without waiting for a reply, she announced to the men, 'I need a cart!'

Tanios was carried, barely conscious, and laid in the back. The *Khouriyya* herself took the reins and drove off down the road that wound round the hill on which the castle stood.

No one dared follow her, but just gazed after her until the dust settled again on the road.

The afternoon was dry and the pistachio trees were covered in pinkish velvet.

She did not stop until she reached the gate of the English school. She herself lifted her nephew and carried him towards the house. The clergyman came out to meet her, followed by Mrs Stolton.

'He's going to die in our hands. I'm leaving him with you. If he sees he is here, with you, he will begin to eat again.'

She placed him in their outstretched arms and left without having crossed their threshold.

Fifth Passage

'Old-Head'

In the days following this sudden arrival, Mrs Stolton and I observed the strangest of phenomena. Tanios's hair, which up till then had been black with auburn lights, began to turn white at a speed which worried us. We were often at his bedside, caring for him, and we were sometimes under the impression that the number of white hairs on his head had increased from one hour to the next. In less than a month, the head of this fifteen-year-old youth was as white as that of an old man.

I do not know if this extraordinary event can be explained by the ordeal of starvation that he had inflicted on himself, or by some other natural cause. But the local people saw in this a sign, for Tanios himself and possibly for the whole region. A good or bad omen? There was no agreement on this point. This superstitious belief had, it seems, quite contradictory interpretations, to which I prefer to lend but half an ear.

However, I thought I understood that there existed in this corner of the Mountains a legend concerning persons whose hair is prematurely white, namely that such persons, since the dawn of time, may occasionally appear during troubled periods, only to disappear again shortly afterwards. They are known as 'old-heads', or sometimes 'wise fools'. According to some folk there is only one such person, who is indefinitely reincarnated. It is true that among the Druse, the belief in metempsychosis is solidly established.

Yearbook of the Reverend Jeremy Stolton for the year
1836

I

If the faithful are promised Paradise on their death, Tanios had obtained, by his foretaste of death, a foretaste of Paradise, without the All-Highest holding it against him for his suicide wish. The Sheikh's castle was vast, it is true, but its universe was limited by high walls and kissing of hands. Writing-cases were hidden ashamedly and worry-beads were in evidence. In the clergyman's home, respect went hand in hand with knowledge. Tanios was still on the lowest rung of the ladder, but he felt capable of climbing to the very top. At hand was the library, its works alive in their precious bindings. He loved to open them, to hear the rustle of their pages, even those he would not be able to understand for some years. One day he would have read them all, of that he was certain.

But his new life was not limited to this library, the Reverend's study, and the vaulted ceiling of the classrooms. From now on, he had his own bedroom on the first floor. Up till then it had been reserved for passing visitors, generally Englishmen or Americans from the Union, but the Stoltons immediately made it clear to their unexpected lodger that this room was now his. It had a bed. A four-poster bed. Tanios had never slept in a bed.

The first days he was too weak, barely sufficiently conscious to be able to appreciate its comfort. However, he quickly became so used to it that he wondered how he would ever be able to sleep on the floor again, in constant fear of snakes, scorpions crawling under the blanket, the pale *bou-braïss* lizard with the painful bite, and, worst of all, his childhood terror, 'Mother-Forty-Four', in other words the centipede which was said to creep into the sleeper's ear and cling to his brain!

In this quiet room at the Stoltons' there was a bookshelf with small books, a cupboard fixed to the wall, a wood-burning stove, and a glazed window overlooking the flower beds of the Reverend's lady.

He had interrupted his fast immediately, as soon as he opened his eyes, found himself in a bed, and saw the clergy-man's wife offering him a cup. The next day, his mother came to spy on him from the corridor, without entering the room, and left reassured. Three days later, when Lamia and the *Khouriyya* knocked once more at the clergyman's door, Tanios himself came to let them in. His mother flung her arms round his neck, smothering him with kisses, while his aunt pulled him outside, as she still would not cross the threshold of these heretics.

'So, you managed to get what you wanted!'

The boy's hands sketched a gesture of mock impotence, as if to say, That's the way I am!

'When *I* am thwarted,' the *Khouriyya* told him, 'I shout louder than everyone else, and they all fall silent, even *Bouna* Boutros . . .'

'When *I* am thwarted, I lower my voice.'

He gave a crafty smile and his aunt shook her head several times, pretending to despair.

'Poor Lamia, you haven't managed to bring up your child properly! If he were with me, with four elder brothers and four younger ones, he'd have learned to scream and shove and to reach for the cooking pot without anyone having to beg him to eat! But he's still alive, and he knows how to fight in his own way, that's the main thing.'

The lad smiled broadly, and Lamia deemed it a suitable moment to say, 'Tomorrow we shall come with your father.'

'Who?'

With this cold word, he turned on his heels and

disappeared down a dark corridor of the house. And the two women went their several ways.

He had quickly resumed his lessons, and all the pupils who had some request to make now came to speak to him first, as if he were 'the son of the house'. Soon the clergyman entrusted him – 'because of his ability, and in return for his board and instruction', as he made clear in his Yearbook – with coaching any pupil who fell behind through absence or difficulty in understanding. Thus he came to act the schoolmaster with fellow-pupils older than himself.

It was no doubt to appear more mature in the exercise of his new duties that he decided to grow a beard; perhaps also to mark his newly acquired independence from the Sheikh, and the whole village. A rather sparse beard for the moment, little more than fluff, but which he trimmed, brushed, combed, kept a check on, to ensure its perfection. As if that were where his soul rested.

'And yet,' Gebrayel told me, 'his features, eyes and hands, too, had a somewhat feminine softness about them. He looked like Lamia, as if he had been born from her alone.'

His mother got into the habit of coming to see him every four or five days, often with her sister. Neither of them dared suggest again that he accompany them back to the village. It was not till several months had elapsed that they attempted a step in this direction, not mentioning it directly to Tanios, but through the intermediary of the clergyman. Who agreed to reason with him; if he was happy to accommodate his most brilliant pupil in his home, and flattered to receive so much literally filial affection from him, the Reverend Stolton was well aware that his mission would be better accepted in the region where it was established when Tanios was reconciled with his family, with the Sheikh and his village.

'I must make it quite clear. I would like you to visit Kfaryabda, and see your father and all your own people. Then for you to come back to live in this house where you would be a boarder, and not a refugee. Thus, the Raad incident would be more or less wiped out, and the situation would be more comfortable for everyone.'

When he rode up to the *Blata* on a donkey, Tanios was under the impression that the villagers addressed him cautiously, even with a certain fear, as if he had returned from the dead. And they all pretended not to notice his white hair.

He bent down over the spring, scooped up the icy water to drink from his hands, and not one of the curious onlookers approached him. Then he climbed up the path to the castle alone, leading his mount.

Lamia was waiting for him at the gate to take him to Gerios, begging him to behave nicely to him and kiss his hand respectfully. A painful moment, for the man had clearly taken to drinking copiously. He reeked of arak, and Tanios wondered whether, under the circumstances, the Sheikh would keep him in his service much longer. Alcohol did not loosen his tongue, he scarcely spoke a word to his prodigal son. He seemed more than ever inhibited, and he looked shrivelled and tormented. The lad felt throughout their meeting a suffocating sense of guilt which made him regret he had come back, that he had left, and perhaps even that he had agreed to eat again.

It was a shadow, but the only shadow. Raad was absent from the village: out hunting or at his grandparents, Tanios did not bother to enquire, only too pleased not to have to encounter him. He was simply told that relations between the Lord and his heir were stormy, and that the latter was even thinking of demanding his share of the domain, as custom permitted.

Then Lamia insisted on taking her son to the Sheikh.

Who took him in his arms, as he did when Tanios was a child, hugged him tightly and then looked him up and down. He seemed moved at seeing him again but could not help saying, 'You should shave off that beard, *yabni*, it's a nasty growth!'

Expecting similar comments, Tanios had promised himself not to show his irritation. He would hear him out and do exactly as he pleased. He preferred to hear comments on his appearance rather than on the clergyman's school. A question which the Sheikh apparently had no intention of raising; no doubt he thought it better after all to maintain this slight link with the English. Moreover, no one seemed inclined to bring up such a thorny subject. Not even *Bouna* Boutros, who simply took his nephew on one side to make him swear he would never let himself be corrupted by heresy.

The day after his return was a Sunday, and the boy attended mass, so that everyone could see that he still crossed himself in the same way in front of the statue of the Virgin and Child. On this matter, they were reassured, he had not let himself be 'Anglized'.

As he came out of church, Tanios saw the pedlar coming towards the square, leading his mule piled high with knick-knacks.

'Godless Nader always manages to catch us when mass is over,' commented the priest's spouse. 'He must have such a weight on his conscience that he no longer dares enter the house of God.'

'You are mistaken, *Khouriyya*, I always do my best to arrive in time, but it's my mule who won't. When she hears the bell in the distance, she refuses to budge. She's the one who must have sins on her conscience.'

'Or else she has witnessed too many things which have horrified her . . . Poor creature, if she could speak, you'd be in prison already. Or in Purgatory.'

'Purgatory! I'm there already. Did you think it was Paradise round here?'

This exchange was traditional, the congregation was as used to it as to the sound of the church bells ringing, on which the powerful arms of the peasants took their exercise on Sundays. And sometimes when the muleteer was doing his rounds far from Kfaryabda, everyone felt that there was something missing at the mass which he ignored.

For him, this desultory dialogue served the same purpose as the church bells, to attract customers, and if sometimes the *Khouriyya* forgot to tease him, he called to her himself to provoke her, until he forced her to reply; only then did the faithful, souls at peace and a smile on their lips, loosen their purse-strings.

Some of them, however, decked in their Sunday best, walked away with their families, offended to see the priest's wife laughing so indulgently with this depraved fellow. But Lamia's sister was quietly philosophical. 'Every village must have an idiot and an unbeliever!'

While the customers crowded around him that day, Nader motioned to Tanios to wait for him; and he patted his mule on the belly to indicate he had a gift for him.

The youth was intrigued. But he had to wait patiently until the muleteer had sold the last scarf with the 'lion's-paw' pattern and the last pinch of tobacco before he could get near him. Then Nader brought out a superb box made of polished wood, which clearly contained some valuable object.

'But you mustn't open it here. Follow me!'

They crossed the village square and made their way towards the cliff overhanging the valley. Towards a rock which had the appearance of a majestic seat. I suppose that it must have had a name at that time, but no one can recall it since it became associated with the memory of Tanios-*kishk*.

The youngster clambered up, followed by Nader, with the box under his arm. He did not open it until they were both seated, leaning against the rock. It was a telescope. When opened out, it was as long as an outstretched arm, with the end the size of a child's fist.

From that 'throne', on the very edge of the cliff, if you turn to the west, where the mountains meet the dark green of the valley, you can see the sea.

'Look, that is a sign. You'd think it was sailing past for your eyes alone!'

Pointing his telescope, Tanios could make out on the water a three-master with its sails unfurled.

That was certainly the scene to which these lines from *Wisdom on Muleback* refer:

> I said to Tanios, when we were alone on the rock, 'If doors were to close again in thy face, tell thyself that it is not thy life which is ending, but only the first of thy lives, and that another one is impatient to begin. Then embark on a ship, a city awaits thee.'
>
> But Tanios no longer spoke of dying, he had a smile in his heart and on his lips a woman's name.

He had murmured 'Asma'. A minute later he was annoyed with himself. To confide thus in Nader, the biggest gossip in the whole mountain region and along the whole coast?

Tanios and Asma.

It was written that their calf-love was not to remain a secret for long, but the muleteer's tongue would not be responsible for that.

II

If Tanios was anxious to keep his secret, it was not only out of understandable shyness. Now that he had only just become reconciled with the Sheikh, with Gerios, with the whole village, how could he admit to them that he loved the daughter of their 'thief', of the man they had outlawed?

Since the day, two years before, when he had met Roukoz with his retinue on the road, and chosen to greet him, there had been moments of mutual affection and other times when they had been more aloof. When Tanios wanted to distance himself from the village and found nothing to choose between his two 'fathers', he had felt close to the former major-domo; on the other hand, at the time of the conflict with the Patriarch over the English school, he felt solidarity with the village and the Sheikh, and the outlaw's words had exasperated him. He had decided to keep away from him, and during the first months of his stay at the clergyman's he had not thought even once of going to see him.

But one afternoon, when he was out for a walk after school, on the road leading from Sahlain to Dayroun, he had seen him in the distance, surrounded as usual by his bodyguards. At first he had been tempted to dive into a path under the trees. Then he had thought better of it. Why should I run away like a jackal who's afraid of his own shadow? And he had continued on his way, determined to be courteous, but show he was in a hurry.

However, Roukoz had caught sight of him and leapt off his horse, running to greet him with open arms.

'Tanios, *yabni*, I'd given up hope of seeing you again.

Fortunately chance has mocked at our reluctance to meet . . .'

He more or less forced him to go back with him, and showed him round his house, which he was still enlarging, and also his new oil press, his two cocooneries and his fields of white mulberry trees, explaining in detail the exact time the leaves must be picked to ensure that the worms gave the best quality silk . . . Tanios had to tear himself away to get home at a reasonable time. Not before he had promised to return the following Sunday for lunch and more visiting . . .

It was common knowledge that Roukoz liked nothing better than to conduct his guests on a tour of his property. With Tanios, however, it was not simply a question of displaying his wealth. The very first time, perhaps, but on the following occasions, with so many patient explanations, particularly around the cocooneries, amid the pestilential smell of rotting worms, it was not merely boasting, showing off, the boy felt he was surrounded by renewed solicitude, to which he was not insensitive.

Asma frequently accompanied them on their walks. From time to time Tanios would offer her his hand to help her over a thorny bush or a puddle; when the cultivated terraces were not too high, she leapt from one to another like the men and landed against her father's chest or Tanios's shoulder. Only for a moment, just enough time to steady herself on her feet.

Tanios was quite happy to go along with all that, but on leaving for home – to the Stoltons' that is – he thought no more about it. He rarely spoke to the girl, and he was careful not to let his eyes linger on her, which would have seemed to betray his host's confidence. Was it because, as the clergyman thought he had noticed, 'this was a society where the highest form of politeness to women consists in ignoring them'? It seems to me that with Tanios it was mainly his youth and his shyness.

It was on the Sunday before his return to the village and his meeting with Nader that Tanios had first seen Asma in a different light. He had gone to visit Roukoz and had not found him at home. But, as a frequent visitor to the place, he had entered just the same and walked from room to room to see how the work was getting on. The former major-domo was having an audience room built worthy of a palace, worthy, above all, of his ambitions, as it was even vaster than the Sheikh's Hall of Pillars, which he wished to outdo. It was still unfinished. The specialists in marquetry had lined the walls with damascened panels, but the floor had not yet been tiled; and the only sign that there was to be a fountain in the middle of the room was an octagon drawn with chalk.

That was where Asma came to join Tanios. Together they began to admire the minute detail of the mother-of-pearl work. The floor was cluttered with buckets, rags, piles of marble tiles and a basket of sharp tools against which the girl nearly struck her foot. Then Tanios took her hand to help her round the obstacle. And as, with every step, she nearly stumbled, he kept a firm hold of her hand.

They had been walking hand-in-hand for a little time, looking up at the ceiling in admiration, when the sound of footsteps reached them from the corridor.

Asma quickly withdrew her hand.

'Someone might see us!'

Tanios turned to her.

She was twelve years old and she was a woman. With finely delineated lips and smelling of wild hyacinths.

They continued their wandering through the unfinished hall, but neither of them had eyes any longer for what they pretended to be admiring. And when the footsteps in the corridor died away, they linked hands again. The hands they held were no longer the same. Asma's seemed to Tanios to be warm and trembling like a little bird's body. Like the little bird fallen out of its nest which he had picked up one day and held in the hollow of his hand and which seemed both frightened of that strange hand and reassured to be no longer abandoned.

They both looked together towards the door. Then at each other. Then dropped their eyes, laughing excitedly. Then their eyes met again. Their lids closed. Their breath groped towards each other in the dark.

Your lips touched lightly, then separated.
As if you had exhausted your share of happiness and already
feared to trespass on others' shares.
You were innocent? From what is innocence preserved?
Even the Creator tells us to slaughter lambs for our feasts
But never wolves . . .

If Tanios, during those days, had been able to read the godless muleteer's verses, he would once more have cursed the 'wisdom of the old owl'. And he would have been right, for he was to know happiness in Asma's home. Transient happiness? All happiness is transient; whether it lasts a week or thirty years, one sheds the same tears when the last day comes, and is ready to risk damnation to have the right to another day.

He loved that girl; she loved him, and her father clearly accepted him. There were words to which he could now give a different interpretation. So, when Roukoz called him 'Son!' it was not 'son' he meant but 'son-in-law', 'future son-in-law'. How had he not seen this earlier? If the former major-domo talked to him about his business in the way he did, it was naturally because he saw him as the future husband of his only daughter. In a year she would be thirteen, and he would be sixteen, nearly seventeen, they could be betrothed, and in another two years marry and sleep in each other's arms.

During the course of the following weeks, his visits to Roukoz only reinforced these impressions. For example, his host said, in a roundabout way, 'When it's your job to manage this business . . .' or even, more directly, 'When you are living in this house . . .' quite casually, as if the matter were agreed upon.

Suddenly his future seemed marked out, and by the most benevolent hand, since it promised him love, endless knowledge, and a fortune as a bonus.

What obstacle still remained in his path? Gerios and Lamia? He would find a way of obtaining their consent, or he would do without it. The Sheikh? It is certain that he would not win his favours by marrying the daughter of his enemy, but why should he need his favours? Roukoz's house was not on his lands, after all, and if the former major-domo had managed to defy him for so many years, what was there to fear?

Tanios was confident; but on observing his 'father-in-law' more closely he again grew anxious.

Impressed by Roukoz's fortune, by his domain that he never ceased extending, by the opulence of his dwelling, by the letters of protection which he exhibited, and perhaps, more than anything, by his violent invectives against feudal lords, the youth had let himself be persuaded that Asma's father was no longer an outlaw seeking for rehabilitation, but a serious rival to the Sheikh, and even his equal.

That was in fact Roukoz's ambition – to become the Sheikh's equal, and meanwhile to appear to be so. By his wealth, he was so already; but the rest did not follow. As the years went by, the Master of Kfaryabda, less greedy for money than for pleasure, had grown slowly impoverished; his coffers were regularly empty, and if the English emissary's timely intervention had allowed him to meet an exceptional demand, it was with the greatest difficulty that the annual taxes could be paid, taxes which in those war years grew steadily more onerous. In the great hall of the castle, certain pillars were now scaling, because of the water which leaked from the roof; while Roukoz, growing daily more prosperous thanks to his silkworms, had sent for the most skilful artisans to create for him a *majlis* worthy of a pasha.

The hall could seat comfortably one hundred and twenty people.

But these visitors were yet to arrive . . . The more Roukoz's reception hall grew, the more obvious it became that it was empty; the more it was embellished, the more superfluous it appeared. Tanios finally realized this, and when one day the former major-domo opened his heart to him, it was still an outlaw's heart.

'The Patriarch protected me from the Sheikh, and now they are reconciled. They went together to the Emir, as if to deprive me of my second protector. Since then, I go to bed every night thinking that it might be my last.'

'And your bodyguards?'

'I doubled their wages last week. But if, out of the twelve apostles, there could be one Judas . . .

'I can now count only on the Pasha of Egypt, may God prolong his life and extend his empire! But he has other matters to worry about than my own person, hasn't he?'

It was at the insistence of *Khweja* Roukoz, the former major-domo of the castle, that the Egyptian army established a command post of two hundred men in Dayroun, requisitioning three large houses with their gardens to billet them; the officers lodged in the houses and the soldiers camped in tents. Up till then the Pasha's armies had never been in the neighbourhood, except for brief incursions, whereas they were already quartered in most of the large towns up in the Mountains.

And now, they patrolled morning and evening through the streets of Dayroun, Sahlain and Kfaryabda . . .

Here the monk Elias reports a version which can still be heard to this day, but which seems barely credible to me. It is true that Roukoz had lived for several years in Egypt, he knew the dialect of the country and had purchased some favours, including the famous letter of protection; but from there, to move the Pasha's armies for his convenience . . .

No. If the Egyptian armies had approached our village, they must have intended to be deployed gradually in every corner of the Mountains, to strengthen their hold.

Having said that, it is clear that Asma's father had seen in this a blessing, the answer to his prayers, his hope of salvation. And perhaps even something more . . .

III

Tanios was on a visit to Asma's father one December day, when he saw Adel *effendi*, the officer in command of the Dayroun garrison, arrive accompanied by two other officers in green felt caps, with thick but well-kept beards. The boy's first reaction was mistrust and anxiety, but his host whispered, all smiles, 'They are friends, not more than three days pass without their coming to see me.'

However, Roukoz had motioned to Asma to slip away, it is never good for a girl to be seen by soldiers.

When he had taken this precaution, he welcomed Tanios warmly. He referred to the officers as 'brothers, and even more than brothers'; and he naturally introduced the lad to them as 'as dear to my heart as if he were my own son'.

'Nothing less than a family reunion,' the Reverend Stolton wrote ironically, in a detailed account of this meeting, an account inspired by what his ward – for reasons we shall shortly understand – was to report to him as soon as he returned to Sahlain.

What Tanios immediately noticed about these officers of the Egyptian army was that not one of them was Egyptian; Adel *effendi* was of Cretan origin, one of his fellow-officers was Austrian, the other Circassian. Nothing surprising in that, since Mehmet Ali was himself born in Macedonia of Albanian parents. All however spoke Arabic with an Egyptian accent, and appeared devoted to their master and his dynasty.

As well as to his ideals. According to them, they were not waging a war of conquest, but a battle for the rebirth of the people of the East. They spoke of modernization, equity, order and dignity. Tanios listened with interest, from time to time nodding his head to indicate his sincere approval. How could it have been otherwise when these energetic men were fighting against Ottoman negligence, and spoke of opening schools everywhere, training doctors, engineers.

He was equally impressed when the major promised to put an end to all discrimination between the religious communities and to abolish all privileges. At this point in the speech, Roukoz drank to the health of the officers, to their master's victory, and swore to pluck out the hairs from the Sheikh's moustache, by way of contribution to the abolition of privileges. Tanios had no scruples about drinking a glass of arak while imagining the scene – he would even have willingly added Raad's goatee – and was raising his glass again when Adel *effendi* promised to abolish, while he was about it, 'all foreigners' privileges'.

The major immediately launched into a passionate diatribe, with many examples; he obviously felt strongly about this.

'Yesterday, I was travelling through all the villages, and wherever my horse led me I felt at home. I could enter any house whatsoever, its door stood open to me. Until the moment when I passed the home of an English clergyman. On the gate was his king's flag. And I felt insulted.'

Suddenly Tanios found he could not swallow his arak, and did not dare raise his eyes, for fear of betraying himself. Apparently the officer did not know, could not suspect, that this house, barred by a foreign flag, was his home.

'Is it normal,' insisted Adel *effendi*, 'for foreigners to be more respected, more favoured, more feared, than the natives of the country?'

Then, remembering that he was not himself exactly a native of the country – neither a son of Egypt, nor especially a son of these Mountains which he had conquered – he deemed it useful to clarify.

'I myself was not born here, you will say.' (No one would have dared to tell him that.) 'But I have put myself at the service of this glorious dynasty, I have adopted the language of the country, its religion, its uniform, I have fought beneath its flag. Whereas the English, while living amongst us, seek only to serve the policies of England and respect only the English flag; they imagine these are above our laws . . .'

Roukoz hastened to say aloud that there was absolutely no reason to compare Adel *effendi* with these foreigners, that the English were a most arrogant bunch, that His Excellency was obviously not a foreigner, but a brother. Tanios said nothing.

'However, my ward was more puzzled than he wished to admit to me,' noted the clergyman:

On the one hand, he felt sincere affection for me and Mrs Stolton, and was attached to our educational work. But at the same time he could not be totally insensible to the fact that foreigners may benefit from privileges to which the people of the land have no access. His sense of justice was given a somewhat rough ride.

Understanding his perplexity, I explained to him that as a general rule privileges were a scandal in a society based on right, but, conversely, in a society where arbitrariness rules, privileges sometimes constitute a protection against despotism, thus becoming, paradoxically, oases of right and equity. This is certainly the case in Eastern societies today, be they Ottoman or Egyptian. What is scandalous is not the fact that soldiers cannot freely enter our Sahlain Mission or an Englishman's home. What is really scandalous is the fact that they demand the right to enter at will any school and any home in the country. What is scandalous is not the fact that they cannot seize the person of a British subject, but that they can dispose at will of all persons who do not enjoy the protection of one of the great Powers.

I concluded by saying that, if people wanted to abolish privileges, the right way to proceed would not be to submit foreigners to the unenviable fate of the local population, but, on the contrary, to treat everyone in the same way as foreigners are treated. For the latter are simply treated as any human being should be . . .

I fear I was somewhat carried away while formulating my reply, and Mrs Stolton reproached me with this, but it seems that my ward was sensible to my point of view.

The clergyman was listened to less attentively when he advised Tanios to avoid visiting in future a house frequented by Egyptian soldiers. That is certainly what wisdom would have ordered. But, to outweigh this wisdom, there was Asma's smile, and the whole future path lit up by that smile. For nothing in the world would Tanios have wanted to give this up.

The delicate subject which had cast a shadow over the first encounter with the officers was not to arise again. On the two or three occasions that Tanios met them again at Roukoz's home, the conversation turned mainly on the fortunes of the war, the Master of Egypt's certain victory over the Ottoman Sultan, and once more the abolition of privileges, but only those of the feudal lords in general, and of Sheikh Francis in particular, with the promised fate of his moustache.

Tanios had not the slightest objection to drinking once more to this joyful prospect. He had arrived at a sort of compromise with himself on the question of privileges: to maintain those of foreign nationals, and abolish those of the sheikhs. Which allowed him to spare both the clergyman's anxieties and the aspirations of Asma's father as well as his own inclinations.

Was there not, in fact, a difference of nature between these two types of privilege? If the concessions granted to the English constituted for the time being – he was pre-pared to admit this – protection against despotism, the outrageous privileges of the feudal families, which had been exercised for generations at the expense of a resigned population, served no identifiable cause.

This compromise suited both his heart and his head, and he felt more at peace with himself when he had arrived at it. So much at peace that he could not see another difference between the two types of privilege, which should have stuck out a mile: against the foreign Powers, the officers of the Viceroy of Egypt could do nothing, save curse and swear and drink. Against the Sheikh, they could. It was easier to pluck the hairs from his moustache than from the mane of the British lion.

Sixth Passage

A Strange Mediatorship

It was written that the misfortunes which struck our village were to culminate in an abominable act, bringing malediction: the assassination of the thrice venerated Patriarch, at hands which moreover seemed in no ways made for crime.

A Mountain Chronicle,
the work of the monk Elias

I

The year thirty-eight was calamitous from the start: on 1 January the earthquake occurred. Its traces – and its memory – are engraved in stone.

For weeks the village had been lying dormant beneath a deep blanket of snow, the tops of the pines were weighed down and the children in the school playground sank down in it up to their knees. But that morning the weather was clear. Not a cloud in the sky. A day when the wintry sun, known locally as 'the bear's sun', brought light, but no warmth.

Towards noon, or a little earlier, there was a rumble. Like a growl from the bowels of the earth, but it was the sky that the villagers began to scrutinize, calling to each other from house to house. Perhaps it was distant thunder, or an avalanche . . .

A few seconds later, another rumble, more violent. Walls shook, and people rushed outside shouting, '*Hazzi! Hazzi!*' Some ran to the church. Others knelt down where they were, praying aloud. While still others were already dying beneath the ruins. And people remembered that the dogs had not stopped howling since dawn, and the jackals, too, from the valley, who were normally silent until evening.

'The people who happened to be near the spring at that time,' states the *Chronicle*, 'witnessed a terrifying sight. The façade of the castle cracked under their eyes, the rift spread, as if slashed by gigantic scissors. Recalling a passage from the Holy Scriptures, several people turned away their gaze, lest they be turned into pillars of salt if their eyes beheld the wrath of God.'

The castle did not collapse that year, nor any of its wings; except for this crack, it did not even suffer very much. Moreover, remarkably, the fissured wall still stands to this day. Standing with its crack, when other walls of the castle, some older, some newer, have crumbled long since. Standing overgrown with weeds, as if, having announced the misfortune, it had been preserved from it. Or as if what it foretold had not yet been fulfilled.

In the village, on the other hand, there were some thirty victims.

'Even more serious,' Gebrayel told me, 'the muleteer's house collapsed. An old building in which he had accumulated thousands of books of all kinds. A treasure, alas! The memory of our Mountains! Nader was away on his rounds, far from Kfaryabda. When he returned a week later, the snow had melted and his whole library was decaying in the mud. Among his books he is said to have had . . .'

I had stopped listening a moment before, pondering his first sentence.

'Even more serious, you said? More serious than thirty victims?'

There was a spark of provocation in his eyes.

'Just as serious, at least. When a catastrophe occurs, I naturally think of people and their suffering, but I fear as much for the relics of the past.'

'Ruins as much as men?'

'When all's said and done, carved stones, pages on which the author or the copyist laboured, mosaics, all those are fragments of humanity as well, in fact just those parts of ourselves which we hope to be immortal. What painter would like to survive his paintings?'

In spite of Gebrayel's strange preferences, it was not the destruction of the muleteer's books which caused that year to be called calamitous. Nor the earthquake either, which was only the premonitory symptom. Nor simply the assassination of the Patriarch. 'The whole year, from beginning to end,' says the *Chronicle*, was nothing but one long procession of misfortunes:

> Unknown diseases, monstrous births, landslides, and above all, famine and extortion. The annual tax was collected twice, in February and then again in November: and as if that were still not enough, means were found of introducing additional taxes, on people, goats, windmills, soap, windows . . . No one had two piastres to rub together any more, or provisions, or cattle to call their own.
>
> And when they learned that the Egyptians intended to confiscate beasts of burden and draught animals, the people of Kfaryabda had no choice but to drive their asses and mules over the cliff . . .

Notwithstanding appearances, this was not an act of spite, nor even of resistance. Only a precaution, as the Chronicler explains, for once the animals had been tracked down and seized, Major Adel *effendi* apprehended the owner and compelled him to follow the 'recruited' beast into captivity. 'The worst of governors is not the one who gives you a beating, it's the one who forces you to beat yourself,' he concludes.

Similarly, the monk Elias points out that the inhabitants of Kfaryabda made it a rule not to leave their homes at certain hours. The Pasha of Egypt's men were everywhere, at the barber's, the grocer's, playing *tawle* in the coffee-house on the *Blata*, and in the evening their drunken gangs came singing and shouting to the square and the adjoining streets, so that no one frequented these areas any more, not out of bravado, but again as a wise precaution. for not a day went by but the soldiers insulted and humiliated a passer-by under some pretext or other.

From mid-February, the Sheikh too decided to shut himself up in his castle, and never set foot on the front steps any more; he had just heard that Said *beyk*, his counterpart

in Sahlain, while out in his own domain, had been inter-
cepted by a patrol and required to declare his identity . . .

This incident had plunged the Master of Kfaryabda into
a deep depression. To his subjects who came up the hill
to see him, bringing their grievances, and begging him to
intervene with the Egyptian commander, he replied with
expressions of sympathy, and occasionally with promises;
but he did not budge. Some saw in this an admission of his
helplessness, others a mark of insensitivity. 'When the son
of a grand house is harassed, the Sheikh deems himself
insulted; when it's ourselves, the peasants, who suffer . . .'

The priest had to reproach him.

'Our Sheikh behaves arrogantly with the Egyptians, and
perhaps they interpret this as contempt, which incites them
to behave daily more savagely.'

'And what should I do, *Bouna?*'

'Invite Adel *effendi* to the castle, show him some
consideration . . .'

'To thank him for all he has done, I suppose? But if that
is what people want, I shall not oppose it. *Khweja* Gerios
shall write him a letter today to tell him I shall be honoured
to receive him and have a discussion with him. Then we'll
see.'

The following day, just before noon, a soldier arrived with
the reply, which Gerios unsealed at a sign from the Master,
and glanced through. In the audience chamber was gathered the solemn crowd of those unhappy days. They all saw
Lamia's husband's face suddenly flush, this time without
arak being the sole cause.

'Adel *effendi* won't come, Sheikh.'

'I suppose he insists on my going to his camp myself.'

'No, he wants our Sheikh to go and see him this
afternoon . . . at Roukoz's house.'

Eyes were now all fixed on the Master's hand, which
tightened on his worry-beads.

'I will not go. If he had suggested I go to Dayroun, I would have told myself, this is an arm-wrestling match, we give way a little, then we straighten up. But as it is, he is not seeking a reconciliation, he only wants to humiliate me.'

The villagers consulted among themselves in silence, then the priest spoke for them.

'If this meeting is necessary to dispel misunderstandings and avoid further suffering . . .'

'Do not insist, *Bouna*, I shall never set foot in that house built with money stolen from me.'

'Even to save the village and the castle?'

It was Raad who asked this question. His father stared at him in deathly silence. His eyes grew severe, then outraged. Then scornful. Then turned away from him to look at the priest again. And, after a while, addressed him in a tired voice.

'I know, *Bouna*, it is pride, or call it what you will, but I cannot act differently. Let my castle, the whole village, be taken from me, I want nothing of life. But let me be left with my pride. I would rather die than cross that thief's threshold. If my attitude endangers the village, let me be killed, let my waistcoat be snatched from me and my son be dressed in it and installed in my place. He will agree to go to Roukoz's house.'

The veins swelled in his forehead. And his expression hardened so much that no one was prepared to speak.

Then Gerios, emboldened by the alcohol which had been mingling with his blood throughout the day, had a brilliant idea.

'Why speak of murder and mourning? May God prolong the life of our Sheikh and maintain him above our heads, but nothing forbids him from delegating his son and heir to replace him at this meeting.'

The Sheikh, still sickened by Raad's intervention, said nothing, and his silence was interpreted as consent. He let them do what they thought fit and retired to his quarters with his worry-beads.

The meeting at Roukoz's house was brief. Its only object had been to tweak the Sheikh's moustache, and his son's arrival was thought by all to be a sufficient humiliation. Raad managed to find seven different ways of saying that the village felt nothing but loyalty for the Viceroy of Egypt and his faithful ally, the Emir. And the officer promised that his men would henceforward behave more leniently with the villagers. Then, after half an hour, he withdrew with the excuse of another engagement.

The young Sheikh, on the other hand, in no hurry to return and confront his father, agreed to be shown round the property on the arm of the 'thief', the 'rogue', the 'outlaw' . . .

Between the two men there was to grow, if not friendship, at least collusion. At the same time, the latent conflict between Raad and his father burst out into the open. For several weeks the castle was the seat of two rival courts, and more than once they nearly came to blows.

However, the situation did not last. Those who sided with the young Sheikh, in the hope that he would prove wiser than his father in his dealings with the Egyptians, were soon disillusioned. His frivolity, his weakness, was only too obvious to all. Soon the youth had at his sides no more than four or five companions in debauchery, drunkards and skirt-chasers whom the majority of the villagers despised. It must also be said that, not only did his ineptitude and unreliability count against him, but also his accent, the abhorred accent of the Jord 'locusts', of which he had never been able to rid himself, and which erected a barrier between his subjects and himself.

Tanios did not exactly take kindly to the relationship between Roukoz and Raad. He was capable of understanding that the latter was an instrument in the struggle against the Sheikh. But he did not wish to understand. His distrust of his former classmate remained inviolate, and he never missed an opportunity of warning Asma's father against him. When he sometimes turned up at the latter's house, after school, and saw Raad's horse outside the house with some of his escort, he went on his way without stopping, even if it would be a week before he saw Asma.

Only once was he caught out. He had come in the morning and found his sweetheart alone in the great hall, where they had remained together for a while. Just as he was about to leave, he came face to face with Roukoz and Raad, their clothes covered in mud, and the latter brandishing a bleeding young fox.

'You've had good hunting apparently.'

Tanios's tone was deliberately contemptuous, and he made this even clearer by walking on as he spoke. But the other two men did not seem at all offended. Roukoz even invited him most amiably to stay and partake of some fruit with them. Tanios excused himself, saying that he was expected back in the village. Then, against all expectations, Raad came up to him and put his hand on his shoulder.

'I'm going back to the castle too. I need a wash and a rest. We can travel together.'

Tanios could not refuse; he even accepted the loan of a horse and found himself riding side by side with Raad and two of the louts from his set.

'I needed to talk to you,' said the young Sheikh, making an effort to sound most agreeable.

Tanios was aware of this and forced himself to smile politely.

'You are *Khweja* Roukoz's friend, and I have become his friend, too, so it's time to forget what came between us when we were kids. You were studious, I was rowdy, but we have both grown older.'

Tanios was seventeen and had a fringe of beard round his chin; Raad was eighteen with a goatee, like the Patriarch's, but black and wiry. It was at this beard that Tanios stared, before he turned to look thoughtfully at the road.

'Roukoz tells me he can always talk to you with great confidence and he thinks about what you have to advise. He reckons I should talk to you also and listen to you.'

Raad was now speaking in a confidential tone of voice, but the men who accompanied him pricked up their ears to try to catch every word of the conversation. Tanios shrugged with resignation.

'Of course, nothing stops us talking sincerely.'

'I'm so pleased we're friends again!'

Friends? Friends again? For months they had gone every morning to the same school, on the same road, and they had hardly ever spoken a word to each other! Moreover, at that moment, Tanios had not one friendly thought in his head. Annoying when he wants to be disagreeable, annoying when he wants to be agreeable, he thought . . . While Raad only smiled contentedly.

'Since we're friends now, you can tell me, is it true you have designs on Roukoz's daughter?'

So that was it – the reason for all these friendly overtures. Tanios had all the less desire to confide in the young Sheikh, in that his men had come even closer, with the expressions of dogs smelling a bone.

'No, I have no designs on the girl. Can we not talk of something else?'

He pulled on the reins and his horse reared.

'Of course,' said Raad, 'we can talk of something else straight away, but I needed your reassurance about Asma. I have just asked her father for her hand.'

II

Tanios's first reaction was to feel scorn and disbelief. He could still see the expression in Asma's eyes and feel the caresses of her fingers. And he also knew what Roukoz, in his heart of hearts, thought of Raad. To use this puppet to undermine his father, yes; to be linked to him for the rest of his life – the former major-domo was too shrewd for that.

However, when the young Sheikh came riding up to him, Tanios could not help asking, in what he hoped was a casual tone of voice, 'And what was his reply?'

'Roukoz? He replied as any commoner must reply when his master does him the honour of showing interest in his daughter.'

Tanios had nothing more to say to this detestable fellow, he leapt off the horse Raad had lent him and turned back. Straight back to talk to Roukoz. Whom he found huddled in his usual seat in his new reception hall, alone, with no visitors, no bodyguards or servants, enveloped in tobacco smoke and steam from his coffee. He appeared sunk in thought, and somewhat disillusioned. But at the sight of Tanios he seemed to cheer up and welcomed him with embraces, although they had parted only three-quarters of an hour before.

'I'm so pleased you've returned! Sheikh Raad dragged you away, when I was anxious to stay quietly with you and talk to you like a son, the son whom God gave me belatedly.'

He took his hand.

'I've great news for you. We have arranged a marriage for your sister Asma.'

Tanios withdrew his hand. He recoiled, leaned back,

almost crushed against the wall. Roukoz's words caused the tobacco smoke to thicken till it nearly choked him.

'I know, you and I have had to suffer at the hands of sheikhs, but this Raad is not like his father. The proof is that he agreed to come to this house for the sake of the village, while his father remained obdurate. We don't have to deal with the old Sheikh, we have the heir on our side, and we have the future.'

The young man pulled himself together. Now he looked straight into the deep-set eyes of Roukoz, who appeared to sag.

'I thought that the future, for you, meant the abolition of the sheikhs . . .'

'Yes, that is my belief, and I shall stick to it. The feudal lords must be abolished and I shall see that they are abolished. But what better way to take a fortress than to assure oneself of allies within?'

On Roukoz's face, Tanios now had eyes only for the pock-marks which seemed to pit it deeper than ever, like vermin holes.

There was a moment's silence. Roukoz puffed on his hookah. Tanios could see the embers glow, then grow dim.

'Asma and I love each other.'

'Don't talk nonsense, you are my son and she is my daughter, I'm really not going to give my daughter in marriage to my son!'

That was too much for Tanios, too much hypocrisy.

'I am not your son, and I want to speak to Asma.'

'You can't speak to her, she's bathing. She's getting herself ready. Tomorrow the people will hear the news and will want to come to congratulate us.'

Tanios rushed out of the reception chamber, across the corridor, to the door which he knew led to Asma's bedroom. A door which he pushed roughly open. Asma was there, sitting naked in her copper bath-tub, while a maidservant poured steaming water over her hair. They shrieked simultaneously. Asma crossed her arms across her chest and the servant bent down to pick up a towel.

Staring at what was still visible of his beloved's skin, Tanios did not move. And when Roukoz and his henchmen came running, and grabbed hold of him to drag him away, he feigned an expression of bliss, did not struggle and did not even attempt to ward off their blows.

'Why are you getting so upset? If we are brother and sister, what harm is there in my seeing her naked? From this evening we shall sleep every night in the same room, as all brothers and sisters do in this country.'

Asma's father seized him by his white hair.

'I did you too much honour in calling you my son. No one has ever known whose son you were. I don't want a bastard for a son, nor for a son-in-law.

'Get him out of here! Don't hurt him, but if any of you ever see him prowling round my property again, you can break his neck!'

As if Asma's naked body had opened his eyes, Tanios recovered his lucidity. Filled with anger at himself, and with remorse, but also with his mind at peace.

He was certainly angry with himself for not having seen this treachery coming. Obsessed with rising on the social scale, Roukoz would not have wanted to finish his career where it had begun – by giving his only daughter to a major-domo's son; or, worse, to a bastard – when he could give her to the son of a 'Great House'. And for Raad, most probably haunted daily by the spectre of ruin, to put his hand on Asma's promised fortune could only be welcome.

On the way back to Kfaryabda, Tanios had first felt some satisfaction in blaming his own blindness. Then he had begun to reflect. Not on some childish revenge, but on the exact way in which he could prevent this marriage.

It did not seem impossible. If Roukoz had only been an upstart like so many other newly rich bourgeois or tenant farmers, the old Sheikh would probably have resigned himself to this misalliance. This was clearly not the case; how could the man who had not been prepared to lower himself to cross the threshold of the 'thief' consent to such a union? Tanios knew he would find in him a cunning and determined ally.

He started walking faster and faster, and every step made his legs, sides, shoulders and even his scalp hurt. But he ignored this, only one thing mattered, and with this he was obsessed: Asma would be his, even if it were over her father's dead body.

On reaching the village, he turned to the right, taking the paths which crossed the fields and then skirted the pine forest, leading up to the castle, avoiding the *Blata*.

When he got there, he did not go to see the Sheikh, but his parents. Whom he asked very solemnly to listen to him, making them promise in advance not to try to argue with him, on pain of seeing him leave for ever.

What he then told them is related more or less in the same terms by the monk Elias in his *Chronicle* and by the Reverend Stolton on a loose sheet inserted in his Yearbook for the year 1838, but probably written much later. I am reproducing the latter, as it must correspond to Tanios's own words:

'You must know that I love this girl and she loves me, and her father had given me to understand that he would grant me her hand. But Roukoz and Raad have both made a fool of me, and I have lost hope. If, by the end of this week, I am not betrothed to Asma, I kill either Raad or myself, and you know I would not hesitate to do that.' 'Anything but that,' said his mother, who had never quite got over her son's hunger strike two years previously. She took her husband's hand, as if to beseech him, and he also spoke to Tanios, in the following words. 'The marriage which you fear will not take place. If I do not succeed in preventing it, I am not your father!'

This emphatic oath was not unusual in the region, but, under the circumstances – the drama which was taking place and that surrounding Tanios's birth – these words, far from being laughable, were pathetic.

'Fate tightened its knots,' states the *Chronicle*, 'and death was on the prowl.'

Tanios was under the impression that death was prowling round him. And he was not certain he wished to drive it away. Whereas Gerios, normally so weak, seemed determined to fight against Providence, and to place himself in its path.

People in the village, who had never had the least pity for him – including 'my' Gebrayel, and many other elders – say that the major-domo would have been much less determined if Tanios's aspirations had not coincided with those of the Sheikh, and if he had had to clash with the latter. This is to ignore the change of heart which had taken place in Gerios, in the autumn of a life of disappointments and upheavals. He felt himself involved in an operation of salvation. The salvation of his son, and also of his own dignity, as a man, a husband, a father, too long derided.

That same evening, soon after Tanios's return and his conversation with him, Gerios went to see the Sheikh, and found him in the great hall of the castle, walking from one pillar to the other, alone, bareheaded, his white hair unkempt. In his hand a string of amber worry-beads, which he ran one by one through his fingers, as if to punctuate his sighs.

The major-domo came and stood near the door. Saying nothing, except by his presence, lit up by a nearby lamp.

'What's the matter, *Khweja* Gerios? You seem as worried as I am.'

'It's my son, Sheikh.'

'Our sons, our hopes, our crosses.'

They went to sit side by side, already exhausted.

'Your son isn't easy either,' the Sheikh continued, 'but at least you feel he understands when you speak to him.'

'He understands, perhaps, but he just goes his own way. And whenever he's crossed, he talks of dying.'

'For what reason, this time?'

'He has fallen in love with Roukoz's daughter, and the dog let him understand he would give him her hand. When he heard that he had also promised her to Sheikh Raad . . .'

'So that's all? Then Tanios can put his mind at rest. You can tell him from me that, as long as I live, that marriage will never take place, and if my son insists, I shall disinherit him. He wants Roukoz's fortune! He can go and become Roukoz's son-in-law. But he won't get my domain. The man who robbed me will never set foot in this castle, neither he nor his daughter. Go and tell your son that, word for word, and he'll get his appetite back.'

'No, Sheikh, I won't tell him that.'

The Master started. Never had this devoted servant answered him in this way. He usually began to express his approval even before the Master's words were out of his mouth; this 'No' had never crossed his lips. He began to observe him, intrigued, almost amused. And at a loss.

'I don't understand you . . .'

Gerios simply kept his eyes on the ground. To confront the Sheikh already cost him an effort, to meet his gaze, in addition, was more than he could manage.

'I am not going to report our Sheikh's words to Tanios, because I know in advance what answer he will give me. He will say, "Raad always succeeds in getting his own way, no matter what his father wishes. He wanted to leave the English school, he succeeded in doing it in the worst possible way, and no one had a word of blame for him. He wanted to go to Roukoz's house to meet the officer and nobody could stop him. For this marriage, it will be the same thing.

He wants this girl, he will get her. And soon our Sheikh will dangle on his knees a grandchild christened Francis, like himself, and who will also be Roukoz's grandchild." '

Gerios fell silent. He was stunned by his own words. He could scarcely believe he had spoken to his Lord and Master in these terms. And he waited, his eyes on the ground and his neck damp with perspiration.

The Sheikh, just as silent, hesitated. Should he rebuff him? Repress this incipient rebellion by anger or by contempt? No, he placed his hand on the anxious shoulder.

'*Khayyi* Gerios, what do you think I should do?'

Did he say '*Khayyi*'? My brother? The major-domo shed two tears of satisfaction, and raised himself imperceptibly to suggest the path which, in his opinion, should be taken.

'Did not the Patriarch warn us he would be coming to the castle on Sunday? He is the only one who can make Roukoz and Sheikh Raad hear reason . . .'

'He is the only one, that is true. Providing he is prepared to . . .'

'Our Sheikh will find the words to persuade him.'

The chatelain nodded his approval, then got to his feet to retire to his quarters. It was growing late. Gerios then stood up too, kissed his Master's hand to take leave of him, and also to thank him for his attitude. He was making his way towards the corridor which led to the wing where he lived, when the Sheikh changed his mind and called him back, asking him to accompany him with a lantern to his bedroom. Where he took a rifle from under his eiderdown. The one which had been given to Raad by Richard Wood. It shone in the lantern's flame like a monstrous jewel.

'This morning I saw it in the hands of one of those louts who are always hanging round my son. He told me Raad had given it to him as a result of some wager or other. I confiscated it, telling him it was castle property, and a gift from the English Consul. I want you to lock it up in the safe with our money. Take care, it is loaded.'

Gerios carried the weapon, clutched tightly. It smelt of hot resin.

III

The village-folk felt as much distrust as veneration for the Patriarch's mitre. And when, in the course of his sermon, he exhorted them to pray for the Emir of the Mountains, as well as for the Viceroy of Egypt, their lips began to move – although God alone knows for what they were praying, what wishes lay concealed beneath the uniform hum of their voices.

The Sheikh remained seated in his pew throughout the mass; he had felt slightly unwell in the night, and he rose to his feet only once, to take communion, to receive on his tongue the bread soaked in wine. Raad followed close behind him, with no show of piety, and came to stand beside him, gazing indecently at the swollen veins on the paternal brow.

After the ceremony, the Sheikh and the Prelate left the church together and made their way to the Hall of Pillars. While he was closing the great doors to leave them in intimate conversation, Gerios had time to hear the Patriarch say, 'I have a request to make, and I know I shall not leave such a noble house disappointed.'

Lamia's husband rubbed his hands, God loves us, he thought. If *Sayyidna* has come to ask a favour, he cannot refuse the one we ask of him! And he looked for Tanios to whisper his hope in his ear.

In the great hall, the Sheikh started, and smoothed his moustache with both hands, for he had had exactly the same thought as his major-domo. While the Patriarch continued, 'I have just returned from Beit ed-Din, where I spent a whole day with our Emir. I found him troubled. The agents of England and the Sublime Porte are at work in the Mountains, and many people have let themselves be subverted. The Emir told me, "It is in these circumstances that the loyal person can be distinguished from the traitor." And as we were speaking of loyalty, the first name mentioned was naturally yours, Sheikh Francis.'

'May God prolong your life, *Sayyidna*!'

'I will not hide from you that the Emir had some misgivings. He was still under the impression that this village had lent an ear to the songs of the English. I assured him that that was a thing of the past, and that we were now brothers as we all ought to have remained.'

The Sheikh nodded, but an anxious look crept into his eyes. What was his wily visitor about to ask, after this ambiguous preamble, a combination of warnings and praises?

'Formerly,' the Prelate went on, 'this village has shown its courage in difficult times, the bravery of its men has always been proverbial. Today, grave matters are in preparation, and our Emir again has need of soldiers. In other villages in the Mountains, men have been recruited by force. Here, there are traditions, I told our Emir that Kfaryabda will send more volunteers than he could raise with his recruiting agents. Am I wrong?'

The Sheikh was not delighted with this prospect, but it would have been tactless to show any reluctance.

'You may tell our Emir that I shall assemble our men as before, and they will be the most valiant of his soldiers.'

'I expected nothing less from our Sheikh. How many men can the Emir count on?'

'All those who are hale and hearty, and I shall lead them myself.'

As the Patriarch rose, he cast an appraising glance at his host. Who seemed recovered, and made it a point of honour to rise to his feet like a young man without taking hold of any support. But leading his army into battle would be another matter, . . .

'May God keep you always as fit and strong,' said the Prelate.

And with his thumb he traced the sign of the cross on his brow.

'Before *Sayyidna* leaves, I too have a favour to ask. It is a matter of no great importance, it is even futile compared with everything that is happening in the country. But it worries me and I would like to see it settled before leaving on this campaign . . .'

On leaving their meeting, the Patriarch warned his escort that he would like 'to go by *Khweja* Roukoz's house', whereupon Gerios kissed his hand with such fervour that certain people who witnessed this were intrigued.

'To go by' was simply a euphemism. The Prelate went right into the house, took a seat in the former major-domo's panelled hall, had Asma brought to him, talked at length with her, and then alone with her father, whom he willingly let show him round the vast property. The visit lasted more than an hour, longer than his recent visit to the castle. And he left beaming.

The time seemed interminable to Tanios, Lamia and Gerios, who could not refrain from gulping down several swigs of arak to allay his anxiety.

On returning to the castle, the Patriarch indicated to the Sheikh with a reassuring gesture that the matter was basically settled, but he asked to be left alone with Raad. When he emerged again, Raad did not accompany him; he had slipped away by a secret door. 'Tomorrow he won't give it another thought,' stated the Prelate.

Then, without sitting down, simply leaning against one of the pillars in the great hall, he whispered to his host the result of his mediation and the ingenious solution he had managed to find.

Lamia had brewed herself some coffee on the glowing embers and was sipping the steaming beverage. Voices, sounds reached her through the half-open door, but she expected to hear only Gerios's footsteps, hoping to read in his face what had happened. From time to time she murmured a short prayer to the Virgin, clasping her crucifix tightly in her hand.

'She was young, was Lamia, and still beautiful, and her throat was like that of a trusting young lamb,' commented Gebrayel.

While Tanios waited for the sentence which would soon be pronounced, he climbed up to the alcove where, as a child, he had known so much peaceful happiness. He unrolled his thin mattress and lay down with a blanket over his legs. Perhaps he intended not to move and to resume his hunger strike if the mediation failed. But perhaps he needed only to daydream to stave off his impatience. Be that as it may, it was not long before he dozed off.

In the great hall, the Patriarch had spoken. Then he had immediately taken his leave, the unexpected detour to visit Roukoz having caused him a delay for which he now had to make up.

The Sheikh had accompanied him to the front porch, but had not descended the steps with him. And the Prelate did not turn round to wave to him. He had been helped on to his horse and his retinue set off.

Gerios was standing near the front door, one foot inside and the other on the steps, his mind becoming more blurred by the minute. The result of the arak he had consumed during the hours of waiting, of the Patriarch's explanations, and also the words which his master had just whispered in his ear.

'I'm wondering if I should laugh or strangle him,' the Sheikh had said, his words dry as an expectoration.

Even to this day, when this unforgotten episode is recounted, people remain divided between indignation and laughter: this venerable Prelate, who had gone to ask for Asma's hand for Tanios, had changed his mind on seeing her, endowed with grace and fortune, and had obtained her hand for . . . his own nephew!

Oh, the saintly man certainly had an explanation: the Sheikh did not want the girl for Raad, and Roukoz wouldn't hear of Tanios; so, as he himself had a nephew to marry off . . .

The Master of Kfaryabda felt he had been made a fool of. When he had gone to such lengths to try to put the former major-domo in his place, and now this 'thief' was to be allied to the family of the Patriarch, the supreme head of the community!

As for Gerios, he was in no state to reason thus in terms of gains and losses. Staring at the Patriarch's grey mount, which was slowly ambling away, he had only one idea in his head, a thorn in his flesh, a source of torture. He breathed the words: 'Tanios will kill himself!'

The Sheikh heard only a grunt. He began to look his major-domo up and down.

'You stink of arak, Gerios! Get out, out of my sight! And don't come back till you've sobered up and made yourself smell more sweetly!'

With a shrug of his shoulders, the Master betook himself to his room. Again he felt a sort of dizziness, and badly needed to rest for a few moments.

At the same time Lamia began to weep. She could not say why, but she was sure she had reason to weep. She leaned out of her window and glimpsed the Prelate's retinue moving off through the trees.

She could not hold out any longer and started out

towards the great hall to find out what had happened. As long as the Patriarch was there she had preferred not to show herself, she knew he had never had any love for her, he was annoyed with the Sheikh because of her; she was afraid that on seeing her his anger would be aroused and Tanios would have to bear the consequences.

Useless precaution, so the author of the *Mountain Chronicle* thought. 'The very birth of this lad had always been intolerable to our Patriarch, because of what was said . . . How could he ask for a girl's hand for him?'

Crossing the corridor which led from the major-domo's wing to the central part of the castle, Lamia saw a strange spectacle. At the other end of the narrow passage she thought she caught sight of a figure, like that of Gerios, running with a gun in his hand. She hurried but he had disappeared. She was not quite sure of having recognized him in the half-light. On the one hand she thought it really was him; she couldn't say by what sign, what gesture she had recognized him, but after all she had been living with him for nearly twenty years, how could she be mistaken? On the other hand, that way of running was so unlike her husband, a man who was always so solemn, so obsequious in the exercise of his duties in the castle, a man who wouldn't allow himself so much as a laugh so as not to lack dignity. To hurry, yes, but to run? And with a gun?

When she reached the Hall of Pillars, it was deserted, whereas it had been crowded with visitors a few minutes before. Nobody in the outer courtyard either.

She went out on to the front steps and thought she saw Gerios disappearing through the trees. An ever briefer, more fleeting sight than before. Should she run after him? She was just tucking up her skirts, then she changed her mind and returned to her quarters. She called Tanios, then, without waiting for him to reply, she climbed the little ladder which led to the alcove where he was sleeping. She shook him.

'Get up! I've just seen your father running like a madman, with a gun. You must catch him!'

'And the Patriarch?'

'I don't know anything, nobody has told me anything yet. But hurry, catch your father, he must know, he'll tell you.'

What was there still to say? Lamia had understood. The silence, the deserted castle, her husband running.

The path down which she had seen Gerios disappearing was one of the least frequented ones between the castle and the village. The people of Kfaryabda – I have already mentioned this – used to climb up the steps which led from the *Blata*, behind the spring; carts and riders, for their part, preferred the wide road – now partially collapsed – which wound the long way round the hill on which the castle stood. And then there was this path, on the south-west slope, the steepest and roughest, but a short cut which joined the main road from the square on the outskirts of the village. Anyone venturing on this path had constantly to catch hold of trees and rocks. In the state he was in, Gerios risked breaking his neck.

As Tanios raced after him, he looked in vain for him every time he was forced to stop to support himself against the rock face. But he didn't catch sight of him until the very last minute, when it was too late to prevent anything; while his eyes took in the whole scene – the men, the animals, their movements, their expressions; the Patriarch riding on, followed by his escort, a dozen men on horseback and as many on foot. And Gerios, behind a rock, bareheaded, the rifle cocked against his shoulder.

The shot rang out. A roar echoed through the mountains and the valleys. The Patriarch fell like a log. Hit in the face, between the eyes. His panic-stricken horse bolted, dragging its rider by the foot for several yards before letting him go.

Gerios emerged from his hiding place – a flat, vertical rock, planted in the earth like an immense splinter of glass, and which has been called 'The Ambush' ever since that day. He was holding the gun above his head in both hands, ready to give himself up. But the Prelate's companions, thinking themselves attacked by a band of rebels in ambush, had fled back towards the castle.

And the assassin remained alone, in the middle of the path, still holding his arms in the air, still holding the gun with the reddish glints, the gifts from the English 'Consul'.

Then Tanios came up to him and took him by the arm.

'*Bayyi!*'

Father! It was many years since Tanios had addressed him thus. Gerios looked at his child gratefully. He had had to become a murderer to deserve to hear that word again. *Bayyi!* At that moment he regretted nothing, and wanted nothing more. He had regained his place, his honour. His crime had redeemed his life. It remained now only to give himself up and show himself worthy at the hour of punishment.

He put the weapon down cautiously, as if afraid it would get scratched. Then he turned to Tanios. He tried to tell him the reason why he had killed. He could not speak. No words could pass his throat.

He clasped the boy to him. Then he turned away from him to walk towards the castle. But Tanios pulled him back.

'*Bayyi!* You and I must stay together. This time, you have chosen to be on my side, and I won't let you go back to the Sheikh!'

Gerios let himself be led away. They left the road and took the steep path that led down to the bottom of the valley. Behind them, the clamour of the village arose. But as they clambered down the hill, from tree to tree, from rock to rock, caught up in the brambles, they could hear nothing.

IV

When he had committed his infamous act, the major-domo Gerios climbed hurriedly down the hill, accompanied by his son. They hid from view of all and the Sheikh had to give up the pursuit.

When they reached the bottom of the valley, they walked till nightfall, and then throughout the night, following the torrent which runs down to the sea.

With the first light of dawn, they crossed the bridge over the Dog River, to reach the port of Beirut. Where, at the quay, two large boats were preparing to set sail. The first for Alexandria, but they were careful not to take this, for the Master of Egypt would have hastened to hand them over to the Emir, so that they could expiate their abominable crime. They preferred to embark on the other, which was leaving for the island of Cyprus, where they landed after a day and a night and a day at sea.

There, passing themselves off as silk merchants, they found lodgings in the port of Famagusta, at an inn run by a man from Aleppo.

These sober lines, extracted from the monk Elias's *Chronicle*, do not do justice to the terror felt by the people of my village, nor to the Sheikh's extreme embarrassment.

The curse was upon them, well and truly this time, stretching out from the road near the ambush rock. And when the corpse was carried into the church, to the tolling of the bell, the faithful wept; because they had detested the deceased, and still detested him, they wept as if they themselves were guilty, and from time to time looked for traces of his blood on their sweating hands.

Guilty, the Sheikh knew that he was, because he too had hated the 'Patriarch of the Locusts', so much so that only minutes before the murder he had expressed his desire to strangle him. And even discounting these imprudent words in Gerios's ear, how could he clear himself of responsibility for a crime perpetrated on his land, by his confidential agent, and with a weapon he had himself entrusted to him? The weapon, let us remember, given by Richard Wood, the English 'Consul', and which had been used for nothing less than to shoot down one of the obstacles in the way of England's policies.

A coincidence! Nothing but coincidences? The Master of Kfaryabda who, by virtue of his privileges, had often been called upon to act as judge, could not help thinking that, if he had heard so much circumstantial evidence against a man, he would certainly have found him guilty as accessory to murder, or of incitement. And yet, God knows he had not wished for this crime, and that he would have beaten Gerios's brains out with his own hands if he had suspected his intentions.

When the Patriarch's companions returned to inform the Sheikh of the tragedy which had just occurred, under their very eyes, he seemed to them at a loss, and even close to despair, as if he had, at that moment, foreseen all the misfortunes which would ensue. But he was not the man to let himself be distracted from his obligations as a chief. Quickly recovering himself, he summoned the men of his domain to organize the man-hunt.

It was his duty, and it was also what wisdom dictated: he had to show the authorities, and more immediately the Prelate's retinue, that he had done everything possible to catch the assassins. Yes, assassins. Gerios, and also Tanios. The young man was innocent, but if he had been caught that night, the Sheikh would have had no choice but to hand him over to the Emir's justice, even if he were to be hanged. Because of the way things appeared.

In such a serious matter, which extended far beyond his domain, and even beyond that of the Emir, the Master of Kfaryabda did not have a free hand, he was forced to respect appearances most scrupulously. But that was in fact what he was reproached with. By some of the Patriarch's companions, then by the Emir and the Egyptian command. Simply to have made a pretence of keeping up appearances.

That night all hell broke loose in the castle; the Sheikh rushed about like a madman, shouting orders, exhortations, oaths, with troops everywhere. But, if we are to believe his detractors, this was simply an outward show. Those who had been with the murdered Prelate claimed that the Sheikh, instead of immediately taking the necessary steps, had begun by interrogating them at length on the circumstances of the assassination, and then had appeared incredulous when they said they thought they had recognized Gerios; and he had even sent his men to the major-domo's quarters to call him; when they returned empty-handed, he had told them, 'Then go and fetch Tanios, I have to speak to him.' Then the Sheikh shut himself up for a moment alone with Lamia in the little saloon adjacent to the Hall of Pillars, to emerge a few minutes later with flushed face and with her in tears; but he had said, feigning the greatest confidence, 'Tanios has gone in search of his father, and will certainly be bringing him back here.'

And as the Patriarch's friends appeared sceptical, he had ordered his men to search everywhere – in the village, the pine forest, the old stables, and even in certain parts of the castle. Why search everywhere instead of sending his men down into the valley, down the path which Gerios and Tanios had in all probability taken? On the pretext of searching everywhere, the Sheikh had searched nowhere, because he had wanted to give the culprits time to escape!

But what interest could he have in that? He had no interest at all, quite the contrary, he was taking the gravest risks with his domain, with his own life and also with the salvation of his soul. Except that, if Tanios were indeed his son . . .

Yes, this same doubt hovered over the Sheikh and Lamia, over the castle, over this corner of the Mountains, like a storm-cloud bringing glutinous, pestilential rains.

Extract from the Reverend Stolton's Yearbook:

> The day following the assassination, a detachment of Egyptian soldiers appeared at our gate, commanded by an officer who asked me for permission to search the Mission grounds. I replied that this was out of the question, but gave him my word, as a man of God, that no one was hiding on my premises. For a few moments, I thought he was not going to be satisfied with my word, for he seemed much put out. But apparently he had orders. So, after prowling around the external fence, peering about for any suspicious presence, he eventually withdrew with his men.
>
> The inhabitants of Kfaryabda did not have a right to the same consideration. The village was invested with a force comprising several hundred men, belonging to the Viceroy's army as well as that of the Emir. First they proclaimed on the main square that they were looking for the murderer and his son – my ward – when everyone knew they must already be far away. Then they made it their duty to undertake a house-to-house search. In none of them, naturally, did they find what they claimed to be looking for, but they left no house empty-handed: the 'culprits' thus apprehended had the following names: jewellery, cloaks, carpets, tablecloths, money, drinks or provisions.
>
> In the castle, the room Gerios used as his office was examined and the safe there was duly forced open, so they were able to make sure that the major-domo was not

hiding in it . . . They also searched the wing of the castle where Tanios's parents lived, but his mother had left the previous day, on Sheikh Francis's advice, to go and stay with her sister, the priest's wife . . .

The extortions made by the keepers of order were numerous . . . Fortunately, if I may say so, the country is at war; the soldiers, needed elsewhere for other glorious tasks, were withdrawn after a week. Not before they had committed the ultimate act of injustice.

In fact, in order to make sure the Sheikh did not relax his efforts to find the culprits and hand them over – 'father and son', so the Emir had made clear – the soldiers took with them a 'suspect', or rather a hostage: Raad. It is true that he was the owner of the murder weapon; he is also said to have spoken indiscreetly to the officer who was interrogating him, namely that the Patriarch, after his strange mediation, had only himself to blame for what had happened.

The relationship between the Sheikh and his son was still as stormy as ever. But seeing him led away by soldiers, in that fashion, with his hands tied behind his back like a crook, the old man was ashamed for his flesh and blood.

Before the end of this calamitous year, the castle was deserted. Gone were its inhabitants, their quarrels, their expectations, their intrigues.

No more than a shell, with its cracked façade and the future in ruins; but the loyal villagers still climbed the hill every morning to 'see' the helpless hand of the Sheikh of Kfaryabda.

Seventh Passage

Oranges on the Stairs

Tanios said to me: 'I knew a woman. I do not speak her language and she does not speak mine, but she waits for me at the top of the stairs. One day I shall return and knock on her door to tell her that our boat is preparing to sail.'

Nader, *Wisdom on Muleback*

I

In Famagusta, at this time, the two fugitives were beginning their new existence in terror and remorse, but their life was also to consist of daring, pleasures and carefree days.

The hostelry owned by the man from Aleppo was a sort of *khan*, a caravanserai for passing merchants, a maze of booths, terraces, rickety balustrades: dilapidated, only half furnished, this inn was nevertheless the least inhospitable in the town. From the balcony of their room, on the third floor, Gerios and Tanios had a view of the customs house, slipways and boats moored by the quayside, but not of the open sea.

During the first weeks they were haunted by the fear of being recognized. They remained hidden from morning to night, and ventured out only under cover of darkness – together, or Tanios alone – to purchase food from some steaming stall. The rest of the time, they sat cross-legged on the balcony, watching the busy streets, the comings and goings of porters and travellers, and chewing brown Cypriot carob beans.

Sometimes Gerios's eyes grew misty and the tears flowed. But he did not speak. Neither of his ruined life, nor of his exile. At the very most, he said with a sigh, 'Your mother! I did not even say goodbye to her.'

Or again, 'Lamia! I shall never see her again!'

Then Tanios put his arms round him, to hear him say, 'My son! If it were not to see you, I would not even wish to open my eyes ever again!'

About the crime itself, neither Gerios nor Tanios ever spoke. Naturally, they both thought of it constantly, the single shot, the bloodstained face, the maddened horse bolting, dragging its rider, then their headlong race down into the valley, to the sea and beyond. They certainly relived all that in the course of their long hours of silence. But it was as if the burden of their fear prevented them from speaking of it.

And no one ever mentioned it in their presence either. They had fled so fast that they had heard no voice shouting, 'The Patriarch is dead, Gerios has killed him!' Nor did they hear the church bells tolling. They had never turned round, never met anyone, until they reached Beirut. Where the news had not yet arrived. At the port, the Egyptian soldiers were not looking for any murderers. And on the boat, the travellers who commented on the latest news spoke of the battles in the mountains of Syria and on the Euphrates, an attack on the Emir's supporters in a Druse village and the position taken by the great Powers. But they never mentioned the Patriarch. Afterwards, in Cyprus, the fugitives had shut themselves in . . .

Without any echo of his act, Gerios sometimes came to doubt its reality. A little as if he had dropped and broken a pitcher, without his hearing the sound of the breakage.

It was first on account of this unbearable silence that they were discovered.

Gerios began to act strangely. His lips moved, more and more frequently, in long, silent conversations. And sometimes audible, incoherent words escaped. Then he started, and turned to Tanios, smiling miserably.

'I was dreaming and talking in my sleep.'

But his eyes had been open all the time.

Fearing to see him go mad, the young man decided to make him get out of the inn.

'Nobody can possibly know who we are. And in any case, we are on Ottoman soil, and the Turks are at war with the Emir. Why should we hide?'

First they took only short, circumspect walks. They were not used to walking through the streets of strange towns, neither of them had known any place except Kfaryabda, Sahlain and Dayroun. Gerios could not help keeping his right hand continually raised as if preparing to touch his brow in greeting to people he met, and he examined the faces of all the passers-by.

His own appearance had somewhat changed and he would not have been recognized at first glance. He had stopped shaving his beard in the course of the preceding weeks, and now he decided to let it grow. Whereas Tanios had got rid of his, as well as his villager's cap, and had wrapped a white silk scarf round his head, for fear his hair should betray him. They had also bought loose-sleeved jackets such as were suitable for merchants.

They were not short of money. When he took the murder weapon from the safe at the castle, the major-domo had also taken a purse which he had deposited there previously – his own savings, not a piastre more. He had intended leaving it for his wife and son, but in his haste he had taken it with him, hidden in his clothes. A considerable nest-egg, nothing but high-grade gold coins, which the money-changers of Famagusta caressed with delight, before giving several handfuls of new coins in exchange for each one. For Gerios, hard-working and little given to luxury, there was sufficient to shelter him from need for two or three years. Enough time for them to see the sun rise on the day of their liberation.

Their walks grew daily longer, and more confident. And one morning they were emboldened to go and sit in a coffee-house. They had noticed the place the day they arrived on the island; men were seated inside, so clearly enjoying themselves that the two fugitives had buried their heads in their shoulders from shame and envy.

There was no signboard outside the Famagusta coffee-house, but it could be seen from afar, even from the boats. The owner, a jovial, obese Greek, by the name of

Eleftherios, sat in the doorway, enthroned on a cane chair, his feet in the road. Behind him, his principal piece of equipment, the brazier, on which four or five pots of coffee were kept permanently hot, and from which he also took the glowing embers to light the hookahs. He served nothing besides coffee, except for cold water from the earthenware pitcher. Anyone who wished for liquorice or tamarind syrup had to hail a passing vendor in the street; the proprietor took no offence.

The customers sat on stools and the regulars were entitled to games of *tawle* identical to those played in Kfaryabda and throughout the Mountains. They often played for money, but the coins passed from hand to hand without ever touching the table.

There was only one coffee-house in Kfaryabda, on the *Blata*, but Gerios had never set foot in it, except possibly in his youth, in any case not since obtaining his post at the castle. And *tawle* had never interested him, any more than other games of chance. But that day, he and Tanios had begun to watch the game being played at the next table so attentively that the proprietor brought them an identical set, in its rectangular box of brown, cracked wood. And they started to throw the dice and move the pieces noisily, uttering oaths and sarcasms.

To their astonishment, they were laughing. They could not remember the last time they had laughed.

The next day they returned very early, to sit at the same table; and again the following day. Gerios seemed to have thrown off his melancholia much quicker than Tanios had reckoned on. They were even about to make friends.

So it was that one day, in the middle of a hotly disputed game, a man came up to them, apologizing for addressing them like this, but explaining that he too came from the Mountains and had recognized their accent. His name was Fahim and his face, especially the shape of his moustache, bore a certain likeness to the Sheikh's. He told them the name of his village, Barouk, in the heart of the Druse country; a region well-known for its hostility to the Emir and his allies, but Gerios, still on his guard, gave a false name and said he was a silk merchant, passing through Cyprus with his son.

'I cannot say as much, alas! I do not know how many years will elapse before I can return home. All the members of my family have been massacred and our house was burnt down. I myself escaped only by a miracle. We were accused of having laid an ambush for the Egyptians. My family had nothing to do with it, but our house had the misfortune to be situated at the entrance to the village; my three brothers were killed. As long as the ogre is still alive, I shall never see the Mountains again!'

'The ogre?'

'Yes, the Emir! That is what his opponents call him, didn't you know?'

'His opponents, you say?'

'There are hundreds of them everywhere, Christians and Druse. They have sworn never to rest until they've destroyed him.' (He lowered his voice.) 'Even in the ogre's entourage, in the bosom of his own family. They are everywhere, acting in the shadows. But one of these fine mornings you will hear of their exploits. And that is when I shall return home.'

'And what's the news from there?' asked Gerios after a pause.

'One of the ogre's close advisors has been killed, the Patriarch . . . but you've surely heard about this.'

'We heard of this murder, the work of his opponents, no doubt.'

'No, it was the Sheikh of Kfaryabda's major-domo, a man named Gerios. A respectable man, so they say, but the Patriarch had wronged him. Up till now he has given them the slip. They say he has gone to Egypt, and the authorities there are looking for him to hand him over. It would be in his best interests, too, not to set foot in the country as long as the ogre is alive.

'But I'm talking too much,' the man said, 'and I've interrupted your game. Please continue, and I'll play the winner. Look out, I'm a formidable player: the last time I lost a game I was the same age as this young man.'

This village-type boasting finally relaxed the atmosphere, and Tanios, who had had enough of the game, willingly gave up his place to the newcomer.

That was the day, while Gerios was playing his first games of *tawle* with Fahim, whose inseparable friend he was to become, that the 'incident of the oranges' occurred, the episode in Tanios's life to which the sources refer only indirectly, although it was a decisive factor, it seems to me, in the rest of his travels and also, I believe, in explaining his enigmatic disappearance.

So Tanios had left the two players and had returned to the *khan* to deposit some object or other in his room. As he was opening the door to go out again, through the gap he caught sight of a young-looking woman draped in a veil which she had drawn over the lower part of her face. Their eyes met. The young man smiled politely and the stranger's eyes smiled back.

She was carrying a pitcher of water in her left hand, and with her right hand lifted her dress, to avoid tripping over it, while she held a basket filled with oranges tucked under her bent elbow. Seeing her juggling with all this on the stairs, Tanios thought to help her. However, he was afraid of seeing a husband emerge from some door or other, ready to take offence, so he contented himself with watching her.

He was on the third floor, and she was continuing her way up when an orange slipped out of the basket, and then another, which rolled down the stairs. The woman made as if to stop, but she was unable to bend down. Eventually the young man ran and picked up the oranges. The woman smiled at him but did not stop. Tanios did not know if she was continuing on her way because she wanted to avoid speaking to a stranger, or if she was inviting him to follow her. In doubt, he followed her, but timidly and somewhat anxiously. Up to the fourth floor, then the fifth, and last.

She finally stopped in front of a door, put down the pitcher and the basket, took out a key from the front of her blouse. The young man was standing a few feet away, holding the oranges well in evidence, so that there was no doubt about his intentions. She opened the door, picked up her goods, then, as she entered, turned back and smiled at him again.

The door remained open. Tanios approached. The stranger pointed to the basket which she had put down on the floor, near a thin mattress. And while he went to restore the oranges to their place, she leaned against the door, as if from exhaustion, thus pushing it closed again. The room was tiny and had no other opening except a dormer window high up near the ceiling; and almost empty, with no chair, no cupboard, nor any ornaments.

Still without a word, the woman indicated to Tanios by gestures that she was out of breath. Taking her visitor's hand, she placed it on her heart. He pulled a solemn face, as if in astonishment to find it beating so rapidly, and kept his hand where she had placed it. She did not remove it either. On the contrary, she slid it imperceptibly under her dress. There arose from her skin a scent of fruit trees, the smell of April walks through orchards.

Tanios was then emboldened to take her hand, in his turn, and place it on his own heart. He blushed at his affrontery, and she understood that for him this was the first time. Then she stood up, removed the scarf wound around his head, ran her hand several times through his prematurely white hair, laughing good-humouredly. Then she pulled his head to her bared bosom.

Tanios had no idea what he had to do. He was convinced that his ignorance was obvious at every stage, and he was not wrong. But the orange woman did not hold it against him. She answered each of his clumsy gestures by a gentle caress.

When they were both naked, she dropped the latch on the door, and then pulled her visitor towards the mattress, to guide him with her fingertips along the cool path of pleasure.

They had still not spoken a single word to each other, neither of them knew what language the other spoke, but they slept as one. The room faced towards the west, and through the dormer window a square sunbeam now shone, in which particles of dust flickered. When he awoke, Tanios could still smell the scent of orchards, and beneath his right cheek he could feel a heart beating slowly, regularly, in a woman's soft breast.

Her hair, no longer hidden by the veil, was auburn, like the ferrous earth around Dayroun. And her skin was pink and freckled. Only her lips and the tips of the nipples were a light brown.

As he gazed at her, she opened her eyes, sat up and looked out of the little window to try to judge the time. She pulled Tanios's belt towards her, then, accompanying the gesture with a contrite smile, she tapped the place where money tinkled. Presuming that this was the way things always happened, the lad began to unroll his belt, looking questioningly at his hostess. She put up three fingers of each hand, to indicate six, and he gave her a silver six-piastre coin.

When he was dressed she gave him an orange. He made as if to refuse, but she slipped it into his pocket. Then she accompanied him to the door, and hid behind it while he went out, as she was still unclad.

When he got back to his own room, he lay down on his back and began to throw the orange into the air and catch it, thinking of the wonderful thing that had just happened to him. Did I have to go into exile, and land without hope in this foreign town, in this hostelry, and climb the stairs to the top floor, following a stranger ... did the waves of

existence have to carry me so far for me to be entitled to
this moment of bliss? Such intense bliss that it could be
the reason for my adventure. And its culmination. And my
redemption.

The other characters in his life passed through his mind,
and he paused long on the memory of Asma. Astonished
that he had thought so little about her since he left. Was it
not because of her that the murder had been committed,
because of her that he had fled? And yet she had dropped
out of his mind as if through a trap-door. Of course, their
childish little games, their fingers and lips lightly touching
and withdrawing like a snail's horns, their furtive meetings,
their glances full of promises – all that bore little resem-
blance to this supreme pleasure that he now knew. But they
had been his happiness in their time. If he admitted to
Gerios that he had quite simply ceased to think about the
girl for whom he had threatened to kill himself, the girl for
whom he had made Gerios become a murderer!

He tried to find an explanation. The last time he had
seen Asma, when he had forced the door of her bedroom,
what was she doing? She was getting ready to receive congratulations on her betrothal to Raad! Doubtless the girl
was obliged to obey her father. All the same, what docility!

And then, when she had seen Tanios rush into her room,
she had screamed. He could not reasonably reproach her
for that either. What girl would have acted differently if
someone had burst into her bedroom, while she was bathing? But the picture of Asma shouting, followed by the
stampeding bodyguards and Roukoz grabbing him and
throwing him out – he could not get this out of his head.
And this was his last memory of the girl he had loved so
much. At the time, overwhelmed by his anger and his
injured pride, he had only one idea in his head: to get
back, by any possible means, what had treacherously been
stolen from him; at present he saw things more clearly:
towards Asma all he felt was bitterness. And to think that,

for her, he had ruined his life and the lives of his whole family!

Ought he not to beg Gerios for forgiveness? No, it would be better to leave him with the illusion that he had committed a noble, unavoidable crime.

II

That day Gerios returned late in the evening. To leave again the next morning, as soon as he was up. That was how it was every day from now on. Tanios watched him with a secret smile, as if to say, 'Instead of losing your wits, now you are losing your cares!'

As he approached his fiftieth year, after a life passed as an obsequious drudge, and with the burden of a huge crime on his conscience, hunted, outlawed, proscribed, condemned, Gerios, the major-domo, had now only one thought every morning: to hurry off to the Greek's coffee-house to play trictrac with his fellow refugee.

At the castle he would occasionally join in a game of *tawle*, when the Sheikh was short of a partner, and called for him; then he pretended to enjoy himself and always arranged to lose. But in Famagusta, he was not the same person. His crime had transfigured him. He enjoyed himself at the coffee-house and played wholeheartedly, and, notwithstanding the boasting of his inseparable companion, Fahim, he usually won. And if he made an unwise move, the dice rolled to his rescue.

The two friends made more din than all the other customers; sometimes a little crowd gathered round them, and the proprietor seemed delighted with the lively scene. Tanios hardly ever played any more. He stayed to watch, but, tiring very quickly, would soon get up to go for a walk. Then Gerios tried to persuade him to stay.

'Your face brings me luck!'

But he would leave, just the same.

However, one October morning, he agreed to resume his

seat. Not to bring his father good luck – had he really brought him so much luck in his life? – but because a man was walking towards them, a very tall man with a silky moustache, dressed in the costume of a notable from the Mountains. To judge by the ink stains on his fingers, he was a learned man. He said his name was Salloum.

'I've been listening to you for a moment or two, and I could not resist the temptation to greet some compatriots. In my village I used to spend whole days playing game after game of *tawle*. But I even more enjoy watching others play, if it doesn't disturb them.'

'Have you been long in Cyprus?' asked Fahim.

'I arrived only the day before yesterday. And I'm already homesick.'

'Will you be staying long with us?'

'God alone knows. Just the time to settle one or two matters.'

'And how are things on our Mountains?'

'As long as God does not abandon us, all will eventually end well.'

A prudent formula. Too prudent. The conversation would go no further. The game could be resumed. Gerios needed a double six. He asked Tanios to blow on the dice. Which rolled. Double six!

'By the ogre's beard!' Fahim swore.

Salloum seemed amused by the expression.

'I have heard all sorts of oaths, but I did not know that one. I did not even suspect that ogres could have beards.'

'The one who lives in the palace at Beit ed-Din has one, a very long one!'

'Our Emir!' murmured Salloum, taking umbrage.

He immediately rose to his feet, white-faced, and took his leave.

'Apparently we have offended him,' commented Gerios, watching him walk away.

'It's my fault,' Fahim admitted. 'I don't know what came

over me, I spoke as if we were alone. In future I shall try to keep a watch on my tongue.'

On the following days Gerios and Fahim met the man on several occasions in the vicinity of the port; they greeted him politely, and he returned their greeting, but from a distance, merely with a slight wave. Tanios even thought he caught sight of him on the stairs at the inn, chatting with the proprietor from Aleppo.

The young man was worried, more worried than his two elders. This Salloum was clearly one of the Emir's supporters. If he discovered their true identity, and the reason for their presence in Cyprus, they would no longer be safe. Should they not be thinking of leaving, going to hide elsewhere? But Fahim reassured him. 'After all, we are on Ottoman soil, and this man could not harm us even if he tried. His Emir has not got such a long arm! Salloum heard me speak words which displeased him, so he avoids us, that's all. And if we imagine we see him everywhere, it's because all the foreign travellers have business in the same streets.'

Gerios let himself be convinced. He had no desire to run from one port of exile to another. 'I shall leave here,' he said, 'only to see my wife and my country again.'

A prospect which seemed to come closer every day. Fahim, by virtue of his contacts with the opponents, reported more and more encouraging news. The Egyptians' hold on the Mountains was growing weaker, and the Emir's enemies were growing stronger. Entire regions were rising up. What is more, the 'ogre' was said to be seriously ill; after all he was seventy-three! 'One day, which is not far off, we shall be welcomed in our villages like heroes!'

While awaiting this apotheosis, the two friends continued rolling their dice in Eleftherios's coffee-house.

Tanios would not have been very pleased either if he had had to seek another place of exile. If he felt some anxiety, he also had a powerful reason to prolong his stay in this city and in this *khan*: the orange woman; who must now be given her name, which Nader's work is, to the best of my knowledge, the only one to mention: Thamar.

In Arabic, this word means 'fruit', but Thamar is also the most prestigious name given to the women of Georgia, since it was the name of that country's great sovereign. When we know that this girl spoke neither Arabic nor Turkish, when we also know that, in the whole of the Ottoman Empire, some of the most beautiful women were former Georgian slaves, we can be left in no more doubt.

Tanios's feelings for the venal woman with the orange hair had at first been purely physical. Aged eighteen, restricted and frustrated by his village existence, still bearing the scars of his disappointment in love, and that of an even older wound, disillusioned, frightened, he had found in the arms of this stranger . . . more or less what he had found in this strange town, on this island, so close to his homeland and yet so distant: a haven where he could lie and wait. Waiting for love, waiting for his return, waiting for real life to begin.

The thing which in this affair might seem sordid – the money that changed hands – must, on the contrary, have seemed reassuring. Witness this sentence in *Wisdom on Muleback*: 'Tanios said to me, "All pleasures must be paid for, do not despise those that state their price." '

Once bitten, twice shy: he had now no wish to promise anything or listen to any promises, still less to contemplate the future. Take, give, leave, then forget – thus had he sworn to do. That had been the case only the first time, and even then not entirely. He had taken what the stranger had offered, he had settled his debt, he had left. But he hadn't been able to forget.

Tanios did not even want to believe that two bodies could give birth to passion. Perhaps he reckoned that the pieces of silver would be enough to quench it.

At first he had had only the rather crude desire to taste the same fruit again. He looked out for her on the stairs, caught sight of her, followed her from a distance. She smiled at him, and when she entered her room she left the door open for him. The same ritual, in a word, without the oranges.

Then they were close, recalling the actions which expressed their love. She was just as gentle, just as silent, and her hands smelled of bergamot and sheltered gardens. Then Tanios said his name, pointing to himself; and she took his hand and placed it on her own brow. 'Thamar,' she said. He repeated the name several times as he stroked her hair.

Then, as if it were the most natural thing in the world, as soon as they had been introduced, he began to talk. He told of his fears, his misfortunes, his plans for distant travels, growing indignant, excited, speaking all the more freely in that Thamar understood not one word. But she listened without any sign of boredom. And she reacted, although only mildly: when he laughed, she smiled faintly; when he swore and thundered, she frowned slightly; and when he banged on the wall and the floor, she gently took his hands as if to associate herself with his anger. And during his whole monologue, she gazed into his eyes, nodding slightly to encourage him.

And yet, when he was ready to leave, when he took a six-piastre coin from his belt, she accepted it, without any pretence of refusing; then she accompanied him to the door, still naked.

When he was back in his room, he began to reflect on the things he had said. There were words, sentences, which he did not think he had in him and which he had poured out in front of this woman; and things too which he did not think he had noticed. The first meeting had left him with – I don't think it unfair to say – a feeling of his body being at peace. From this second encounter, he had returned with his mind at peace.

He thought he had attained the ultimate pleasure, and now he had just discovered a still heightened pleasure, even more delight in physical gratification. No doubt he would not have opened his heart to his companion if she had been able to understand him; in any case, he would not have been able to speak as he had done of the murder committed by Gerios, the reasons that had led him to this act, nor of the rumours around his own birth. But now he thought he would like, one day, to talk to her again of all that in a language which she could understand.

He began to find the time he spent without her hanging heavily on his hands. When he realized the need that had grown within him, he was alarmed. Could it be that he was now so attached to this woman? After all, she was – he would not have wanted to utter the correct word – but, let us say, she was what he knew she was!

Then he began to watch out for her comings and goings on the stairs, thinking that he would surprise her with other men; but he would have wept his heart out if he had seen her smile at another as she had smiled at him, and let anyone else follow her into her room, for a man's dirty hand to be placed on her heart. There must have been others, many others, how could he imagine otherwise? But Tanios never succeeded in seeing them. Moreover, Thamar did not climb the stairs as often as he had supposed; perhaps she had another house where she led a different life?

Perhaps a veiled echo of those days of anguish and confusion can be found on this page of Nader's book:

The woman of your dreams is the wife of another, but he has driven her from his dreams.

The woman of your dreams is the slave of a seaman. He was drunk the day he bought her at the market of Erzurum, and on waking he no longer knew her.

The woman of your dreams is a fugitive, as you were, and you sought refuge with each other.

His two visits to Thamar had taken place at the siesta hour; but one night, when he could not get to sleep, Tanios had the idea of going to knock on her door. Reassured by Gerios's snores, he slipped out of the room, and climbed the stairs in the dark, clinging on to the balustrade.

He tapped twice sharply on the door, then twice again, and the door opened. There was no light in the room and he could not see the expression of the face which received him. But as soon as he uttered one word, their fingers met, recognized each other, and he entered with a tranquil heart.

When he started to caress her, she firmly pushed his hands away, then pulled him to her, with his head in the hollow of her shoulder.

He opened his eyes at dawn, and Thamar was sitting up, waiting for him. She had things to say to him. Or, rather, one thing. Which she tried to mime, relying on words in her own language to help her hands to express the appropriate gestures. She seemed to be saying, 'When you leave, I shall leave with you. To travel as far as possible. I shall embark on the boat that takes you away. Do you want that?'

Tanios promised her that one day they would leave together. A reply simply to please her? Perhaps. But the moment he said 'Yes', he believed it with all his exile's heart. And, placing his hand on the orange-coloured hair, he swore to do so.

They were entwined. Then he detached himself and put his hands on her shoulders, holding her at arm's length, to gaze at her. She must have been the same age as himself, but this was not her first life. In her eyes he could make out a dawning distress, and it was as if she had never before undressed like that.

Her beauty was not as perfect as he had thought when she was only the woman of his masculine desires. Her chin was a little too long and she had a scar at the bottom of one cheek. Tanios stroked the long chin and passed his thumb over the scar.

She wept two tears of joy, as if the recognition of her defects was a declaration of love. And she said, still more by gestures than by words, 'There, across the seas, you will be my man and I shall be your woman.'

Again Tanios said, 'Yes', then he took her arm and slowly walked round the room with her, as if for a wedding ceremony.

She lent herself to the pretence with a sad smile, then broke free, herself took the young man's hand and led him to a corner of the room where she loosened a tile with her fingernails to unearth an old Turkish tobacco jar from a hiding place. She slowly lifted the lid. Inside were dozens of gold and silver coins, as well as bracelets and earrings. Wrapped in a hem-stitched handkerchief she had kept the two six-piastre pieces which Tanios had given her on his previous visits. She showed them to him and slipped them into his pocket, still wrapped in the handkerchief, closed the tobacco jar and replaced the tile.

At the time, the young man did not react. It was only when he got back to his room, where Gerios was still snoring, and thought back over the scene, that he realized the enormous trust Thamar had just shown in him. She had put her treasure and her life in the hands of a stranger. He was sure she had never acted like that with a man before. He was flattered and moved. He promised himself he would never let her down. He who had suffered so much from treachery, never would he betray her!

However:

> *When the boat awaited you at the port, you searched for her to say 'Farewell!'*
> *But that farewell, your lover did not want.*

III

When, very early one morning, there was a knock on their bedroom door, at first Gerios and Tanios were alarmed. But they soon recognized Fahim's voice.

'When you hear what brings me here, you'll not be angry with me!'

'Speak!'

'The ogre is dead!'

Gerios was on his feet, clinging with both hands to his friend's sleeves.

'Say that again, to be sure I've understood correctly!'

'You heard me, the ogre is dead. The monster has breathed his last, he can do no more harm, his long beard is soaked in his own blood. It happened five days ago, and I was brought the news last night. The Sultan had ordered an offensive against the Egyptian army, which was forced to evacuate the Mountains. When the opponents heard this, they leapt at the Emir's throat, they massacred him and all his supporters, and proclaimed a general amnesty. But perhaps I was wrong to wake you for such a trifle ... Try to go back to sleep in peace, I'll be off.'

'Wait. Sit down for a moment. If what you say is true, then we can return home.'

'*Yawash, yawash!* Slow down! You can't leave like that, on an impulse. And then there's no saying there'll be a boat in the next few days. It's November!'

'We've been on this island for nearly a year!' said Gerios, suddenly weary, suddenly impatient. 'A year, Lamia has been alone.'

'Let's go for a coffee,' said Fahim, 'then we can stroll around the port. Afterwards we'll think what to do.'

That morning they were the Greek's first customers. It was cool, the ground was damp and they sat inside, as near as possible to the hot coals. Gerios and Tanios asked for their coffee to be sweetened, Fahim took his without sugar. The daylight slowly flooded the streets, porters arrived, carrying ropes on their shoulders, their backs bent. Some of them stopped first at Eleftherios's, who gave them their first coffee of the day for nothing, the one before they were paid.

Suddenly, among the passers-by, a familiar face.

'Look who's here,' murmured Tanios.

'Let's invite him,' said Fahim. 'We'll have some fun. *Khweja* Salloum, come and join us.'

The man approached, touched his forehead.

'You'll surely have a coffee!'

'I don't feel I can swallow a thing this morning. Excuse me, I must go.'

'Something is worrying you, it seems.'

'It's clear you've not heard.'

'Heard what?'

'The Emir, our great Emir, is dead. The country will never recover from this disaster. They've killed him, they've proclaimed an amnesty, soon we shall see all the criminals strutting about at liberty. The age of justice and order is over. It will be chaos, nothing will be respected any more!'

'A great misfortune,' said Fahim, restraining his laughter.

'May God be merciful to us,' added Gerios, in a suddenly sing-song voice.

'I was to leave this morning, there's a boat going to Latakia. But now I'm not sure.'

'You're right. There's no hurry.'

'No, there's no hurry,' repeated Salloum, thoughtfully.

'But the weather is going to break and God alone knows when I shall be able to sail again.'

He went on his way, his head down, while Fahim clung tightly to his companions' arms.

'Hold me, or I shall burst out laughing before he's turned his back!'

He rose.

'I don't know what you intend to do, but I'm going to take the boat that's leaving this morning. After what this man has just said, and seeing his face when he uttered the word "amnesty", I've no more hesitations. I'm going to Latakia. I'll stay there for one or two nights, enough time to make sure the news from the Mountains is good, then I'll travel by road to my village. I think you should do the same. I have a friend who has a house in Slanfeh, up in the hills, he'll be happy to welcome all three of us!'

Gerios no longer hesitated.

'We'll come with you.'

He now imagined he could see Lamia's face and the village sunshine. Perhaps he was also afraid of spending the winter in Famagusta without his trictrac partner. Tanios was in two minds. But the final decision did not rest with him, a lad of eighteen.

So it was agreed they would meet in an hour's time on the quayside. Fahim would see to booking the passages on the boat, while his friends returned to the inn to empty their room and settle the innkeeper's account.

They had only one light bundle each to carry, and Gerios divided his remaining money between them.

'In case I drown . . .' he said.

But he did not seem depressed. And set out for the port.

They had not gone more than a few yards when Tanios stopped, pretending he had forgotten something.

'I must go back to the room for a moment. You go on, I'll catch you up.'

Gerios opened his mouth to protest, but the boy had already gone. So he went on his way, without hurrying, looking back from time to time.

Tanios ran up the stairs two at a time, past the third floor, and stopped, out of breath, only at the fifth, and knocked sharply. Twice, then twice again. A door opened on the landing. Not Thamar's. A stranger's eyes were watching him. But he knocked again. Then he glued his ear to the door. Not a sound. He glued his eye to the keyhole. Not a shadow. He went down again, slowly, one step at a time, still hoping to meet his sweetheart on the stairs, their stairs.

He continued looking for her down in the courtyard of the *khan*, among the booths, among all the customers. Right out into the street. Thamar had chosen to be absent that morning.

Tanios was still lingering, oblivious of the time, when the sound of a ship's siren reached him from the port. He started to run. The wind blew off the scarf he wore wrapped round his young-old-man's head. He caught it, kept it in his hand; he would put it on later, he thought, later, on the boat.

Gerios and Fahim were standing impatiently at the bottom of the gangway, beckoning to him. Salloum was there too, a few yards away; he had apparently decided to leave as well.

People were already embarking. There was a crowd of porters, sometimes in groups of two or three, manhandling heavy trunks bound with iron hoops.

When it was Fahim's and Gerios's turn to go aboard, Tanios was separated from them by a score of passengers; Gerios drew the Turkish customs officer's attention to the youngster, pointing out his name on the ticket, so that his son would be allowed to follow him.

The two men had just reached the deck of the boat when a procession arrived, interrupting the boarding. A rich merchant was rushing up, surrounded by a host of servants, scattering orders and oaths to right and to left.

The customs officer asked the other passengers to make way.

He exchanged a long embrace with the new arrival, they whispered together, then both looked over the crowd around them with the same expression of contempt and suspicion. And some amusement. And yet there was nothing particularly funny in the appearance of these worthy passengers who were already worrying about the November sea; the only thing that might have seemed amusing was the proximity of this enormous merchant, more enormous than the most enormous of the trunks, and the weak, bony little customs officer, with a moustache reaching round to his ears, and wearing an immense plumed cap. But nobody among the onlookers would have dared laugh at the pair.

Everyone had to wait until the merchant had walked the length of the gangway with his retinue, and only then could the other travellers set their modest feet thereon once more.

When it was Tanios's turn, the officer indicated that he must go on waiting. The boy thought it was because of his youth, and he let the older men behind him go first. Until the very last had embarked. But the customs officer still barred the way.

'I told you to wait, so you will wait! How old are you?'

'Eighteen.'

More porters were arriving behind him and Tanios made way for them. From the boat, Gerios and Fahim were shouting to him to hurry, but he gestured to them that he could do nothing, discreetly pointing to the officer.

Suddenly Tanios saw that they were raising the gangway. He shouted, but the Turk calmly said, 'You can take the next boat.'

Fahim and Gerios gesticulated more wildly than ever, and the young man pointed to them, trying to explain, in his approximate Turkish, that his father was on the boat, and there was no reason for he himself to be held on land. The customs officer did not reply, he called over one of his men, whispered a few words in his ear, and the other man came to explain to Tanios, in Arabic.

'His Honour says that if you continue to behave insolently, you'll be beaten and thrown into prison for insulting one of the Sultan's officers. On the other hand, if you do as you are told you can go free, you can catch the next boat and, what is more, his Honour invites you to coffee in his office.'

His Honour confirmed the offer with a smile. Tanios had no choice, as the gangway had already been removed. To Gerios and Fahim, who stood bewildered, he made a final gesture signifying 'later'. Then, as ordered, he followed the detestable little fellow with the big moustache.

On the way, the man stopped several times to give an order, inspect a packet, listen to a request. From time to time, Tanios gazed after the boat, which was slowly moving off, its sails unfurled. He waved again to the passengers, not knowing if they could still see him.

In the customs office, he finally received the explanation he was waiting for. He could not grasp everything that was said to him – it is true he had learned Turkish from books, but not enough to keep up a conversation. However, he could understand the essential: that the merchant they had seen, who was one of the richest and most influential people on the island, was extremely superstitious; to go to sea in the company of a young man with white hair was, according to him, to be certain of shipwreck.

The officer laughed wholeheartedly, and Tanios was also invited to find the matter amusing.

'Stupid beliefs, aren't they?' suggested his host.

Tanios thought it unwise to agree. So he preferred to say, 'Your Honour acted wisely.'

'Stupid beliefs all the same,' the other insisted.

Adding that, for his part, he found prematurely white hair an extremely good omen. Approaching the lad, he slowly passed one hand after the other through his hair, with evident pleasure. Then he dismissed him.

When he left the port buildings Tanios went to ask the

innkeeper to give him back his room for a few nights more. He told him of his misadventure, and this man also found it amusing.

'I hope your father left you enough money to pay me!'

Tanios tapped his belt confidently.

'Well then,' said the innkeeper, 'you can thank Heaven you've been left behind here, you'll be able to renew some pleasant associations.'

He laughed slyly and Tanios realized that his visits to the top floor had not gone unnoticed. He lowered his eyes, promising himself to keep a closer look-out the next time he went to knock at Thamar's door.

'You'll certainly have a better time here than in your Mountains,' the man insisted, with the same sly smile. 'They're still fighting there, aren't they? And your great Emir is still the best of friends with the Pasha of Egypt!'

'No,' the young man corrected him. 'The Emir has been killed, and the Pasha's army has evacuated the Mountains.'

'What are you telling me?'

'That's the latest news, we just heard it this morning, and that's why my father has returned home.'

Tanios went up to his room and back to sleep. His night had been too short, he felt the need of a calmer awakening.

He did not open his eyes again until lunchtime. From his balcony he could see a merchant selling fritters. The smoke made him feel hungry. He selected the correct amount of money, which he held in his hand so as not to have to unfasten his belt in the street, then he went down.

At the bottom of the stairs he met the innkeeper, who was in fact coming up to see him.

'Curses on you! You nearly caused me terrible trouble. I was wrong to believe a youngster's lies!'

He explained that some Turkish officers whom he knew had dropped by to see him and he thought he would please them by congratulating them on the victories over the Egyptians. But they had taken this very amiss.

'For two pins, they'd have arrested me. I had to swear I

wasn't making fun of them. Because the truth is that, far from winning, the Turkish army has suffered more reverses. And your Emir is no more dead than you and I.'

'Perhaps these officers haven't heard the latest news . . .'

'I not only talked to these officers, I also spoke to some travellers who've just arrived from Beirut. Either all these people are liars and ignoramuses, or else . . .'

'Or else,' Tanios repeated, and began to tremble in every limb, as if he had been struck down with epilepsy, where he stood.

IV

'Fahim,' so states the *Mountain Chronicle*, 'was the assumed name of Mahmoud Bourass, one of the Emir's most cunning bloodhounds':

He was a member of the *diwan*, the Emir's eyes and ears, headed by Salloum Kramah, who acted under his own name. The stratagem by which they had succeeded in bringing back the Patriarch's assassin was their most remarkable exploit.

This success raised the Emir's prestige among the inhabitants and also among the Egyptians. To those who claimed that power was slipping from his hands, that his arm was weakening, that old age was overcoming him, he had just shown that he could still extend a powerful arm even beyond the Mountains, beyond the seas.

On his arrival in Latakia, Gerios was apprehended by soldiers of the Egyptian army, then transferred to Beit ed-Din to be hanged. He is said to have faced the betrayal and his death with the utmost resignation.

On learning of his major-domo's fate, Sheikh Francis set out immediately for Beit ed-Din, to obtain the freedom of Sheikh Raad, his son. He was kept waiting for a whole day with the common people, without regard for his rank and birth. The Emir refused to receive him, but let him know that, if he returned the next day, he would be able to leave with his son.

Thus, at the appointed time, he presented himself at the palace gates; whereupon two soldiers came and deposited Raad's dead body at his feet. He had been hanged at dawn that same day and his throat was not yet cold.

When Sheikh Francis went in tears to ask the *diwan* the reason for this, he received the following reply: 'Our Emir had said that for this crime he had to punish a father and a son. Now the debt is settled!'

The man who uttered these words was none other than *Khweja* Salloum, whose part in Gerios's capture was already known to the Sheikh – if we are to believe the author of the *Chronicle*. And he is said to have replied, 'You, who are his bloodhound, go tell your Emir, that he would do better to kill me too, if he wants to sleep in peace.'

And Salloum is said to have retorted, in the calmest possible voice, 'I have already told him so, but he insisted on letting you go free. He is the Master . . .'

'I know no other Master than God!'

It is said that, on leaving the palace, the Sheikh entered an old church on the outskirts of Beit ed-Din. And he kneeled in front of the altar to say this prayer.

'O Lord, life and its pleasures have no more meaning for me. But do not let me die before I have had my revenge!'

If Salloum and Fahim were the Emir's agents, the Turkish customs officer, the wealthy superstitious merchant, and also the orange woman were, beyond a shadow of doubt, the agents of Providence.

But, during those anxious days, Tanios was not thinking of himself, nor of Death, who had made an appointment with him but which appointment he had not kept. He still tried to convince himself that he had not been lied to, that the 'ogre' had really been killed, that the news would soon spread. Fahim, he was sure, really did belong to an underground network of opponents; he could have been informed of certain events which ordinary people would get to know only the next day, or the next week.

Then he hung around Eleftherios's café, the souks, the quays, the taverns near the port, trying to pick out, by their appearance or accents, people from the Mountains or the coast, sailors, merchants, travellers. No one could reassure him.

In the evening he went back to his room, to spend the whole night on the balcony. Watching the lights of Famagusta go out, one by one. Listening to the rumble of the waves and the footsteps of the soldiers on patrol. Then, at dawn, when the shadows of the first passers-by were seen in the streets, he fell asleep to the sounds of the city, his head resting against the balustrade. Until the sun, halfway up the heavens, scorched his eyes. Then, stiff and aching in every limb, with a bitter feeling in his belly, he got up to resume his search.

Just as he was leaving the inn, he saw a carriage pass, flying the English flag. He almost flung himself at it, shouting in English, 'Sir, sir, I need to talk to you.'

The carriage halted, and the person within appeared at the door, frowning in perplexity.

'Are you by chance a British subject?'

The accent Tanios adopted might have let him think so, but his appearance spoke otherwise. In any case, the man seemed disposed to listen to him, and Tanios asked if he knew of any serious events said to have taken place in the Mountains.

The man scrutinized him as he was speaking. And when he finished, instead of replying, he announced triumphantly, 'My name is Hovsepian, I'm the English Consul's dragoman. And you must be Tanios.'

He gave the young man just time to gaze at him in astonishment.

'There is someone looking for you, Tanios. He has given your description to the Consulate. A clergyman.'

'The Reverend Stolton! Where is he? I would so like to see him again!'

'Unfortunately he sailed only yesterday, from Limassol.'

The Reverend Jeremy Stolton's Yearbook, last notes for the year 1839:

I had intended to make my way to Constantinople in the month of November, to discuss with our ambassador, Lord Ponsonby, the temporary closure of our school, a decision which I had been obliged to make in view of the increased tension in the Mountains, and particularly in Sahlain . . .

But now, in the weeks preceding my departure, I had heard rumours that Tanios and his father had taken refuge in Cyprus. So I had wondered whether, on my way, I should not stop over on that island.

I had great hesitations. On the one hand, in my capacity as a minister of the Protestant Church, I would not wish to show the slightest indulgence to the assassin of a Catholic patriarch. But, on the other hand, I could not decide to let the most brilliant of my pupils, the most talented, and who had become for Mrs Stolton and myself something of an adopted son, finish his days hanging at the end of a rope, for no other crime than that of pity for a misguided father.

So I resolved to make this detour by Cyprus, with the sole aim of separating the boy's fate from that of his father. Unaware that matters were developing, at that very moment, thanks to the wise intervention of the Almighty, and without recourse to the pathetic intermediary of my humble self.

By a sort of naivety for which I blush today, but which my great optimism excuses, I was convinced that on my arrival on the island, by putting the necessary questions to people, I would myself find my ward in a matter of hours. He had one characteristic which made him easy to identify – his prematurely white hair – and, as I thought, unless he had had the unfortunate but prudent idea of dying it, I would have been able to be led to him.

Things turned out to be more complicated. The island is vast – about forty times bigger than Malta, with which

I was better acquainted – and has numerous ports. And then, no sooner had I begun to ask questions around me, than I realized with alarm the danger to which I was unwittingly exposing my protégé. After all, I was not the only one looking for him, and if I had been successful in my investigations, I might perhaps have facilitated the task of those who wished for his destruction.

So, after two days, I resigned myself to entrusting this delicate mission to a most skilful man, Mr Hovsepian, our Consulate's Armenian dragoman, before continuing my journey.

The very next day after my departure, Tanios was discovered, not in Limassol, where I had been looking for him, but in Famagusta. Mr Hovsepian advised him not to leave the inn where he lodged, promising to get a message to me about him. Which message was indeed communicated to me, three weeks later, by Lord Ponsonby's secretary . . .

If the encounter with the dragoman had allowed Tanios to establish this precious contact, he had hardly been reassured as to the essential: the news from his country. Quite clearly, the Emir was not dead. Discontent, it is true, was spreading, and there was talk of an uprising in the Mountains: moreover, the great Powers, notably England, Austria, Russia, were having consultations on the best means of protecting the Sultan from the intrigues of his Egyptian rival; military intervention was no longer completely ruled out: all the things which were leading in the direction wished for by the wretched Gerios. But no upheaval took place, nothing which could have justified his precipitous return.

Tanios turned over and over in his mind the conversations with Fahim, with Salloum; he could hear their words, see their gestures which now he understood differently. Then he imagined Gerios arriving at the port, being seized by soldiers, discovering the truth, in chains, beaten, humiliated, led to the gallows, offering his neck to the hangman, then swinging in the light dawn breeze.

When this image formed in his mind, Tanios felt profoundly guilty. If it had not been for his whims, his blindness, his threats of suicide, the major-domo would never have turned into an assassin. 'How shall I ever be able to face my mother again, and the villagers' whispers?' Then he thought of leaving, going far away, as far as possible.

But he thought better of it, he thought of Gerios, he saw his frightened eyes the day of the Patriarch's murder, he imagined him with the same look as he faced the noose, faced treachery. And, as on that day, he whispered to him the word, 'Father'.

Eighth Passage

On his Knees for Fame

Then I took Tanios aside, as my duty bade me do, and I told him, 'Reflect, you have no part to play in this war. Whether the Egyptians or the Turks control your Mountains, whether the French get the better of the English or vice-versa, nothing will change for you.' But he simply replied, 'They killed my father!'

The Reverend Jeremy Stolton's Yearbook, the year 1840

I

For what reason had the Emir let the sorrowing Sheikh go free? It could not have been negligence, still less compassion.

However, the old monarch had said. 'He must be allowed to weep over the body of his son.'

And his long, too long lashes had begun to quiver, like the legs of an invisible spider.

On his return to Kfaryabda, the Sheikh had spoken of organizing for Raad the most impressive obsequies that the Mountains had ever known. A poor consolation, but he felt he owed this ultimate homage to his son, to his race and, to the Emir, this ultimate defiance.

'You will see, the population of whole villages will come pouring in. And the noblest just like the humblest will come to express their sadness, their just anger and their hatred of the tyrant.'

But he was dissuaded. The villagers consulted among themselves, and, as usual, the priest went up to the castle, to express their anxiety.

'Has our Sheikh not wondered why the Emir spared him?'

'That is the question I have been asking myself ever since I left Beit ed-Din. I have no answer.'

'And what if the tyrant simply wanted our Sheikh to rally his faithful friends, all the opponents, all those who wish for change? All of them would gather in Kfaryabda, and the Emir's agents would infiltrate them. They would get to know their names, they would remember their words; then, in the following days, all your friends, one after the other, would be silenced.'

'Perhaps you are right, *Bouna*. But, all the same, I cannot bury my son hurriedly, like a dog.'

'Not like a dog, Sheikh, simply like a believer who has faith in Redemption and in the Creator's justice.'

'Your words comfort me. You speak for religion, and also for wisdom. And yet, what a victory for the Emir if he can even prevent us sharing our grief with those who love us!'

'No, Sheikh, that he cannot do, Emir that he is. We can send men to all the villages, asking them to pray at the same time as us, but without coming here. Thus, everyone will be able to show his sympathy without giving the Emir any hold over them.'

Nevertheless, on the day of the funeral, when only the villagers were supposed to gather, Said *beyk* was seen to arrive. 'The Lord of Sahlain had recently sustained a fall,' states the *Chronicle*, 'but he had insisted on coming, leaning on the arm of his eldest son, Kahtane *beyk*.'

'Sheikh Francis has asked his many friends not to come, under the circumstances, to avoid embarrassing them – that is his noble character and to his honour. But my own honour demanded that I come all the same!'

'Those words were to cost him his life,' notes the author of the *Chronicle*, 'and our village renewed sufferings.'

The two old chiefs stood shoulder to shoulder, together for the last time. Over Raad's grave *Bouna* Boutros intoned a long prayer, into which he slipped a word for Gerios, that his crime might be pardoned in Heaven. The major-domo's remains were never to be recovered: to the best of my knowledge, he never received a proper burial.

Two weeks had not elapsed when an important detachment of Egyptian troops, together with some of the Emir's soldiers, infested Kfaryabda at dawn on all sides simultaneously, as if it were an enemy fortress. Soldiers spread over the *Blata*, through all the surrounding streets, on the roads leading to the village, and pitched their tents all round the castle. Adel *effendi* led them, but at his side he had *khweja* Salloum, appointed by the Emir.

The two men demanded to meet the Sheikh. Who immediately shut himself up in his private apartments, letting them know that, if they had the slightest respect for his grief, they would not have come to importune him before the fortieth day of the mourning period. But they forced his door and compelled him to listen to a message from 'the tyrant'. The latter reminded him that the Patriarch had come to ask him to provide men for the army, and they wished to know whether he was disposed to do so. The Sheikh made the same reply. 'Come and see me after the fortieth day, and I will speak to you.'

But they had come intent on provocation and with a mission which they had to accomplish. And while Salloum went through the motions of parleying at the castle, his men went from house to house, calling on the inhabitants to gather on the *Blata*, to listen to a proclamation.

The villagers began to approach, suspicious, but curious, and gradually filled the square, from the courtyard of the parish school, right up to the arches of the coffee-house. Carefree urchins even plunged their hands into the icy water of the spring, before being sent flying with a box on the ears from their parents.

Up in the Sheikh's apartments, Adel *effendi* stood near the door, silent, with crossed arms, while Salloum was harassing his host, his prey.

'The men of Kfaryabda are reputed for their bravery, and as soon as they are under arms, our Emir has thought of a mission for them.'

Perhaps he wanted to be asked what the mission would be. But the Sheikh let him continue.

'The people of Sahlain are becoming more and more arrogant. Only yesterday they laid an ambush for a patrol of our allies, and wounded three men. It is time to inflict an exemplary punishment on them.'

'And you want to lead my men against Said *beyk*'s men?'

'We, lead your men, Sheikh Francis? Never! There are traditions in Kfaryabda. You yourself will lead them, and no one else. Have you not always led your men into battle?'

The chief of the spies seemed to relish his role – with a lance in his hand, slowly probing the flesh of a wounded beast. The Sheikh glanced towards the door of his bed-chamber. A dozen soldiers were waiting, arms at the ready. He turned towards his torturer, and sighed scornfully.

'Go and tell your master that no drop of blood has ever been shed between Said *beyk*'s family and my own, and there never will be as long as I live. On the other hand, between the Emir and myself there is now the blood of my innocent son, which will be redeemed as it must be. Your master thinks he is sitting at present at the peak of his power, but the highest mountains overlook the deepest valleys. Now, if either of you still possesses an ounce of dignity, go, leave my chamber and my castle!'

'This castle is no longer yours,' Salloum then said, without a glance at the Sheikh. 'I have orders to seize it.'

Adel *effendi* pushed open the door to let in his men, who were growing impatient.

A few minutes later, Sheikh Francis, blindfolded, with his hands tied behind his back, descended the steps from the castle down to the spring, supported by two soldiers holding him by the arms. His head was bare, revealing silvery locks standing up around a small bald patch. But he still wore his apple-green waistcoat, with gold embroidery, the last vestige of his authority.

The inhabitants of the village stood there, silent, motion-less. Breathing to the rhythm of the old man's advance, starting every time his foot slipped on a step and he was pulled upright.

Then Salloum motioned to the soldiers to halt and make their prisoner sit down on the ground. He himself and Adel *effendi* came and stood just in front of the Sheikh, so that the crowd could no longer see him.

The Emir's counsellor then made this speech:

'People of Kfaryabda,

'Neither this Sheikh, nor his ancestors, nor his descendants have ever had the slightest consideration for you, for the honour of your wives, nor the rights of the tenant farmers. With the excuse of collecting taxes, they have raised unwarranted sums which were used to maintain their luxurious, dissolute existence in this castle.

'But this individual you see here on the ground behind me has done worse. He has allied himself with heresy, he has been guilty of the death of a venerable Patriarch, he has drawn down on this village and its inhabitants the wrath of Heaven and the authorities.

'I have come to announce to you that the feudal age is over. Yes, the time has passed when one proud man could arrogate to himself abusive rights over women and girls.

'This village no longer belongs to the Sheikh, it belongs to its inhabitants. All the feudal properties are, from this day, confiscated for your profit, and entrusted to the management of *Khweja* Roukoz, who is present here, and he will ensure that they are managed diligently, for the good of all.'

The former major-domo had been there for a minute, on horseback, surrounded by his bodyguards, a little apart from the crowd. Faces were turned to him briefly. He smoothed his magnificent beard and smiled slightly. While Salloum concluded.

'Today, by the will of the All-Highest, by the wise benevolence of our beloved Emir, and with the support of our victorious allies, a page is turned in the history of this land. The detested feudal lord is brought low. The people rejoice.'

During all this time, the people had remained silent. As

silent as the Sheikh. One man, one only, had uttered a cry of joy. To regret it immediately. Nader. It seems that he had arrived at the square towards the end of Salloum's speech, and, remembering perhaps 'his' French Revolution, had simply shouted, 'Abolition of privileges!'

A hundred burning glances turned towards him, and, notwithstanding the presence of Adel *effendi* and his soldiers, of Roukoz with his bodyguards, and of the Emir's counsellor, the muleteer took fright. He left Kfaryabda that same day, swearing he would never set foot there again.

With this exception, nowhere in the crowd was there any trace to be seen of the happiness which was supposed to accompany this proclamation. Tears ran down the faces of men and women, which were not tears of joy. The Egyptian soldiers exchanged glances of incomprehension. And Salloum looked threateningly at all these ungrateful people.

When the Sheikh was pulled to his feet and dragged away, the sound of weeping and groaning arose, as at the funeral of a loved one. Among the women who lamented there was more than one whom the Sheikh had known, and then abandoned, and others who had had to use all their wiles to avoid his advances. But they all wept. And Lamia more than any, standing near the church, dressed in black, still beautiful and slender despite all her misfortunes.

And suddenly, the church bell tolled. Once. Then silence. And then again, more loudly, its echo resounding like a rumble of thunder. The mountains sent back the echo, which was still ringing in their ears when it tolled a third time. It was the *Khouriyya*'s sturdy arms that clung to the rope, pulling, letting go, catching and pulling on it again.

The soldiers, momentarily taken aback, moved off again. In their midst, the Sheikh had drawn himself up to his full height.

This is not how I ought to have presented the great social revolution which took place in my village at that time. And yet, that is how my sources revealed it to me, and that is the way it has remained in the memory of the old people.

Perhaps I should have doctored the events a bit, as others have done before me. I would no doubt have gained in respectability. But the rest of my story would have become incomprehensible.

II

The day after this ceremony, Roukoz abandoned his sumptuous property, as one discards a garment that no longer fits and is unworthy of one's position. To take up residence in the castle, with his daughter, his bodyguards, his fears and his pettiness. He also brought a portrait of himself, which he had had painted by a passing Venetian artist, and which he lost no time in hanging in the Hall of Pillars, in place of the panel tracing the genealogy of the dispossessed Sheikh. A very good likeness, so it is said, except that on the features as painted there was no trace of pockmarks.

Asma was installed in the room formerly occupied by the Sheikha, which it seems she rarely left. As for the wing where the major-domo of the castle lived, and which Roukoz himself had occupied many years before, it remained empty. Lamia still lived with her sister, the *Khouriyya*. She was rarely seen. At the most, she went to church on Sundays, passing through the sacristy. A delicate, black-clad figure on whom the congregation looked affectionately, but who seemed scarcely to see anything herself.

'Did she never feel any remorse?' I asked old Gebrayel one day.

He wrinkled up his eyes, as if he had not understood the meaning of my question.

'You and all the old people of the village have given me to understand that, on a certain September afternoon, in the Sheikh's chamber, she yielded to temptation, and that her fault had drawn down a succession of misfortunes on the village. And yet, every time you have spoken of Tanios's mother, she is all innocence and beauty and grace, "a trusting lamb"; you never find her guilty and never once have you spoken of her remorse.'

Gebrayel seemed delighted with my anger, as if I were granting him the privilege of defending this lady's honour. We were sitting in the drawing room of his old sandstone house. He took my hand and led me out on to a terrace where there still grew a mulberry tree from former times.

'Look up at our Mountains. Their gentle slopes, secret valleys, their caves, rocks, scented breezes, and the changing colours of their garments. Beautiful, like a woman. Beautiful, like Lamia. And they, too, bear their beauty like a cross.

'Coveted, violated, rough-handled, often captured, sometimes loved and loving. What do adultery, virtue, bastardy signify in the course of centuries? They are nothing but tricks to ensure the process of birth.

'You would have preferred Lamia to remain in hiding? While Roukoz governed, she did remain in hiding. And our village was then like an inverted cyclamen: its flower buried underground and its hairy, muddy tuber turned to the sky.'

'Hairy tuber' was the least offensive, the least savage of the comparisons which occurred to the old people of my village, as soon as Roukoz's name was mentioned. No doubt this aversion was not undeserved. However, it has sometimes seemed excessive to me. There was something sordid about this man, it is true, but something pathetic, too: ambition was for him what gambling or avarice is for others, a vice from which he suffered, even while he could not help indulging it. Is that to say that his fault, the day he betrayed Tanios, was equal to that of a big-time gambler, who squanders money stolen from a person dear to him? I wouldn't go so far as to say that; yet I think that, when he surrounded the youth with solicitude, it was not simply out of cold calculation, he had a sincere desire to feel that Tanios loved and admired him.

If I mention this characteristic, it is not to exonerate him – wherever he is now, he no longer needs that – but because, with the villagers, the people under his administration, he was to behave in the same way.

He had, it is true, endlessly schemed, compromised, distributed baksheesh to right and left, in order to ensure that his fallen rival's fief be entrusted to him. But he was not able to enjoy the revenge for which he had been waiting and preparing for so many years. Because of the people who wept at the sight of their humiliated overlord. That day, Asma's father had scowled haughtily but he was sickened. And he had sworn to gain the affection of this crowd, before long, and by every means.

He began by abolishing the hand-kissing, the symbol of feudal vanity. Then he let the peasants know that he would not demand the slightest piastre until the end of the year, 'to give them time to recover after the difficulties of the recent seasons', and, if there were taxes to be paid, he would settle them out of his own pocket.

He also decided to repair the church bell, which was threatening to collapse, and to clean out the basin of the fountain. He also got into the habit of distributing coins to right and left, whenever he passed through the village, in the hope that people would rejoice to see him pass, and would acclaim him. In vain. People stooped to pick up the coins, then stood up and turned their backs on him.

When, on the first Sunday after his accession, Roukoz made his way to church, he deemed it his right to occupy the seat covered with a rug, which up till then had been reserved for the Sheikh. But the seat had disappeared. Spirited away by the priest's care. The priest who, that day, chose the following words from the Gospels as the text for his sermon: 'It is easier for a camel to go through the eye of a needle, than for a rich man to enter into the kingdom of God.'

Which, in this village, where the attribution of a nickname was the equivalent of a second christening, had its immediate effect ... not the one I would have expected. Roukoz was not nicknamed 'the camel' – they had too much affection for these creatures, too much respect for their loyalty, their endurance, their character, as well as for their usefulness – it was the castle which was nicknamed 'the needle', as I have already mentioned.

This was only the very first stone of a veritable landslide of vehement, often cruel, anecdotes.

Here is one, for example, which Gebrayel still enjoyed telling:

'A villager goes to Roukoz and begs him to lend him his portrait for a day. The former major-domo is all the more flattered when his visitor explains that with this portrait he will quickly make a fortune.

' "How?"

' "I shall hang it on the wall, the villagers will file by and I shall make them pay."

' "You will make them pay?"

' "Three piastres for an insult, and six piastres to spit." '

Infuriated by all the stories told against him, Roukoz finally reacted in such a farcical way that he certainly did himself more harm than did all his detractors' mockery. He persuaded himself, in fact, that the anecdotes did not arise spontaneously, but that conspirators met every evening in a certain house to invent the one which would be circulated the next day. And that there was an English agent, in disguise, in their midst. The *Khweja* asked his men to scatter through the village to find 'the anecdote workshop' at all costs!

I could have sworn that this was just one of the many stories invented by his enemies, and certainly not the most credible, if Nader – scarcely guilty of hostility to Roukoz – had not himself mentioned this as un undeniable fact.

'By their indulgence they had turned the Sheikh into a

capricious tyrant; by their ill will, they drove his successor mad.

'He asked only to please them and to obtain their forgiveness, he would have given away his whole fortune to hear a word of gratitude from their lips.

'He ended up drunk in the night, looking for the "anedcdote workshop", and their laughter rang out from all the darkened houses.

'I myself left the village so as not to join in their laughter, but one day I shall join in their tears.'

It is true that there has always been something disconcerting in the behaviour of the people of my village towards those who govern them. In some of these, they recognize themselves; in others, not. To speak of a legitimate chief and a usurper is to place the problem elsewhere. It is not the length of time which is, in their eyes, a guarantee of legitimacy, it is not novelty in itself which they reject. As far as the Sheikh was concerned, they had the feeling that he was one of them, that his behaviour reflected their wishes, their fears, their anger – even though it meant having to put up with his. Whereas his rival obeyed pashas, army officers, the Emir . . . Roukoz could have given them his entire fortune. They would have taken it disdainfully, while thumbing their noses at him.

Moreover, the former major-domo was to confirm their worst suspicions. Had he not been promoted by his masters so that he would prove a more docile servant than the Sheikh? After three short weeks of respite, those behind him came to seek him out, presenting him, so to speak, with the unpaid bills.

The Sheikh had been unwilling to march against Sahlain; Roukoz had promised to do so; Adel *effendi* came to demand he keep his promise. The new Master of Kfaryabda had not yet lost all hope of winning over the people he administered, and he knew that, by asking them to fight against the neighbouring village, he would be discredited for good. So there was, between him and the officer, this unfriendly exchange.

'I have just taken this region in hand, wait till my power is consolidated,' Roukoz begged.

'We are your power!'

'In the mountain villages, when they begin to settle scores, they continue from generation to generation, and nothing can stop them . . .'

The officer had then interrupted him as follows, recorded word for word by the monk Elias's virtuous pen: 'When I go to see a brothel-keeper it is not to hear him talk about the virtues of virginity!'

Then he had added, 'Tomorrow I shall be here at dawn with my men. We shall not even stop to drink coffee with you. You will be outside with the villagers you have recruited. We shall count them, then we shall decide on your fate.'

The *Chronicle* relates what then ensued:

At dawn on that thrice-accursed day, Adel *effendi* arrived at the village with forty horsemen and three times that number of foot-soldiers. They went up to the castle where Roukoz was waiting for them in the courtyard. He had with him his own bodyguards, thirty horsemen armed with new rifles.

The officer said, 'These men I know, but where are the others?'

Then Roukoz pointed to ten men [here follow the names of six of them] whom he had succeeded in recruiting in return for a fee.

'Are these all that this village, reputed for its bravery, can raise?' asked the officer in astonishment.

And he swore to deal with Kfaryabda accordingly, as soon as he had finished with the people of Sahlain. Then he ordered his soldiers to march through the pine forest, followed by Roukoz's men.

When they reached that village, they easily disarmed Said *beyk*'s guards, killing eight of them, then they entered the palace, laying about them with their swords. The Master of Sahlain received a severe blow on the head and died three days later. His eldest son, Kahtane, was beaten and left for dead, but he recovered as we shall see. The village itself was pillaged, all the men encountered were killed and the women humiliated. There were twenty-six dead, including the *beyk*, a good man, loved by Christians and Druse alike, may God keep his soul and may the makers of discord be cursed for all eternity.

It is reported that, on the way back, Roukoz again expressed his scruples to the officer.

'What we have just done will set all the Mountains ablaze for a hundred years.'

And the officer is said to have replied, 'You are nothing but two races of scorpions, and if you sting each other to death, the world will be all the better for it.'

Then he is said to have added, 'If these damned Mountains had not been in his path, our Pasha would now be Sultan in Istanbul.'

'That day will come, God willing.'

Apparently, God was not willing, or was no longer willing. The officer was aware of this, and his disillusioned tone caused Roukoz extreme disquiet. He was quite prepared to serve the army of occupation, on condition that it was victorious. If, tomorrow, the Egyptians evacuated the Mountains, Adel *effendi* could become Governor of Gaza, or Aswan, but what would become of him, Roukoz? He realized that day that he had committed himself too far, especially with this expedition to Sahlain, which would never be forgiven him.

However, for the time being, he had to preserve his good relations with his protectors.

'This evening, Adel *effendi*, to celebrate the victory and

reward all your men who have fought so valiantly, I shall give a feast at the castle . . .'

'So that my soldiers can get drunk and be massacred!'

'God forbid! Who would dare attack them?'

'If you give a single one of my men one drop of arak, I'll have you hanged for treason.'

'*Effendi*, I thought we were friends!'

'I have no time for friends. Besides, we have never had friends in these Mountains. Neither among the men, the animals, the trees, or the rocks. Everything is hostile to us, everything is watching us.

'And now, listen to me carefully, Roukoz! I am an officer and I know only two words – obedience or death. Which do you choose?'

'Command, I shall obey.'

'This evening, the men will rest. In their tents, outside the village. And tomorrow we disarm the whole population, house by house.'

'These people wish you no harm.'

'They are scorpions, I tell you, and I shall not feel at peace until they have neither sting nor poison left. In every house I shall confiscate a weapon.'

'And those that have none?'

'Our Pasha has said that every house in these Mountains contains a firearm – do you think he lied?'

'No. He surely spoke the truth.'

The next day, at dawn, Roukoz's men, closely watched by Adel *effendi*'s soldiers, began the search of all the houses in the village. The first one was that of Roufayel, the barber, situated near the *Blata*.

When they knocked at his door and asked him to hand over his weapons, he seemed amused.

'I have no weapons except my razors, I'll bring you one.'

Roukoz's men were about to enter the house to carry out a search, but their master, who was standing nearby with the Egyptian officer, called Roufayel over to speak to him. All around, people were at their windows, or on the roof-tops, eyes and ears alert. Roukoz said in a loud voice, 'Rou-fayel, I know you've got a gun. Go and fetch it, otherwise you'll be sorry.'

The barber replied, 'I swear by the earth that covers my mother's coffin that there are no weapons in this house. Your men can search it.'

'If they begin to search, they'll not leave a stone standing, neither in your house nor in your shop. They'll even search under the plants in your garden and the feathers of your cockerel. And under your wife's gown. Do you understand, or would you prefer to see all that with your own eyes?'

The man was now afraid.

'Do you think I would let all that happen for the sake of a gun which I wouldn't even know how to use? I have no weapons, I've sworn on my mother's grave, what else must I swear on to be believed?'

'Our master, the Pasha of Egypt, has said that there is a weapon in every house in the Mountains. Do you think he was lying?'

'God forbid. If he said that, it is surely true.'

'Then listen to me. We are going to continue our search, and we shall be back at your house in a quarter of an hour, that will give you time to reflect.'

The man did not understand. Then Roukoz said, very loudly, so that everyone in the vicinity could hear, 'If you have no weapon, buy one and hand it over, then we'll leave you in peace.'

The people all around sniggered, the men softly, the women more boldly, but Roukoz simply smiled. In him, as they say in the village, 'the nerve of decency had snapped'. One of his henchmen approached the barber and offered to sell him his rifle. Two hundred piastres.

'Give it to me without any ammunition,' Roufayel said. 'Then I won't be tempted to fire at anyone!'

The barber went back into his house. And came back

with the required sum of money, which he tipped out in a heap. The vendor entrusted the rifle to him while he counted the coins. Then he nodded, took back the weapon and proclaimed, 'Good, we have seized a gun in this house.'

The disarming of the village proved so lucrative that the following days a similar collection took place in the neighbouring villages, and in Dayroun as well, among the wealthier merchants.

Some people, however, were unwilling to hand over either their arms or their money. They were known as *frariyya*, 'rebels', and on the day they heard that the search had begun near the *Blata*, they had gone to hide in the wooded hills, with guns, swords and provisions, leaving at home only women, boys under nine years old, and the disabled; that day was known as *yom al-frariyya*, the day of the rebels.

How many were they? From Kfaryabda itself, more than sixty, and as many from the neighbouring hamlets. They soon linked up with those who had already fled from Sahlain, some even a long time ago; on the following days, still more arrived from Dayroun and its dependencies. They agreed to help each other, but they would all follow their own chiefs.

During the same period, a similar phenomenon occurred in different parts of the Mountains. The insurgents had not all left under the same circumstances, but their reasons were similar: the presence of the Egyptian troops was burdensome, because of the taxes, forced recruitment and disarming of the population.

The insurgents were immediately approached – this has been established – by English and Turkish agents, who showered them with weapons, ammunition, money, and also encouragement, so as to make life difficult for the Pasha's army and the Emir, his ally. They assured them that the Powers would not leave them long to face the Egyptians alone.

From time to time rumours spread of the imminent arrival of an English fleet. And the insurgents on the

Mountains, filled with hope, screened their eyes from the sun, to gaze out to sea.

III

Tanios had had no news of the village for months; he knew nothing of its gaolers, or the rebels. But the upheavals in the Levant were soon to be the talking point in London, Paris, Vienna, as well as Cairo and Istanbul. And also, naturally, in Famagusta, at the inn, in the narrow commercial alleyways, at the Greek's coffee-house. The decisive battle seemed to be engaged; and, as Lord Ponsonby had predicted, it was taking place in the Mountains. As well as along the coast they overlooked, between Byblos and Tyre.

The European Powers had finally decided to send their gunboats and troops to put an end to the ambitions of the Viceroy of Egypt, whose soldiers were being constantly harassed by hundreds of bands of rebels.

Tanios knew with which side his heart lay. On some days he was seized with the desire to cross the straits, arm himself and go to join the rebels. To fight against the Egyptians? In his mind, it was mainly against the Emir. The man whose agents had duped Gerios and taken him to his death. It was Fahim and Salloum he would have liked to see at the end of his gun. That, yes, that was what he dreamed of. And he clenched his fists. And then, in his mind's eye, he again saw the picture of Gerios hanged. The dream changed into a waking nightmare, anger was transformed into disgust. And immediately he lost his desire to fight. He could think of nothing except leaving. In the opposite direction. To the West. To Genoa, Marseilles, Bristol. And beyond, to America.

Between two worlds, Tanios? Between two forms of revenge, rather. The one by bloodshed, the other by contempt. Torn between the two, he remained where he was, in Famagusta, near Thamar. Their dreams entwined, like their bodies. Thamar, his companion, his consolation, his sister, an outcast like himself.

At the same time, he kept ceaseless wait for the Reverend Stolton's return. But he did not receive a message from him until the beginning of the summer, through the intermediary of Mr Hovsepian, telling him that he would definitely be passing through Cyprus to see him. And three months later the clergyman arrived on the island. In Limassol, where Tanios, informed by the dragoman, went to meet him. It was 15 October 1840. Three weeks later, Tanios-*kishk* had become a legendary figure. An actor in a brief epic, the hero of a riddle.

First there was the reunion in Limassol, on a vast estate by the sea, the residence of a British merchant. Seen from the outside, an oasis of serenity. Within, more swarming with activity and people than a caravanserai. Seamen, officers in three-cornered hats, weapons, boots, drink. Recalling certain English plays which he had read, Tanios felt he had wandered by mistake into the wings of a theatre, during a rehearsal.

He was taken to an office, smoke-filled but quiet. The clergyman was there, with six other people seated round an oval table. They were all in European dress, although one of them was quite clearly a high-ranking Turk. It did not take Tanios long to realize that they were emissaries accredited to the great Powers.

Stolton left his seat, hurried over to him and embraced him like a father. The diplomats simply nodded slightly to the newcomer and resumed their conversations in a low voice, puffing harder on their pipes. Except for one man, who stood up, smiling broadly, and held out his hand.

It took Tanios a few moments to recognize him. The man had grown a full brown beard, which was rather unkempt and was out of keeping with his elegant attire. Richard Wood. The same whom the villagers had insisted on christening the English 'Consul', when he was not yet that, but who, since then, had become much more, namely the mastermind of the English policy, its virtuoso agent, the 'Byron' of the Mountains, the invisible leader of the rebels, their supplier of gold, arms and promises.

Tanios had not met him since the day he came to the castle in Kfaryabda, bearing gifts, and had presented him with his silver writing-case, and Raad with his gun ...

'We already met, four or five years ago ...'

'Of course,' Tanios said politely.

But his gaze was shrouded by painful images.

'My visit to our young friend's village will remain the most surprising memory of my first stay in the Mountains.'

Wood addressed this explanation to his colleagues, speaking in French, which was doubtless customary among diplomats, but paradoxical under the circumstances since, of all the European Powers, France was the only one not represented.

But what was the Reverend Stolton doing in the midst of all these people, Tanios wondered. And why had he insisted on meeting him in their presence? His ward would have expected him to take him on one side to enlighten him. But it was Wood who suggested they go for a walk together in the garden.

The surroundings lent themselves to their conversation. The avenue of palm trees, drawn up in two military lines, reached down to the sea; between the green turf and the blue water, no ochre frontier.

'You are aware that British vessels are anchored off the coast of Beirut, with orders to shell the city's fortifications whenever it is necessary. Other ships have already landed British, Austrian and Turkish units on the coast, near Nahr al-Kalb. We hoped that the Viceroy Mehmet Ali would understand our warnings; it seems he did not take them seriously, or he thought he was capable of facing up to them. He was wrong, and the French will not come to his help.'

Wood spoke in English, but gave the local names the pronunciation of the Mountain people.

'I was anxious to mention, in the first place, the military operations which are taking place at this moment, but that is not the only thing. The actions taken by the Great Powers have many aspects, judicial and diplomatic, and others, which it has been necessary to negotiate in detail for many months. And one of these aspects concerns you, Tanios.'

The young man did not dare utter a sound of approval, for fear this should all prove a dream and he would wake up before seeing how it would end.

'At a certain moment, for one of the tasks which we have set ourselves, and not the easiest I must say, we have agreed that someone from the Mountains should be with us, to play a certain role in a certain place. Forgive me if I have to talk in riddles, I promise to be more explicit when we are at sea. I simply wanted to tell you that we have chosen you. It happens that you have learned our language, it also happens that the Reverend Stolton and I know you, and think much of you; chance finally has seen to it that you are in Cyprus, which was on our route . . .

'I shall not conceal the fact that I did have one hesitation. Not on account of the murder of the Patriarch, of which everyone knows you were innocent; but because of the fate which befell your father. What you are going to do will fall in with your legitimate wish for . . . shall we say, reparation. But during your mission you will have to forget any personal grudges. Are you capable of promising me this? And, if that is so, would you be ready to come with us?'

Tanios nodded his agreement, while his consent could also be read in his eyes. Wood then held out his hand and they sealed the agreement with a hearty handshake.

'I must now tell you that Mr Stolton has some scruples. When we go back into the office, he will want to take you on one side and ask you to reflect fully before committing yourself. Do you think you can give me your assurance that, when you have reflected, your decision will still be the same?'

Tanios found Mr Wood's way of expressing himself amusing and he laughed heartily. And the devil of an Irishman joined in.

'I shall leave with you,' the young man said finally, wiping all trace of amusement off his face to give his decision some solemnity.

'I am very pleased. But by no means surprised, I must say. I have got to know the Mountains and their people.

'*HMS Courageous* will weigh anchor in two hours' time. If you still have any things left behind in Famagusta, or bills you still have to settle, tell me, and our friend Hovsepian will send someone to deal with them.'

Tanios had nothing to collect, nothing to pay. All his money was kept permanently in his belt, and the room was paid for a week in advance. There was only Thamar. He had promised to leave with her, and now he was departing unexpectedly, without even saying goodbye. But that was something the dragoman could not do for him.

He swore that, in the not too distant future, he would go back to the *khan* in Famagusta, climb the stairs to the top floor, tap twice sharply on the door, then twice again . . . Would she be there to open to him?

It was at that time, perhaps the same day as the meeting in Limassol, or the day before, that a fire destroyed the huge pine forest, as well as some thirty houses on the outskirts of my village and in the neighbouring hamlets. For a short while the castle was thought to be threatened, and Roukoz was preparing to evacuate it when the south-west wind rose suddenly, blowing the fire back towards the lands already burnt.

To this day, evidence still remains of the disaster, a piece of the hillside where no vegetation ever grows; and echoes of a controversy also remain in books and memories.

I had always heard tell in the village of a great fire which had occurred 'long ago', 'a very long time ago' – it was while trying to put Tanios's story together that I learned the date and the circumstances of this fire.

Throughout the month of September, some youngsters from Kfaryabda, who had taken to the hills when the weapons were being collected, had been making daring raids on the village. Some of them came to get provisions from their families, and two or three even made so bold as to strut about on the *Blata* and in front of the church.

Nearly everywhere in the Mountains, the Egyptian troops were now on the defensive, and sometimes were even in disarray; but in Kfaryabda and the neighbourhood, Major Adel *effendi* had managed to keep the situation well in hand. So he had decided to settle scores with the rebels. His soldiers penetrated deep into the forest. The rebels fired a few shots where the trees were thickest and the soldiers rushed in that direction.

The rebels numbered only about fifteen, but they had taken up their positions in different places, so that, on an agreed signal, they could light several fires, in order to bar the enemy's escape. And, as the round-up was taking place in daylight, it was some time before the soldiers detected the flames. When they finally realized they had been lured into a trap, they were encircled by a wall of fire.

The conflagration spread simultaneously towards the centre of the forest, tightening the grip round the troops, and also outward, towards the village. In Kfaryabda itself, the people had time to flee, but in certain nearby hamlets, on some isolated farms, the flames arrived from all sides at once. According to the monk Elias's *Chronicle*, some fifty civilians died, and thirty or more soldiers.

A controversy followed. Had anyone the right, in order to trap the army of occupation, to take so little account of the lives of the villagers, their homes, and even their precious

forest? Were the fifteen young *frariyya* heroes? Daring freedom fighters? Or thoughtless firebrands? They were doubtless all these at once: criminal freedom fighters,
irresponsible heroes . . .

The fire is said to have continued to rage for four days
and two weeks later, a black cloud still hung over the site
of the tragedy.

It could be seen from afar, no doubt visible from the
English ships which were patrolling close to the shore. That
was even more than likely, since her Majesty's vessels could
be seen distinctly from the village, and a few days earlier
they had been heard shelling the fortifications of Beirut,
which were being defended, in the name of the Viceroy
of Egypt, by one Sulayman-Pasha-the-Frenchman, alias, de
Sèves.

Could Tanios have seen the smoke? I do not think so, for
HMS Courageous must have made directly for Sidon, too far
to the south, in relation to Kfaryabda.

On board, out of the people who had met in Limassol,
there was only the English representative – Wood – and the
Turk, with their respective retinues; the other diplomats
had left for other destinations. As for the Reverend Stolton,
after a long conversation with his ward, he had preferred
to embark on another British vessel, sailing to Beirut, which
allowed him to reach Sahlain more directly; he was
impatient to get back to his school and resume classes after
a year's break.

Wood waited until they were on the high seas before
informing Tanios of the mission which had been assigned
to him.

'We are to go to the palace in Beit ed-Din, to meet the
Emir.'

The young man felt his legs about to give way under him.
But he put a brave face on it and remained quiet and
attentive.

'The Powers have decided that the Emir must relinquish his position. Unless he agrees to break with the Egyptians and join the coalition. But that is highly unlikely, we have sounded him out discreetly. So we have to notify him of his destitution and our decision to send him into exile.'

'To what destination?'

'As far as that is concerned, he will be allowed his say. You will leave the choice to him. Within certain limits, naturally . . .'

Tanios was not sure he had understood aright. Had Wood actually said 'you'?

'It has been agreed among the representatives of the Powers that the Emir should be notified of their decision by the voice of one of the people under his jurisdiction. Preferably a Christian, like himself, to avoid treading on toes. It simply remained to select the person . . .

'This is the text which you have to translate. Then to read to him.'

Tanios went off to walk alone on the deck, facing into the wind. What strange trick was fate playing on him again? He, who had fled from his country to escape from the redoubtable Emir, he whose father had been executed by order of the tyrant, here he was making his way to the palace in Beit ed-Din to meet him and tell him he must depart into exile! He, Tanios, nineteen years old, must stand before the Emir, with his long white beard and bushy eyebrows, the Emir who had been causing all the people in the Mountains, peasants and sheikhs alike, to tremble with fear for half a century, and he was going to tell him, 'My mission is to drive you out of this palace!'

'Here, on this English vessel, I am already trembling. What shall I do when I am face to face with him?'

When the ship berthed in Sidon, the town was in complete disarray. Deserted by the Egyptians, it had not yet been occupied by their enemies. The *souks* were closed, for fear of looting; the people rarely left their homes. The arrival of the *Courageous* was considered a major event. Foreign nationals with their consuls, turbaned dignitaries, all that remained of the authorities and a good number of the inhabitants were there to welcome the delegation. And when the Turkish diplomat explained that he had not come to take possession of the town, and that he was simply passing through before continuing his journey to Beit ed-Din, those to whom he spoke seemed disappointed.

The presence of a young man with white hair, quite clearly a native of the country, did not pass unnoticed, particularly as he walked among the representatives of the great Powers, his head held high, like an equal. He was presumed to be the leader of the rebels, and his youth only increased the admiration which surrounded him.

They had landed in Sidon in the afternoon, and spent the night at the English consular agent's residence on a hill overlooking the town and its marine citadel. At Wood's request Tanios was provided with new clothes, of the type normally worn by notables in the Mountains; baggy trousers, white silk shirt, red embroidered waistcoat, terracotta-coloured cap with a black scarf to wind around it.

The next day they took the coast road as far as the River Damour, where they halted to change horses before setting out on the mountain road for Beit ed-Din.

IV

Everything about the Emir's palace spoke of the collapse of his reign. Its arcades had a chilly grandeur; in the garden mules reached high in the trees to feed. Visitors were rare and the corridors silent. The delegation was received by dignitaries of the Emir's *diwan*. Attentive, as always with representatives of the Great Powers, but grave and dignified.

Tanios had the impression that no one had noticed him. No one addressed him, no one requested him to be so good as to follow him. But when he followed close behind Richard Wood, no one asked him to stay where he was either. From time to time, his two companions exchanged a glance, a few words; but for him, nothing. They too seemed to ignore him. Perhaps he should have dressed differently, in European garments. He felt now as if he were in disguise, dressed in the Mountain clothes which he had always worn, and which so many people they met on the way were also wearing. But was not his role, in fact, in the delegation of the Great Powers, to adopt the appearance of the region and to speak its language?

The Turkish envoy walked in the lead, and was the recipient of awed demonstrations of respect: the sultans had established their mastery over the Mountains more than three centuries before, and if the Viceroy of Egypt had temporarily swept them aside, they now seemed about to recover their authority; at the sight of the bowing and scraping with which the Turk was received, this could no longer remain in doubt.

But the other emissary was the object of no less

consideration. England was in everyone's eyes the foremost of the Powers, and Wood had, in addition, his own prestige.

An important dignitary of the palace, who had been walking at the Turk's side from the moment they reached the top of the steps, now invited him to take coffee with him in his office, while waiting for the Emir to be ready to receive him. Another dignitary invited Wood similarly into another office. The two men disappeared at almost the same moment. Tanios was left standing. Anxious, scowling, perplexed. When a third official, of lesser rank, but no matter, came and invited him to accompany him. Flattered that someone was taking an interest in him for the first time, he hurried after the man, down a corridor, and found himself seated in a little office, with a cup of steaming coffee in his hand.

Presuming that this was the normal procedure with official visitors, he began to sip his coffee noisily after the fashion of the villagers, when the door of the room opened and he saw enter the one person whom more than anyone he feared to meet. Salloum.

Tanios leapt to his feet, nearly upsetting his coffee. He wanted to rush through the corridors, shouting, 'Mr Wood, Mr Wood!' as if to shake off a nightmare. But from terror, or a sense of his own dignity, he did not move.

The other gave him a foxy smile.

'You finally decided to leave your island' and come back to our beautiful land.'

Tanios hopped from one foot to the other. Could he, too, possibly have fallen into a trap?

'Your poor father!' Salloum continued. 'He stood right there, where you are standing. And I sent him coffee, just like you.'

Tanios's legs could no longer support him. This could not really be happening. All this scenario could not have been set up – the delegates from the great Powers, the English vessel, the welcome committee in Sidon – just to trap him! It was ridiculous, he knew, and he repeated this to himself. But he was afraid, his jaw quivered and he could not trust his judgement.

'Sit down,' Salloum said.

He sat down. Heavily. And only then did he look towards the door. A soldier was guarding it. He would not be able to get out.

No sooner was he seated than Salloum left the room. Without a word of explanation he went out through the only door and a second soldier entered, who could have been the twin brother of the first one: the same moustache, the same build, the same dagger with the bare point thrust into his belt.

Tanios's eyes rested on him for a moment. Then he slipped his hand inside his waistcoat to take out the text which he had laboriously translated on the ship, and which he soon had to 'recite'. He searched and searched again. He got up. Felt his chest, sides, back, legs, right down to his heels. No trace of the document.

Then he began to panic. As if that piece of paper gave reality to his mission, and its disappearance made it an illusion. He began to swear, walk round in circles, unbutton his garments. The soldiers stared at him, their hands flat on their wide belts.

Then the door opened and Salloum returned, holding a yellowing document, rolled up and tied with tape.

'I found this on the floor in the corridor, you dropped it.'

Tanios thrust out his hand. A childish gesture which simply met with a handful of air and a scornful glance. How could he have managed to drop the document? Or did Salloum perhaps have light-fingered agents in his service?

'I have just seen our Emir. I told him who you are and the circumstances under which we met. He replied, "The Patriarch's murder has been duly punished, we have no more quarrel with the family of the guilty man. Tell the young man he can leave the palace as free as when he entered it." '

Rightly or wrongly, Tanios understood by this that Salloum had intended to hold him prisoner, but that his master had prevented it.

'Our Emir has seen the text which I have in my hand. I suppose it was you who translated it, and that you are to read it to him.'

Tanios acquiesced, only too happy to be once more considered, not as the son of a condemned man, but as a member of the delegation.

'Perhaps we ought to go to that meeting,' he said, straightening his cap on his head and taking a step towards the door.

The soldiers barred his way and Salloum still kept the paper in his hand.

'There is one sentence which upset our Emir. I promised him it would be modified.'

'You must talk to Mr Wood about that.'

Salloum did not listen to the objection. He went to the writing-table, sat down on a cushion and unrolled the document.

'Where you say, "He must go into exile", that formula is a bit abrupt, don't you think?'

'I didn't compose this,' the young man insisted, 'I only translated it.'

'Our Emir will take into consideration only the words which he hears from your mouth. If you modify the text slightly, he will be very grateful. Otherwise, I cannot guarantee anything.'

The two soldiers cleared their throats simultaneously.

'Come and sit beside me, Tanios, you will be more at ease to write.'

The youngster obeyed, and even let a pen be placed in his hand.

'After "He must go into exile", you must add, "to any country of his choice".'

Tanios had to do as he was bid.

While he was writing the last word, Salloum patted him on the shoulder.

'You will see, the Englishman will not even notice.'

Then he directed the soldiers to take him to the Emir's antechamber. Where Wood seemed annoyed.

'Where did you get to, Tanios? You've kept us waiting.'

Then, lowering his voice, he added, 'I wondered whether you'd been thrown into a dungeon!'

'I met an acquaintance.'

'You look shaken. Have you at least had time to read through your text?'

Tanios had squashed the document into his belt, like the soldiers' daggers, folding the top to form a handle which he grasped with his left hand.

'You'll need courage to read it to this old devil. Keep constantly in mind that he is defeated, and that you are addressing him in the name of his conquerors. If you are to have any feelings for him, let them be of pity. Neither hatred nor fear. Only pity.'

Strengthened by these words, Tanios walked more firmly into the *majlis*, a vast hall, with numerous arches and walls painted in bright colours, blue, white and ochre, in wide horizontal stripes. The Emir was sitting cross-legged on a little dais, smoking a long pipe, whose bowl rested on a silver dish on the floor. Wood, followed by Tanios and the Turkish emissary, greeted him from a distance, touching their foreheads and then placing their hands on their hearts, while bowing slightly.

The Master of the Mountains went through the same motions. He was in his seventy-fourth year, and the fifty-first of his reign. However, nothing in his face or words gave any sign of exhaustion. He motioned to the diplomats to take their seats on the two stools which had been placed before him for this purpose. Then he casually indicated to Tanios the rug at his feet, between himself and the Briton. And the young man had no choice but to kneel down there; he sensed in the potentate's eyes, still sharp under his bushy eyebrows, cold hostility towards himself; perhaps he took it amiss that he had greeted him from a distance, standing, like the foreign dignitaries, instead of kissing his hand as the local people did.

Tanios turned anxiously towards Wood, who nodded to him reassuringly.

After a string of polite formulas, the British delegate got to the point. Speaking first in Arabic, and then in the local tongue. But the Emir bent forward, straining his ears, screwing up his eyes. Wood realized that his pronunciation was unintelligible; without any other transition than a slight cough, he quickly changed over to English. Tanios understood that he had to translate.

'The representatives of the great Powers have deliberated at length over the Mountains and their future. They all appreciate the order and prosperity which Your Highness's wise government has for many years assured this region. And yet they could not but express their disappointment with regard to the support which your palace has given to the Viceroy of Egypt's enterprise. But even at this late date, if you were to take an unambiguous stand in favour of the Sublime Porte, and to approve the decisions of the Powers, we would be prepared to renew our trust in you and confirm your authority.'

Tanios expected to see the Emir comforted by the offer of this loophole. But when he had translated the last sentence, he saw his eyes filled with an expression of deeper distress than had been visible when they entered, when the Master of the Mountains thought his fate already sealed, and he had no other choice than that of his place of exile.

He stared at Tanios, who was forced to lower his eyes.

'How old are you, my boy?'

'Nineteen.'

'Three of my grandsons are more or less your age, and all three are held in the Pasha's camp, as are several members of my family.'

He had spoken softly, as if in confidence. But he indicated to Tanios that he should translate his words. Which he did. Wood listened, nodding his head a few times, while the Turkish emissary remained impassive.

The Emir resumed, a little louder.

'The Mountains enjoyed order and prosperity when peace reigned all around. But when powers fight powers, decisions no longer lie in our own hands. Then we try to allay the ambition of the one, to divert the damage done by the other. For seven years the Pasha's armies have overrun this land, even to the neighbourhood of this palace, and sometimes even encroaching within these walls. There have been times when my authority has reached no further than this carpet on which I place my feet.

'I have done my best all along to preserve this house, so that, the day the war of the powers is over, honourable people like yourselves can find someone on these Mountains to whom they can talk . . . It seems that this is not enough for you.'

A tear formed in those terrible eyes. Tanios saw this and his own eyes grew misty. Had not Wood authorized him to feel pity? But he had not thought he would have to use this permission . . .

The Emir drew on his long pipe for the first time, then exhaled the smoke upward to the high ceiling.

'I can proclaim my neutrality in this conflict which is drawing to a close, by calling on my subjects to let the great Powers act. And to pray to the Almighty to grant long life to our master, the Sultan.'

Wood seemed interested in this compromise. He consulted the Turk, who shook his head vigorously, and said harshly in Arabic, 'To pray for our Master's long life, even the Pasha of Egypt is ready to do that! It is no longer the time for prevarication! The Emir has taken up his stand against us for seven years, the least he could do would be to declare himself clearly in our favour for seven days. Is it too much to ask him to recall his men from the Egyptian camp and put them under our flag?'

'My grandsons would be here with us now, if they still were at liberty to come and go.'

The Emir made a gesture of impotence and Wood judged that this question was now closed.

'Since Your Highness cannot give us satisfaction on this point, I fear we are obliged to notify him of the decision reached by the Powers. Our young friend here has translated this, and he is instructed to read it.'

Tanios judged it necessary to stand, and to assume the posture and tone of a narrator.

'The representatives of the great Powers . . . meeting in London, then in Istanbul . . . after examining . . . must go into exile . . .'

When he reached the contentious clause, he hesitated for a brief, a very brief moment. Then finally introduced the correction insisted upon by Salloum.

On hearing the words 'the country of your choice', the Turkish emissary started, looked at Tanios, then at Wood, as if to say he had been deceived. And when the reading was finished, he demanded, with a warning note in his voice, 'And for what destination will the Emir leave?'

'I need to reflect, and to consult those near to me.'

'My government insists that the matter be decided here and now, without the slightest delay.'

Feeling the tension rising, the Emir said hastily, 'I choose to go to Paris.'

'Paris, out of the question! And I am sure that Mr Wood will not contradict me.'

'No, indeed. It has been agreed that the place of exile will be neither France nor Egypt.'

'Then let it be Rome,' said the Emir, using an expression intended to convey that this would be his final compromise.

'I am afraid that will scarcely be possible,' said Wood apologetically. 'You must understand that the Powers whom we represent prefer it to be on their territory.'

'If that is their decision, then I must accept it.'

He reflected for a few moments.

'Then I shall go to Vienna!'

'Not Vienna either,' said the Turk, rising to his feet as if to withdraw. 'We are the victors, and we shall decide. You will come to Istanbul, and you will be treated according to your rank.'

He took a couple of steps towards the door.

Istanbul was just what the Emir wished to avoid at all costs. Salloum's whole manoeuvre was aimed at preventing him finding himself in the hands of his bitterest enemies. Later, when things had calmed down, he would go and kiss the Sultan's gown and beg for forgiveness. But if he went there immediately, he would first be divested of all his possessions, then they would have him strangled.

Tanios could read fear of death in his eyes. Then the young man's mind became confused, or perhaps one should say a strange shift in his feelings occurred.

So he had before him this old man, and could now see nothing save his long white beard and eyebrows and lips and, above all, his eyes, those of a formidable old man who, at this moment, was himself afraid, defenceless. And, at the same time, the young man thought of Gerios, of the expression on his face before the certainty of death. Suddenly Tanios no longer knew if this old man was the one who had had his father hanged, or was himself a fellow sufferer; the man who had put the rope in the hangman's hands, or another neck offered to the noose.

In this moment of hesitation, the Emir leaned towards him and said, in a choking voice, 'Say a word, my son!'

'And the native of Kfaryabda,' so the *Chronicle* reports, 'hearing the voice of the humiliated old man, put aside his desire for revenge, as if he had satisfied it a thousand times, and said aloud, "His Highness could go to Malta!" '

What had made him think of Malta? No doubt because the Reverend Stolton, who had stayed long on that island, had often spoken to him about it.

Wood immediately fell in with this suggestion, all the more willingly in that Malta had been a British possession since the beginning of the century. And the Turk, caught unawares, eventually agreed also, with a gesture of irritation; the idea did not greatly please him, but England was the heart of the coalition of the great Powers, and he dared not risk a conflict for which those in high places might hold him responsible.

'The Emir gave little sign of his relief, for fear the Sultan's envoy might change his mind; but his expression as he looked at the young man from Kfaryabda was one of surprise and gratitude.'

Final Passage

Guilty of Compassion

Thou, Tanios, with thy child's face and thy six-thousand-year-old head

Thou hast crossed rivers of blood and mire, and hast emerged immaculate

Thou hast entered the body of a woman, and ye have parted from one another as virgins

Today, what has been destined for thee is over, thy life can finally begin

Come down from thy rock and plunge into the sea, let thy skin at least take on the taste of salt!

Nader, *Wisdom on Muleback*

I

Rather than turn his weapons at the eleventh hour against his Egyptian protector, the Emir has chosen to go into exile. So this week he embarked for Malta, accompanied by his wife, Hosn-Jihane, a former Circassian slave, purchased, so I am told, on the Constantinople market, but who became a lady unanimously respected; the fallen potentate's retinue also included a hundred or so other members of his household, children, grandchildren, advisors, guards, servants . . .

By a curious misunderstanding – or let us say by a form of boastful exaggeration in which Orientals are not loathe to indulge – a role of the most unimaginable distinction is attributed to Tanios, that of having forced the Emir to leave the country, while generously saving his life, as if the European Powers and the Ottoman Empire, with their armies, fleets, diplomats and agents, were but onlookers in a dramatic arm-wrestling match between the infant prodigy from Kfaryabda and the despot who had condemned his father to death.

This fanciful interpretation is so widespread in every circle, whether Christian or Druse, that my ward's prestige reflects on me, his mentor. And people come every day to congratulate me for having caused such a rare flower to bloom in my garden. I accept the congratulations without attempting to deny this interpretation of the facts, and I must say that, when all is said and done, both Mrs Stolton and myself are flattered . . .

That is what the clergyman wrote in his Yearbook for 2 November 1840, adding on the following day:

> ... And while the Emir was embarking in Sidon on the same vessel which had brought Mr Wood and Tanios, the latter was returning by road to Kfaryabda, greeted in every village he passed through by eager crowds who congregated to see the hero, to sprinkle him with rose water and rice like a young bridegroom, and to touch his hands and also, when they could get close enough, his white hair, as if this were the most apparent sign of the miracle which had been achieved by his intervention.
>
> The lad accepted all this, speechless and incredulous, visibly overwhelmed by the excessive kindnesses which Providence was showering on him, smiling blissfully like a dreamer who wonders when he will awake to the realities of the world ...
>
> After so much sudden glory, is there still some room in this fragile creature for the ordinary life to which his birth seemed to intend him?

When he arrived at the village square, acclaimed there as elsewhere as a hero, he was carried shoulder-high up to the castle, where he was officially installed on the seat formerly occupied by the Sheikh and more recently by the usurper. Tanios would have liked to be alone with his mother for a moment, and to hear from her lips the sufferings she had endured. Instead of which he was forced to listen to a thousand grievances, a thousand complaints, all voiced at once. Then he found himself set up as supreme judge to decide on the fate of the traitors. No one knew the Sheikh's whereabouts. According to some, he was a prisoner in a citadel in Wadi al-Taym, at the foot of Mount Hermon; according to others, he had died in detention. In his absence, who was more worthy to occupy his place than the hero of the hour?

Although in a state of near exhaustion, Tanios did not

appear insensible of this honour. If Providence offered him revenge for his past, why should he be unwilling to accept it? Seated on the Sheikh's cushion, he found himself imitating the Sheikh, his slow, majestic gestures, his abrupt speech, his forthright gaze. He was already thinking that it was not by chance he had been born in a castle, and was wondering if he would ever be able to turn his back on this place and melt into the crowd... When the said crowd made way suddenly to allow a man in chains, blindfolded and with swollen, lacerated face, to be cast at the hero's feet. Roukoz. When the Egyptians left, he had been attempting to flee, but the 'rebels' had caught him. He was to pay for all the ordeals the village had endured, for all the dead, including those who died in the fire, for the looting that took place when the weapons were being collected, for the humiliations inflicted on the Sheikh, for a thousand other extortions, so obvious that there was no need to make any preliminary investigations before a trial could take place. Tanios had only to pronounce the sentence which would be carried out without delay.

Roukoz began to groan loudly, and the hero, losing patience, cried, 'Quiet! Or I'll beat your brains out with my own hands!'

Roukoz imediately fell silent. And Tanios was given an ovation. And yet, far from experiencing any satisfaction, he felt a pain like a stab wound low down in his chest. If he was so infuriated, it was because he felt himself unable to pronounce the sentence, and Roukoz, by his moaning, was challenging him.

The people were waiting. They whispered to each other, 'Silence! Tanios is about to speak! Listen to what he has to say!'

And he was still wondering what he was going to say, when a new wave of noises and murmurs disturbed the gathering. Asma had just entered. She ran to kneel at the feet of the conqueror, took his hand and kissed it, begging, 'Have pity on us, Tanios!'

Now every word, every look, every breath he heard increased the young man's suffering.

Bouna Boutros, seated at his side, murmured, as if to himself, 'O Lord, let this cup pass from me!'

Tanios turned to him.

'I suffered less when I was starving myself to death!'

'God is near, my son. Do not let these people lead you according to the dictates of their hatred, do only those things for which you would not blush when face to face with yourself and with your Creator!'

Then Tanios cleared his throat and said, 'I returned from across the seas to tell the Emir he must leave these Mountains which he had been unable to preserve from misfortunes. I shall not punish the servant more severely than the master.'

For a few seconds he had the impression that his words had carried. The gathering remained silent, Roukoz's daughter kissed his hand feverishly. He withdrew it with some irritation. He had spoken like a king – or so he believed. A brief moment. Before the revolt broke out. First it was the young *frariyya*, who had returned from the hills, still armed, and who did not intend to let themselves be moved to pity.

'If we let Roukoz leave with his gold, so that he can go and make another fortune in Egypt and come back to take his revenge in ten years' time, we shall be cowards and fools. Several of his men are already dead, why should the worst one of all be spared? He has killed, he must expiate his sins. It must be understood that all those who harm this village will pay for it.'

An old tenant farmer in the hall shouted, 'You *frariyya* have done more harm to Kfaryabda than this man. You burnt down a third of the village, caused dozens of deaths, and destroyed the pine forest. Why should you not be judged also?'

The confusion grew. At first Tanios was alarmed, but he

immediately realized the advantage he could derive from this.

'Listen to me! There have been crimes in recent days, many serious errors, the deaths of many innocent people. If everyone began to punish those who have done wrong, those who have caused the death of one of his kin, the village would never recover. If you wish me to decide, these are my orders: Roukoz must be dispossessed of all his property, which will be used to compensate those who have suffered from his extortions. Then he will be banished from this region.

'And now, I am dead tired, I am going to rest. If anyone wishes to occupy the place left by the Sheikh, let him do so, I shall not prevent him.'

At that moment, at the back of the hall, a man whom no one had noticed, spoke up. He had covered his head with a chequered scarf, but now he removed it.

'I am Kahtane, the son of Said *beyk.* I waited until you had finished your deliberations before I intervened. You have decided to banish Roukoz for the crimes which he committed against you. That is your right. Now it is my turn to judge. He killed my father, who was a good man, and I ask for him to be handed over to me, to answer for this crime.'

Tanios tried not to show he was shaken.

'The punishment has already been pronounced on this criminal. The matter is closed.'

'You cannot dispose of those who have committed crimes against us, as you have disposed of those who have harmed you. This man killed my father and it is for me to decide if I wish to be merciful to him or ruthless.'

The 'judge' turned towards the priest. Who was no less embarrassed than himself.

'You cannot say no to him. And at the same time, you cannot hand this man over to him. Try to gain time.'

While they were deliberating, Said *beyk's* son elbowed his way through the crowds to join in their discussion.

'If you came with me to Sahlain, you would understand why I spoke as I did. There is no question of my father's murderer going unpunished. If I pardoned him myself, my brothers and cousins would not pardon him, and would never forgive me for my leniency. *Bouna* Boutros, you knew my father well, did you not?'

'Certainly, I knew him and respected him. He was the wisest and most just of men!'

'I try myself to follow the path he set me. There is no room in my heart for hatred and dissent. In this business, I have only one piece of advice to give you. I am supposed to ask you to hand over this man, but if this Christian were killed by the Druse, the matter would have undesirable consequences. So forget what I said aloud, and listen to the only counsel of reason: condemn him yourselves, let everyone punish their own community's criminals; let the Druse settle their scores with the Druse criminals, and the Christians with the Christians. Execute this man, and I shall go to tell my people that your justice has preceded ours. Execute him today, because I shall not be able to control my men until tomorrow.'

Then the priest said, 'Kahtane *beyk* is right. I am loathe to give such advice, but the most God-fearing sovereigns must sometimes pronounce the death sentence. In our imperfect world, this detestable punishment is sometimes the only just and wise one.'

Bouna Boutros's gaze fell on Asma, still on her knees, wild-eyed, devastated; he motioned to the *Khouriyya* to drag her to her feet and take her away. Perhaps the inevitable sentence would then be easier to pronounce.

II

In this strange way did the trial of Roukoz take place in the castle. The hall was filled with judges and executioners, and seated in the only judge's place was a devastated witness. Who could manage to show no mercy only to himself. In his mind, during those moments, he ceaselessly castigated himself: What did you return to this country to do, if you are incapable of punishing the Emir, who had your father hanged, incapable of killing the scoundrel who betrayed you and betrayed the village? Why did you agree to take your seat in this place if you are incapable of letting your sword fall on the neck of a criminal?

And in this wise he let himself be filled with remorse. In the midst of this crowd, faced with their murmurs and looks, he could not breathe, he thought only of fleeing. Oh Lord, how serene Famagusta was, in his memory! And how sweet it was to climb the stairs of the inn!

'Speak, Tanios, the people are restless and Kahtane *beyk* grows impatient.'

Bouna Boutros's whispered words were suddenly drowned by the shouts of a man who came running.

'The Sheikh is alive! He is on his way! He will spend the night in Tarshish and be here tomorrow!'

The crowd shouted for joy, and Tanios could smile again. Happy, apparently, at the master's return; but in his innermost heart, happy that Heaven had so promptly saved him from his predicament. He let a few moments of jubilation pass, then called for silence, which was granted him, as if his last wish.

'It is a joy for us all that the Lord of this castle returns among us, after enduring suffering and humiliations. When he has taken the place which is rightly his, I shall let him know the sentence which I have pronounced in his absence. If he approves, Roukoz will be dispossessed and banished for ever from this land. If he decides otherwise, he will have the last word.'

He pointed to four young men in the front row, classmates from his days in the parish school.

'You will be responsible for guarding Roukoz until tomorrow. Take him to the old stables!'

Having accomplished this last act of authority with dignity, he withdrew. The priest and Kahtane *beyk* tried in vain to detain him, he had slipped away, almost running.

Outside it was already twilight. Tanios would have liked to walk along the paths away from the houses, away from the murmurs, alone, as in the old days. But the villagers were everywhere that evening, around the approaches to the castle, in the squares, the alleyways. Every one of them would have liked to talk to him, touch him, embrace him. After all, he was the hero of the celebrations. But in his heart, he was nothing but the fatted calf.

He crept through the unlit corridors to the wing where he used to live with his parents. Not a single door was locked. A reddish glow shone from the window overlooking the valley. The principal room was nearly empty; on the floor a few dusty cushions, a chest, a rusty brazier. He touched nothing. But he went and stooped over the brazier. For, of all the memories, painful or happy, which crowded in on him between these walls, the one which stood out was the most trivial, the one he had nearly forgotten: one winter's day, when alone, he had pulled out a thick woollen thread from a blanket, he had dipped it in a bowl of milk and suspended it over the hot coals, and then dropped it, to watch it twist, turn black, then red, to listen to it crackling, and to smell the mixture of burnt milk and wool and hot coals. It was that smell, and no other, that he was smelling since his return.

He remained for a moment stooping over the brazier, then stood up and moved, with half-closed eyes, into another room. The one in which Lamia and Gerios used to sleep on the floor. And he himself, a little higher up, in his alcove. It was scarcely more than a ledge under an arch, but in winter it received all the warmth of the house, and in summer it was cool. It was there that he had spent his childhood nights, there that he had begun his hunger-strike; there, too, that he had awaited the result of the Patriarch's mediation . . .

Since then he had often seen in his memory the ladder with its five rungs, that Gerios had put together, and which was still standing against the wall. He placed one foot on it, cautiously, convinced it would not now support his weight. But it did not break.

He found his thin mattress, rolled up in an old torn sheet. He opened it out, slowly smoothed its surface, then lay down, his feet now reaching right up to the wall. Reconciled with his childhood and praying that the world would forget him.

An hour went by in the black silence. Then a door opened, closed again. Another opened. Tanios pricked up his ears, feeling no anxiety. Only one person could guess his hiding place, and follow him like this in the darkness. Lamia. And that was the one person he wished to speak to.

She approached on tiptoe, climbed halfway up the ladder. Smoothed his brow. She climbed down again, went over to the old chest to fetch a blanket, came and spread it over his stomach and legs, as when he was a child. Then she sat down on a low stool, leaning against the wall. They could not see each other, but they could talk without raising their voices. As in the old days.

He had bushels of questions to ask her, how she had lived, how the best and the worst news had reached her . . .

But she insisted on first telling him the rumours which were buzzing around in the village.

'The people never stop talking, Tanios. I've a hundred cicadas in my ears.'

The young man had come to take refuge here with the express purpose of avoiding hearing all this. However, he could not remain deaf to his mother's anxiety.

'What do these cicadas say?'

'The people are saying that if you had suffered like them from Roukoz's extortions, you would have been less lenient to him.'

'You can tell these people that they do not know the meaning of suffering. Do they think that I, Tanios, did not suffer from Roukoz's treachery, his duplicity, his false promises and his overwhelming ambition? Is it not without any doubt because of Roukoz's trickery that my father became a murderer and my mother finds herself a widow . . .?'

'Wait, calm down, I have reported their words badly. They mean only that if you had been in the village when Roukoz and his gang were dealing so harshly with everyone, you would have had nothing but contempt for the man.'

'And if I had had nothing but contempt for him, I would have done my job as a judge better, I suppose?'

'They also say that it is on account of his daughter that you let him live.'

'Asma? She came and knelt at my feet, and I scarcely spared her a glance! Believe me, Mother, if at the moment of pronouncing sentence I had recalled all the love that I used to have for that girl, I would have killed Roukoz with my own hands!'

Lamia suddenly changed her tone. As if she had accomplished her mission as messenger, and she was now speaking for herself.

'You have said what I wanted to hear. I do not want you

to have blood on your hands. Your unfortunate father's crime is enough. And if you let Roukoz live because of Asma, no one will blame you.'

Tanios raised himself up on his elbows.

'It was not because of her, I told you . . .'

But his mother spoke before he could finish the sentence.

'She came to see me.'

He said nothing. And Lamia continued, in a voice which she forced herself, with every word, to make expressionless.

'She left the castle only twice, and on each occasion it was to come and see me. She told me her father was still trying to marry her off, but she would never agree. Then she told me about you and herself, and she wept. She wanted me to come back to live in the castle, as before. But I preferred to remain with my sister.'

Lamia expected her son to ask her to tell him more, but the only sound that reached her from the alcove was a distressed child's breathing. Afraid that he would be embarrassed, she continued. 'When you were sitting in the great hall, in the Sheikh's place, I was watching you from a distance and I thought: let him not pronounce the death sentence; Roukoz is nothing but a fat lout, but his daughter's soul is pure.'

She fell silent. Waiting. Tanios was not yet in a condition to speak. Then she added, as if to herself, 'It's just that the people are worried.'

He spoke again, his voice still harsh.

'What are they worried about?'

'They are whispering that Roukoz will surely bribe the young men who are guarding him, to let him escape. Then who will be able to appease the people of Sahlain?'

'Mother, my head is as heavy as a mill-stone. Leave me now. We will talk again tomorrow.'

'Sleep. I will say no more.'

'No, go and sleep at the *Khouriyya*'s; she must be expecting you. I want to be alone.'

She rose to her feet; in the silence, each of her footsteps

and the creaking of the door hinges could be heard. He had hoped for comfort from his mother, she had brought him nothing but further torments.

About Asma first. During his two years' exile he had not thought of her except to heap reproaches upon her. And eventually he had seen in her only the feminine replica of her father. A soul as perfidious, under an angel's mask. She had cried out in her chamber that day, and Roukoz's henchmen had come and seized him, beaten him black and blue and chased him away. Because of this picture, which was engraved on his memory, he had cursed Asma, he had banished her from his mind. And when she had come to kneel at his feet, to ask him to spare her father, he had ignored her. And yet she had come to console Lamia in his absence and speak of him again . . .

Had he been unjust to the girl? Long-forgotten images flooded back into his mind: the day when he had first kissed her in the unfinished audience chamber; those moments of intense bliss when their fingers touched shyly. He did not know whether he had been wrong in his love or in his hatred.

He fell asleep with his troubled mind. And his troubled mind woke him. A few seconds had elapsed, or a few hours.

He sat up, resting on his elbows, turned around, felt his feet suspended in the air, ready to jump. But he remained where he was, his back arched, as if on the look-out. Perhaps he had heard sounds. Perhaps he was thinking of the villagers' worries. Be that as it may, after a few moments of perplexity he jumped down and ran outside, crossed the courtyard of the castle and took the path to the left which led to the old stables. It must have been five o'clock in the morning. The only thing to be seen on the ground were white stones and shadows, as if at full moon.

In this pale light, the last day in the existence of Tanios-*Kishk* began – what was known of his existence, at least.

However, I find myself compelled to interrupt the account of his flight and return to that of his last night. I have attempted to reconstruct it as well as I could. At all events, another version of that same night exists. Which nothing in the written sources corroborates and which – even more serious according to my criteria – does not have the merit of probability either.

If I nevertheless mention it, it is because old Gebrayel would not forgive me if I omitted it. I can still remember how annoyed he was at my doubts. 'Nothing but a legend, you say? You want nothing but facts? Facts are perishable, believe me, only legends remain, like the soul after the body, or the perfume in the wake of a woman.' I had to promise him to mention the other version.

What does it say? That the hero, after slipping away from the crowds to go and lie on his childhood bed, had fallen asleep before being awakened the first time by Lamia's caresses. He had had with her the conversation that we know of, then he had begged her to leave him to rest.

Then he had again been woken by caresses.

'Mother,' he said, 'I thought you had left.'

But these were not Lamia's caresses. She was in the habit of placing her hand flat on his forehead, then smoothing his hair, as if to tidy it. Her invariable action, when he was two just as when he was twenty. This new caress was different. A hand was stroking his forehead, then round his eyes, his cheeks, his chin.

When he said, 'Asma,' two fingers were pressed against his lips, and the girl said, 'Don't speak, and shut your eyes.'

Then she lay down beside him, her head in the hollow of his shoulder.

He put his arms round her. Her shoulders were bare. They curled up passionately, close to each other, without saying a word. And they wept over all their misfortunes, without a glance at each other.

Then she rose. He did not try to stop her. As she climbed down the ladder, she merely said, 'Don't let my father die.'

He was about to reply, but Asma's fingers again closed his lips with a gesture of trust. Then he heard the rustle of her dress in the dark. Once again he smelled the scent of wild hyacinths.

He dried his eyes on his sleeve, then sat up. Jumped to his feet. And began to race towards the old stables.

Was it to make sure Roukoz had not bribed his guards to let him escape? Or perhaps, on the contrary, to free him himself before the Sheikh arrived? In a moment the question would not be of the slightest relevance.

The old stables were some way from the castle. That is probably why they had been disused from long before the Sheikh's time, and new ones had been built closer. Since then the old ones had mostly been used as a sheepfold, but sometimes also briefly to detain maniacs, raving lunatics or criminals reputed to be dangerous.

The closing mechanism was simple and solid: heavy chains embedded in a thick wall, a heavy half-moon door, two gratings built into the stone.

As he approached, Tanios imagined he saw the figure of one of the guards sitting against the door, his head on his shoulder, and another one lying on the ground. At first he stepped more softly, thinking to surprise them asleep. Then he thought better of it and began to stamp loudly and clear his throat, to avoid having to upbraid them. They did not stir. Then he noticed the door; it was wide open.

The guards were dead. Those first two, and the other two a little further away. Bending over each one, he was able to feel their wounds with his fingers; their throats had been cut.

'Curses on you, Roukoz!' he roared, convinced that his accomplices had come to free him. But on entering the building he saw a body lying under the arch, the feet still in chains. Tanios recognized Roukoz by his clothes and his corpulence. The assailants had carried off his head by way of a trophy.

The Reverend Stolton reports that it was paraded that same day in the streets of Sahlain, on the point of a bayonet. He had some harsh words to say:

> In order to obtain the head of a criminal, they killed four innocent men. Kahtane *beyk* told me he did not wish this. But he allowed it to be done. Tomorrow the people of Kfaryabda will come and slaughter other innocent folk by way of reprisals. All of them will, for many long years, find excellent reasons to justify their successive acts of vengeance.
>
> God did not say to man, 'Thou shalt not kill without good reason.' He simply said, 'Thou shalt not kill.'

And he added, two paragraphs lower down:

> Persecuted communities have for centuries come to settle on the sides of the same mountain. If, in this place of refuge, they tear each other to pieces, slavery will rise up towards them from all around and submerge them, just as the sea washes over the rocks.
>
> Who, in this business, bears the greatest responsibility? The Pasha of Egypt most certainly, who set the mountain dwellers against each other. We too, the British and the French, who came here to prolong the Napoleonic Wars. And the Turks, by their negligence and bouts of fanaticism. But, in my eyes, because I have come to love these Mountains as if I had been born here, the only ones who cannot be forgiven are the local people, Christians and Druse . . .

As if he could have read his former guardian's words, Tanios, 'local man' that he was, held himself the sole guilty person. Had he not been told that, if he failed to execute Roukoz, a tragedy like this would not fail to occur? Even the priest had foreseen this. But he had refused to listen. He was the one who, with a gesture which he intended to be authoritative, had marked out these four young men for death, and, by this inability to act ruthlessly, provoked the massacres which might follow. Guilty of indecision. Guilty of leniency, because of traces of affection, a residue of love. Guilty of pity.

He was so convinced of his own guilt that he dared not return immediately to the village to tell what had occurred. He went to walk in the pine forest, so recently burnt down. Some of the charred trees were still standing. He caught himself stroking them, as if they alone could understand his mood. With his feet in the blackened grass, he sought in vain for the path which he used to take on his way to school in Sahlain. The acrid smoke made his eyes smart.

Gradually the sky grew lighter. In Kfaryabda, the sun is on its way before it actually appears, for, to the east, not far off, rises one of the highest peaks in the Mountains – the celestial body takes long to climb it. At sunset, the opposite takes place, it is already dark and lanterns are being lit in the houses, while from their windows the sun's orb can still be seen on the horizon, glowing red, then turning blue, until it lights up only the depths of the sea into which it sinks.

That morning, many things happened before the appearance of the sun. Tanios was still wandering in the charred forest when the church bell began to toll. It rang once, then silence. It tolled a second time, then silence. Tanios was troubled. 'They have discovered the bodies.'

But the bell began to peal wildly. What he had taken for the death-knell were the preliminary notes of a joyous carillon. The Sheikh had just arrived. He was walking through the *Blata*. People were rushing up, shouting, surrounding him. From where he stood, Tanios could even make him out in the middle of the crowd. However, he could not hear the murmur which spread: 'He can't see! They have put out his eyes!'

III

The Sheikh detected the villagers's astonishment, and was himself astonished. He thought that the news had spread; in the first week of his imprisonment his eyes had been put out with the red-hot iron.

The people tried not to restrain their joy, but as they jostled round the Master, to 'see' his hand, they could not help staring at him as they would never have dared to do when he had his eyes.

Everything about him had changed. His white moustache was now unkempt, his hair in disarray, his gait unsteady, of course, but strange too was the way his hands gesticulated, the stiff way he held himself, the way he moved his head, twitched his face, and also the slight hesitation in his voice, as if it too needed to see his path. Only his apple-green waistcoat was still in place, even his gaolers had not dared remove that.

A black-clad woman approached, took his hand, as all the others were doing.

'You are Lamia.'

He clasped her head in his hands and placed a kiss on her forehead.

'Do not go away. Come and sit on my left. You shall be my eyes. Never did I have such beautiful eyes.'

He laughed. Everyone around him wiped away tears, Lamia more than them all.

'Where is Tanios? I cannot wait to speak with him!'

'When he hears that our Sheikh is back we shall see him come running.'

'This lad is our pride and the jewel of the village.'

Lamia was beginning a reply, wishing him long life and good health, when howls rang out, followed by the crackle of guns firing in the air. Then people began to scramble in all directions.

'What is happening?' asked the Sheikh.

Several breathless voices shouted at once.

'I don't understand. Let one of you speak and the others keep quiet!'

'Let me,' said one.

'Who are you?'

'I am Toubiyya, Sheikh!'

'Good. Speak, Toubiyya, what is happening?'

'The people of Sahlain attacked us during the night. They killed Roukoz and the four young men who were guarding him. The whole village must take up arms and go to make them pay for this!'

'Toubiyya, I did not ask you to tell me what I must do, only to tell me what has happened! Now, how do you know it was the people from Sahlain?'

The priest motioned to Toubiyya to let him speak. He stooped over the Sheikh to whisper in his ear a brief account of what had occurred the previous day at the castle, the decision taken by Tanios, Kahtane *beyk*'s intervention... *Bouna* Boutros avoided criticizing Lamia's son, but around him the people were angry and threatening.

'Tanios had been installed in our Sheikh's place for only one day and already there is fire and bloodshed in the village.'

The Master remained impassive.

'Everyone be silent, I have heard enough. Let us go up to the castle, I need to be seated. We will talk some more when we are there.'

The church bells stopped pealing at the precise moment when the Sheikh once more crossed the threshold of the stately dwelling. Someone had gone to warn the bell-ringer that the hour for rejoicing had passed.

*

And yet, as he resumed his usual place in the Hall of Pillars, the Master turned to the wall and asked, 'Is the thief's portrait behind me?'

'No,' was the answer, 'we took it down and burnt it!'

'A pity, it would have helped us fill our coffers.'

He kept a straight face, but there were smiles among the gathering, and even some slight laughs. So, the Sheikh knew about the jokes which the villagers had made up about the usurper. Overlord and subjects were united in their memories, ready to face the ordeal.

'What has occurred between Kfaryabda and Sahlain saddens me more than the loss of my eyes. I have never departed from the path of good neighbourliness and fraternity! And in spite of the innocent blood which has just been shed, we must avoid war.'

Several murmurs arose.

'Let those who do not appreciate my words leave my home immediately, before I find it necessary to drive them out!'

No one stirred.

'Otherwise, let them keep silent! And if anyone wishes to go off and make war against my will, he must know that I shall have him hanged before the Druse have time to kill him.'

There was general silence.

'Is Tanios here?'

The young man had arrived after the Sheikh and, refusing the seats offered him, stood leaning against one of the pillars. At the mention of his name, he started, approached and bent over the hand which the Sheikh held out to him.

Lamia rose to give up her seat to her son, but the Sheikh prevented her.

'I need you, do not go away, Tanios was all right where he was.'

Lamia sat down again, somewhat ill at ease; but the young man went back to lean against his pillar, without seeming to have taken offence.

'Yesterday,' the Master continued, 'when it was not yet known whether I would return, you gathered here under the authority of this young man, to judge Roukoz. Tanios pronounced a judgement, which turned out to be unfortunate, disastrous even. Some of you have told me that he lacked wisdom and firmness. I agree with them. Others have whispered in my ears that Tanios lacked courage. To these I say: "Know that to confront the Emir and notify him of his destitution and banishment needed a hundred times more courage than to cut the throat of a man in chains." '

He uttered these words in a powerful and indignant voice. Lamia straightened herself up on her seat. Tanios kept his eyes lowered.

'With experience and age, this young man's wisdom will be equal to his courage and his intelligence. Then he will be worthy to sit in this place. For it is my intention and my wish that he succeed me, the day when I am no longer here.

'I begged Heaven not to let me die before I had seen the downfall of the tyrant who unjustly killed my son. The Almighty has listened to my prayer, and has chosen Tanios as the instrument of His wrath and His justice. This boy has become my son, my only son, and I appoint him as my heir. I was anxious to say this today, before you all, so that no one should think of contesting it.'

All eyes were turned to the chosen one, who still seemed as abstracted as before. Was this his way of receiving these honours, a sign of modesty, after all, and excessive politeness? All the sources agree that Tanios's behaviour that morning disconcerted those present. Insensible to criticism, insensible to praise, hopelessly speechless. The explanation seems simple to me. Of all the people present, not one, not even Lamia, knew the essential fact: that Tanios had discovered the bodies of the four young men, and he could not erase the picture of their bloodstained corpses from his mind, and was obsessed with his own guilt, and incapable of thinking of anything else, especially of the Sheikh's Will and Testament and his own brilliant future.

And when, a few minutes later, the Master of the castle said, 'Now let me rest for a while; come back and see me this afternoon, when we will speak of what is to be done with our neighbours from Sahlain,' and as the villagers began to withdraw, Tanios remained leaning against his pillar, as if inconsolable, while they filed past him, staring at him as if he were a statue.

The noise of their footsteps eventually died away. Then the Sheikh asked Lamia, who was supporting him by the arm, 'Have they all gone?'

She said, 'Yes,' although her son was still standing in the same place, and she was watching him with growing anxiety.

The two of them walked away towards the Sheikh's private apartments, at the slow pace dictated by his infirmity. Only then did Tanios raise his head, watching them move away, arm in arm, as if embracing, and he was suddenly certain that it was his parents whom he was contemplating.

This thought shook him out of his torpor. His gaze became sharper. What was there in this gaze? Affection? Reproaches? The feeling that he had at last the key to the riddle which had burdened his whole life?

At the same moment, Lamia turned round. Their eyes met. Then, as if ashamed, she released the Sheikh's arm, came back to Tanios and placed a hand on his shoulder.

'I was thinking of Roukoz's daughter. I am sure that no one in the village will go to express their condolences. You should not leave her alone on a day like this.'

The young man nodded in agreement. But he did not move immediately. His mother went back to the Sheikh who was waiting for her at the same spot. She took his arm again, but holding him less closely. Then they disappeared round a bend in the corridor.

Tanios made for the door, a strange smile on his lips.

*

Again I quote from the Reverend Stolton's Yearbook:

I am told that, on his way to visit *Khweja* Roukoz's daughter, to present his condolences, Tanios noticed a crowd
gathered not far from the *Blata*. Young men from the
village were rough-handling Nader, the pedlar, accusing
him of having slandered the Sheikh and of having been
in league with Roukoz and the Egyptians; the man was
struggling to get away, swearing he had come back only
to congratulate the Sheikh on his return. His face was
streaming with blood and his wares were scattered on the
ground. Tanios intervened, using what prestige he still
had, and accompanied the man with his mule to the
outskirts of the village. A distance of three miles, at
the very most, there and back, but it was four hours later
when my ward returned. He spoke to no one and climbed
up to sit on a rock. Then, as if by a miracle, he disappeared. [*He vanished* is what it said in the English text.]

In the night, his mother and the priest's wife came
back to ask me if I had seen Tanios, if I had news of him.
No man accompanied them, on account of the extreme
tension which reigns between Kfaryabda and Sahlain at
present.

As for the *Mountain Chronicle*, this is what it says:

Tanios accompanied Nader as far as the *khraj* [the territory just beyond the limits of the village], made sure he
was safe, then returned and immediately climbed up to
sit on the rock which today bears his name. He stayed
there for some time, leaning back, without moving. From
time to time, the villagers approached to watch him, then
went on their way.

When the Sheikh woke from his siesta, he called for
him. People then came to the foot of the rock to call him,
and Tanios told them he would join them in a moment.
An hour later he still had not come to the castle. Then

the Sheikh seemed put out and sent other messengers to call him. He was no longer on his rock. But neither had anyone seen him climb down and depart.

Then people started to search for him, shouting his name, the whole village was afoot, men, women and children. They even thought the worst, and they went to look at the foot of the cliff, in case he had fallen in a fit of giddiness, but there was no trace of him there either.

Nader was never to set foot in the village again. Moreover, he gave up criss-crossing the Mountains with his wares, preferring to set up a more sedentary business in Beirut. He lived there for twenty good, lucrative, and extremely talkative years. But when the folk from Kfaryabda went to visit him from time to time, and questioned him about Lamia's son, he told them only what everyone knew – that they had parted on the outskirts of the village, that he himself had gone on his way and Tanios had retraced his steps.

His share in the secret he noted down in an exercise-book which, one day in the 1920s, a lecturer at the American University of Beirut was to discover by chance, among all the jumble in an attic. Annotated and published, with an English translation, entitled *Wisdom on Muleback* (which I have freely rendered as *La sagesse du muletier*), it had only a limited circulation among people who were not in a position to make the connection with Tanios's disappearance.

And yet, if you are prepared to look closely at these maxims, with their poetical pretensions, you can find quite clear echoes of the long conversation which took place that day between Nader and Tanios on the edge of the village, and also certain keys to understanding what could have occurred subsequently.

Sentences such as: 'Today, what has been destined for thee is over, thy life can finally begin', which I have quoted as the epigraph to this chapter; or again: 'Thy rock is weary of bearing thee, Tanios, and the sea has grown tired of thy sterile gaze'; but even more this passage that old Gebrayel – may he live and maintain a clear head beyond his hundredth year – gave me to read one evening, stressing every word with his gnarled forefinger:

For all the others, thou art the absent one, but I am the friend who knows.

Unbeknownst to them thou hastened down the path, that the murderer, thy father, took towards the coast.

She waits for thee, the girl with the treasure, on her island; and her hair is still the colour of the setting sun.

When I first read these words, so crystal clear, I thought I had before me the real story. Perhaps it is. Perhaps not. Perhaps these lines reveal what the muleteer 'knew'. But on re-reading them, perhaps they contain only what he hoped to learn one day of the fate of his vanished friend.

In any case, there remain many obscure areas, of which time has only deepened the mystery. And firstly this one: why did Tanios, after leaving the village with the muleteer, return to sit on this rock?

It is possible to imagine that, after his conversation with Nader, who might once again have urged him to leave his Mountains, the young man was still undecided. One could even list the reasons which could have encouraged him to leave, and the ones which, on the contrary, ought to have made him stay . . . What would be the use? That is not the way a decision to depart is made. You don't evaluate, you don't draw up a list of advantages and disadvantages. You alternate, from one moment to the next, now this way, now that. Towards another life, towards another death. Towards glory or oblivion. Who can ever tell because of what look, what word, what sneer, a man suddenly finds himself an outsider in the midst of his own people? So that he feels this sudden, urgent need to go far away, or disappear.

Following in the invisible footsteps of Tanios, how many men have left the village since! For the same reasons? From the same impulse, rather, and under the same pressure. My Mountains are like that. Attachment to the soil and aspiration towards departure. Place of refuge, place of passage. Land of milk and honey and of blood. Neither paradise nor hell. Purgatory.

At this point in my surmises, I had somewhat forgotten Tanios's distress in the presence of my own distress. Had I not been searching for the truth beyond the legend? When I had thought to reach the heart of the truth, it consisted of legend.

I even convinced myself that there was, perhaps, after all, some spell connected with the rock of Tanios. When he came back to sit there, I told myself, it was not in order to reflect, nor to weigh up the advantages and disadvantages. He needed something quite different. Meditation? Contemplation? More than that – to pour out his soul. And he knew instinctively that by going to sit on that rocky throne, by abandoning himself to the influence of the site, his fate would be sealed.

I understood now why I had been forbidden to climb that rock. But just because I understood, because I had let myself be persuaded – against my reason – that the superstitions, the distrust, were not without foundation, the temptation was all the greater to defy the prohibition.

Was I still bound by the promise I had made? So many things had happened, the village had known so many upheavals since my grandfather's not-so-distant time, so much destruction, so much bruising, that one day I finally yielded. I murmured my apologies to all the ancestors and climbed up in my turn to sit on the rock.

What words can I find to express my feelings, my mood?

The weightlessness of time, weightlessness of the heart and of the mind.

At my back, the mountains so close. At my feet, the valley from which at nightfall the familiar howling of jackals would rise up. And yonder, in the distance, I could see the sea, my narrow strip of sea, narrow and long, stretching out to the horizon like a road.

Note

This book is freely inspired by a true story: the murder of a patriarch, committed in the nineteenth century by a certain Abou-*kishk*-Maalouf. The assassin took refuge in Cyprus with his son, from where he was brought back to his home country by the cunning of one of the Emir's agents, and there executed.

The rest – the narrator, his village, his sources, his characters – all the rest is nothing but impure fiction.